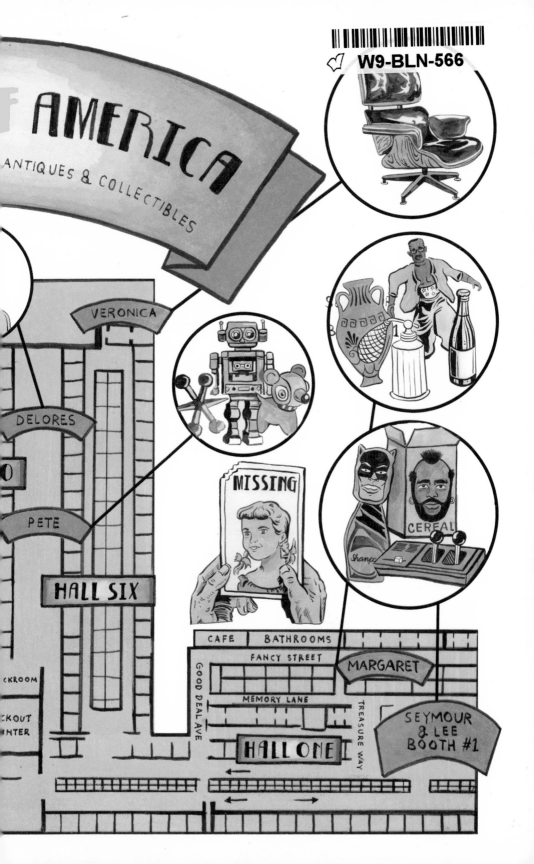

HEART

OF

JUNK

LUKE GEDDES

Simon & Schuster

New York   London   Toronto   Sydney   New Delhi

Simon & Schuster
1230 Avenue of the Americas
New York, NY 10020

First Simon & Schuster hardcover edition January 2020

SIMON & SCHUSTER and colophon are registered trademarks of Simon & Schuster, Inc.

For information about special discounts for bulk purchases, please contact Simon & Schuster Special Sales at 1-866-506-1949 or business@simonandschuster.com.

The Simon & Schuster Speakers Bureau can bring authors to your live event. For more information or to book an event, contact the Simon & Schuster Speakers Bureau at 1-866-248-3049 or visit our website at www.simonspeakers.com.

Interior design by Carly Loman

Manufactured in the United States of America

10 9 8 7 6 5 4 3 2 1

Library of Congress Cataloging-in-Publication Data

Names: Geddes, Luke, author.
Title: Heart of junk / Luke Geddes.
Description: New York : Simon & Schuster, [2020]
Identifiers: LCCN 2019027853 (print) | LCCN 2019027854 (ebook) | ISBN 9781982106669 (hardcover) | ISBN 9781982106683 (ebook) ·
Subjects: LCSH: Kidnapping—Fiction. | GSAFD: Mystery fiction.
Classification: LCC PS3607.E3612 H43 2020 (print) | LCC PS3607.E3612 (ebook) | DDC 813/.6—dc23
LC record available at https://lccn.loc.gov/2019027853
LC ebook record available at https://lccn.loc.gov/2019027854

ISBN 978-1-9821-0666-9
ISBN 978-1-9821-0668-3 (ebook)

For Steph

What is it that will last?
All things are taken from us, and become
Portions and parcels of the dreadful past.

—ALFRED, LORD TENNYSON, "The Lotos-Eaters"

Hello, I am seeking a nice room mate to share my 2 bedroom home. You won't have to pay utilities or do any chores so it's perfect for a young person or a student. But I cannot have anybody touching or moving my stuff because it would set off a chain reaction of emotions and feelings towards you and towards my things. Hoarding is not a mental illness, it is something environmentally responsible because I don't like to throw anything away. But the Department of public health said my living conditions were unsafe and came in and forcibly removed my things I have been collecting for over 40 years. It traumatized me and I have been rebuilding my collection ever since.

—craigslist.org, posted August 23, 2009, at 12:03 a.m.

THURSDAY

DEALER ASSOCIATION MEETING DAY

1

MARGARET

Margaret Byrd watched the two new vendors who had taken her dear friend Patricia's vacated booth (#1-146) lug in their boxes of inventory, thinking: There were antiques and then there were collectibles. She ought to poke her head out from behind her immaculate, organized-by-color shelves of perfume bottles, some of which—on the top row, of course, locked behind thick, bulletproof glass, the storage unit screwed securely to the wall, and, of course of course *of course*, the entire set insured to its precise value—dated back to the eighteenth century, and introduce herself, welcome the gentlemen to the Heart of America Antique Mall family, perhaps show them to the café and treat them to a package of Nilla wafers and a Pepsi from the vending machines. Yes, she certainly should, and in a little while she would. But for now she only watched, making note of the many *collectibles* (which consisted of any crafted or manufactured items *less than* one hundred years old, unlike *antiques*) the two men removed from overstuffed cardboard boxes and set haphazardly on the fiberglass shelving units they probably assumed the mall had provided but which had actually belonged to Patricia. Margaret had thought her leaving them there was a sign she'd return one day, she hadn't really meant the unpleasant things she'd said two months ago, before she dropped, quite deliberately, Margaret's Royal Flemish biscuit jar with gold and amethyst butterfly embellishment, shattering it into a thousand glittering pieces—but no, in retrospect, an accident, just an accident, Margaret was certain, unequivocally so—and stormed out, sending her three brutish sons to collect her inventory days later. They'd forgotten Patricia's beautiful hand-painted porcelain doll, and although it didn't fit, Margaret had been keeping it safe behind a shelf in her own booth. Margaret called her, sometimes twice a day, ready to explain away the simple misunderstanding that had led to all this trouble. She'd written her spiel down on a telephone pad, just in case she got flustered or nervous—though why should she be nervous? The calls went unanswered, the messages unreturned.

One could make out dust rings on the shelves left by Patricia's exquisite Josef Hoffmann–style candlesticks and already these two were moving right on in, proudly displaying *Dallas* and *The Beverly Hillbillies* board games where Patricia's gilt nineteenth century hand mirrors once sat, fanning back issues of *Playboy* and *Oui* and *Mad* magazine on the lowest shelves where anyone's children could get at them, and stacking tin lunch boxes whose brightly colored visages—the Fonz, grinning; a tense Lee Majors, standing impassively in a fluorescent sea of flames; soaring, dead-eyed cartoon superheroes; potbellied, silver-jumpsuited casts of science fiction television programs long forgotten—mocked everything booth #1-146 had once been. And even though their ten-by-twenty-square-foot space was stuffed thick and musty with the accumulated ephemera of a thousand Generation X childhoods, they left for the parking lot and returned with still more things.

Margaret's heart began to hiccup as they continued to unpack. There were artifacts and then there were knickknacks. There were knickknacks and then there was junk. With the emergence of each item, she was surer that these two were nothing more than half-rate junk dealers. When one of them pulled out an unopened box of Mr. T breakfast cereal, she began to choke. She needed some coffee, with a lot of cream and half a spoonful of sugar, and maybe some popcorn or those Nilla wafers. How-

ever, the only route to the café was past the dreaded twosome. Oh, what the heck, she thought. She may as well satisfy her own morbid curiosity. She couldn't help it. She was human, too, always slowed down with the rest of them to take a gander at a grisly accident at the side of the highway, though she did it out of concern, in case someone would happen to flag her down for help; she wasn't some thrill-seeking gawker.

She waited until their backs were turned to slip out of her booth and down the aisle, named, according to the wood-carved street sign hanging from the ceiling, Memory Lane, but one of the men—the blond, mustachioed one—cornered her and stuck out a visibly moist palm. "Hello there." She nodded, tried to smile, took his hand daintily. "We're new," he said unnecessarily.

The dark-haired one, his hands tangled in a bundle of video game joysticks, turned and said hello, but not so friendlily as the other. He looked at his partner in a way to suggest that the blond always talked to strangers in terms too intimate and that, although the dark-haired man didn't like it, he was helpless to stop him. There was something obscenely paternal in that look, especially given that the dark-haired one, judging by his receding hairline and the thin skin around his eyes, appeared significantly older than the blond. Wasn't that the way it worked with these homosexuals? Their relationships hinged on bizarre power struggles that reversed themselves in the privacy of their bedroom, culminating in unimaginable acts of perversion. Anyway, something was off about these two. They were both so tall and thin. As a couple, they seemed unbalanced. Wasn't one of them supposed to be short and stout, the Laurel and Hardy dynamic? They were gays of a type that used to be popular on raunchy television sitcoms that Margaret, as a rule, refused to enjoy: Hawaiian-shirt-wearers who drank flamboyantly named martinis like fuzzy navels, sex on the beaches, and pink flamingos, who called themselves bitches and meant it as a compliment, who used words like po-mo and kitsch and camp as if anyone knew what they meant.

"I don't think we have room for this, Lee," Blond said to Dark Hair, motioning to a large Styrofoam hamburger, the vestige of a defunct and better-off-forgotten novelty diner. He turned to Margaret and said, "You mind if we keep it in your booth?" Margaret must have blanched, because he touched her shoulder and said, "Only kidding, dear," and then, "Seymour," more like an exclamation than a way of identifying himself.

"Margaret," Margaret said uncertainly. "Booth one-dash-one-thirty-eight, corner of Memory Lane and Treasure Way." Seymour didn't say anything, so she added, "Welcome aboard." The words tasted sour, camp counselorish, and unnatural. Already these men's tackiness was affecting her. After a few weeks' exposure, she'd be decorating her mantel with plastic fast-food prizes and those googly-eyed fuzzballs with sticker feet, wearing shirts that jingled with myriad gaudy charms and buttons sewn in willy-nilly patterns, eating Lucky Charms for breakfast out of a Tiffany bowl.

Seymour said, "Don't mind us. We're just settling in. Got this booth here and one in Hall Three for our vinyl."

She prayed that by *vinyl* he meant record albums and not some sort of depraved sex apparel. You just never knew when it came to these people. They had been here less than a day and already they'd staked their claim to multiple halls! As much as it would anguish her, Margaret would have to investigate their other booth later. As the Heart of America's senior-most dealer, it was her duty.

"Nice to meet you," Lee said without sincerity and then left, probably to gather even more junk. Frankly, she preferred his rudeness to Seymour's *hello there aren't I cute* brand of social charm. He was presently digging through the boxes and humming. Having made himself known, he evidently had no interest in continuing the conversation, no desire to ask Margaret what sorts of antiques (official dictionary definition) interested her, how long she'd been in the industry, or if she would introduce him to the community of dealers who made the Heart of America their home away from home. Just as she was preparing to sigh pointedly and leave for the café, he yanked out of a box an object so vile and blatantly violative to the mall's clear policy guidelines that Margaret swore she could taste—she could actually taste—a wisp of vomit in the back of her throat.

It was a doll, not just any doll, but one fashioned in the likeness of a man named MC Hammer, whom Margaret—though she'd never cared for popular music, preferring opera and classical—recalled as a rap musician she'd watched, despite herself, perform his clangorous so-called songs on many late-night talk shows in the nineties. The man, with his ridiculous circus pants and a swagger that intimated violence, had been inescapable. Margaret especially did not care for rap music or whatever nonsense name it was called by now. The doll was of compatible dimensions with the Barbies and Kens that Delores Kovacs sold in Hall Two, and manufactured by the same company. With horror she pictured it, in its distasteful sparkling outfit, cavorting with the clean-cut figures of her childhood: staring out of those still, white eyes and flashing that menacing grin as he reclined on the DreamHouse sofa, his arm around Barbie, stripped down to her black-and-white underthing, a nearby boom box quaking with the cacophonous beat of the bonus cassingle the box boasted was included inside, while poor Ken lay dead on the floor, shot up by the rapper himself.

Seymour must have noticed her looking, because he held the doll close to her face. "I know," he said. "Isn't it hysterical?"

Margaret pinched her lips and nodded. There was junk and there was—even in her thoughts she pardoned her French—shit. The Pac-Man beer stein was one thing, the *My Secret Princess* play set quite another, but this—this was just too much. Something would have to be done about it. She would see to it that something *was* done. She nodded a curt goodbye to Seymour, walked down Memory Lane, turned the corner at Good Deal Avenue, and stopped in the lounge/café area at the intersection of Good Deal and Fancy Street.

The mall was so immense—nearly two hundred thousand square feet, featured upon its opening in *Martha Stewart Living* magazine as the largest year-round antiques market in the state of Kansas—that, for the benefit of fatigued customers, rest areas such as this had been strategically placed around the building near the bathrooms. There sat a large TV on mute tuned to the listings channel, an old couch and a couple of recliners (not antique, not collectible, but flannel thrift store cast-offs), a couple of humming vending machines, an "old fashioned" popcorn cart, and—thank heavens—Heart of America co-owner Keith Stoller, hunched over the surface of a wobbly card table with the focus of a monk as he collated a mess of papers into neat stapled packets.

"Keith," Margaret said as she took the seat across from him, "I'm so glad you're here."

"Just getting some stuff ready for the meeting." Keith, an astonishingly short man with a pale comb-over on an even paler scalp, whose clothes were forever haunted by stains of mysterious origin, and whom frankly Margaret could sometimes scarcely bear to look at, kept his eyes trained on the papers. "Lindy Bobo Action Plan," the cover sheet read, referring to the local toddler, a beauty pageant champion already something of a regional celebrity, who had recently gone missing. Margaret felt for the little girl and her family, she truly did. The world could be so wicked. But the Heart of America was supposed to be a haven from the wicked outside world, offering respite from the stresses and calamities of modern life. Littering the rest area with such stark reminders of the brutality people came here to escape ruined the ambience, to say the least.

"We have a problem," Margaret said to Keith's bald spot. When he didn't look up, when he continued to *slap slap slap* the stapler with machine-like efficiency, when it became clear he was ignoring her, she added, at a volume that surprised even her: "A big problem!" Keith recoiled and knocked some papers onto the floor. Margaret made no move to pick them up. Now that she had his attention, she continued. "As you may or may not know, you've got a pair of new vendors under your charge. They've taken over—completely—Patricia's booth."

"Her old booth, yes. Lee and Seymour. Nice guys."

Of course, she didn't have anything against gays in general. She enjoyed many reality television shows they hosted and appreciated their zest for life and eye for color. She especially liked decorating and remodeling programs and used to watch them together with Patricia as they talked on the phone, her TV across town tuned to the same channel, her laughter blowing through the receiver like a soft breeze in Margaret's ear.

"Perfectly friendly gentlemen whom I have no personal feeling toward one way or the other. However"—Margaret's eyes drifted to the television screen behind Keith, a commercial for a racy movie thriller that alternated images of bare flesh, guns, and explosions—"a doll they are selling and putting on prominent display in their booth is in violation of policy guidelines."

"Do we have to do this right now? Maybe we should save this for the meeting. Veronica wants these booklets ready before—"

"I would *love* to talk about it at the meeting, Keith, but I think it's crucial you get the whole story beforehand so you know I'm right. Now, as you and I and *most* dealers are aware, there are different policies for different areas of the building. What works for one hall may not work for—may in fact actively *work against*—the aims of another hall. Over in Hall One, the logical starting point for most customers and thus the hall with the heaviest foot traffic, we have a rule—a very generous rule, I think—that all items displayed must be made before the year 1989."

"And you think this doll is from after that time."

"I am almost certain."

Keith shifted in his seat. He had thumbprint smudges on the oversized lenses of his glasses. Margaret sensed he was going to tell her something she didn't want to hear. He was positively radiating meekness. He was the abstract concept of ineffectuality made concrete. "Look," he said, "it's just one doll. Let it go. I've got more important things to—"

"It's not just one doll. There's more. Computer game apparatuses, I think. A *My Secret Princess* play set that looked suspiciously contemporary." She clenched her fists. She should have known not to bother with him. It was his wife, Stacey, who sported the figurative pants when it came to antiques—Keith didn't know cameo from cloisonné—but she and Margaret, through no fault of Margaret's own, had a somewhat strained relationship. "The doll's name is McHammer," she said.

"A McDonald's thing?" Keith fiddled with the stapler. "Oh!" he said. "*MC* Hammer."

"You of all people should be aware that this is no time to be upsetting the equilibrium of Hall One, what with Mark and Grant coming on Monday. Unless you *want* to look like some dirty old flea market on national TV." The past couple of years had not been kind to the Heart of America, and stalwart Hall One, itself larger than many entire antique malls, was their only shot at making a good impression on the "Peddlin' Pair" (as the promos called them). If Keith and Stacey knew what was good for them, they'd direct the camera crews to Hall One and Hall One only, as it was the only of the mall's six sections at anything close to capacity; some of the others—Hall Five in particular—were frankly in shambles.

Keith pushed back his chair and stood. "If it matters so much to you, all right. We'll look it up."

Margaret followed him down Fancy Street to the lobby, noting but not in any way appreciating or even meaning to look at the yellow-white strip of ripped underwear briefs his sagging pants revealed. On the bulletin board a neon flyer adorned with the missing girl's image was pinned so it overlapped with the laminated announcement of her own booth having been voted "customer's choice" at last month's sales event. At the register, Keith's teenage daughter, Ellie, paged idly through a textbook, ignoring the customer who stood before her and cleared his throat for attention.

"Customer, Ellie," Keith said.

"What am I supposed to do about it?"

"Your job," Keith said tremulously. "Please, sweetheart."

Ellie slammed her book shut with such force the customer startled. Through gritted teeth she said, "How may I help you, *sir*?" Far be it from Margaret to poke her nose in other people's family affairs, but the Stollers ought to do something about that girl of theirs.

In the EMPLOYEES ONLY area in the back room behind the counter, among storage lockers, a kitchenette, and a series of desks and bookshelves that functioned as a dealer reference library, was an old computer that purred like a motorcycle whenever you turned it on and an assortment of illustrated antiques and collectibles price guides to satisfy every niche. Keith selected a heavy tome whose cover read *TOYS: From Victorian Dolls to the Electronic Games of the Future.* Holding it close to his chin so that Margaret couldn't look over his shoulder, he turned the pages thoughtfully. "Well," he said, "the *My Secret Princess* thing is definitely okay." Margaret pictured the heavy book colliding swiftly with Keith's skull, though in her mind's eye she couldn't tell who'd swung it; she guessed with slight embarrassment that she had. "But the Hammer thing is from 1991. You're right."

"Of course."

Keith bit his lip, removed his glasses, and wiped them on his shirt. When he put them back on they were somehow even more smudged than before. "Are you really sure this is worth me having to talk to them about it?"

"Yes," Margaret said, "I am." After all, she wanted to add, it took less than a doll to fell Rome, though she wasn't sure what that even meant.

•

Having done her due diligence, Margaret thought it prudent to let Keith confront the men discreetly, so she left to attend to some errands and did not return to the Heart of America until later in the afternoon.

The Dealer Association meeting was not to take place until after closing, but as usual many dealers had arrived early with plans to update their stock or redecorate their booths. They shuffled in, unusually listless, the small talk strained and automatic. A couple of men from Hall Six flicked cigarettes past the outdoor ashtray and traded macabre gossip about the Bobo case.

"I heard they already found her body in a dumpster behind Big Lots."

"Nah, the mother went psycho and staged the kidnapping, only she tied the rope too tight and the kid choked."

"Says who?"

"Guy in the comments of the *Eagle* article, but it seems legit."

Nevertheless, once Margaret made her way past those boors into the mall proper, she found herself overcome with a sense of comfort and belonging. How nice, even amid all the ugliness of the world outside, to know she belonged to a true-blue community. It was just too bad that the Dealer Association continually failed to elect her president, despite her expertise and seniority. She had been selling at Heart since before *antique* was a verb, years before current president Peter Deen began cluttering up Hall Two with his little playthings.

Margaret dreaded running into the new dealers. Perhaps it'd been unnecessary to raise such a fuss over a single item, even if it was by date of manufacture verboten vis-à-vis official Hall One policy. She hoped Keith hadn't mentioned specifically that it was she who'd reported them. It wasn't as if Margaret were some humorless shrew who lived and died by arbitrary principles, who never jaywalked even across empty streets, who never let loose or enjoyed half of a vodka gimlet to celebrate special occasions. And it wasn't as if the power that came with being the senior-most dealer had gone to her head. She wasn't out to disallow anyone the freedom to sell whatever merchandise he or she wished. This was the Heart of *America*, after all. She was, in fact, the driving force, so many years back, in the successful petition for looser merchandise restrictions in Hall One; before she changed things around, the area was limited to antiques and antiques only, but she hadn't been able to see why she shouldn't be allowed to include her fine Depression-era glass with the rest of her collection. And all the other dealers—most of them gone now, moved on to other malls and flea markets, or else they'd since dropped out of the business entirely—agreed with her. No one could accuse her of sticklerness. She had her fun, kooky side, too. If one doubted that, one could be directed to her second booth, in Hall Three, containing the most expansive selection of Hazel-Atlas juice glasses in the state, if not the entire nation.

Still, as she returned to her little corner of Hall One, she was relieved to see the offending item had been removed. She hoped—though she didn't care one way or the other what most people thought of her, not really—that the men wouldn't hold against her the fact that she'd, with no personal animosity but only a humble respect for the policies to which even she herself was held accountable, seen to the excision of the doll.

Now that it was gone—and *sincerely* she appreciated the men's compliance—other sights poked her in the eyes: a big-headed Batman shampoo bottle, demonic stuffed creatures she vaguely recognized from TV ads, an illuminated beer sign with a picture of a scantily clad woman leaning over a pool table, a framed illustration of a crude Charlie Brown smoking a marijuana joint, a statuette done in the Precious Memories style of a grotesquely shrunken man with a base that read "Dirty Old Men Need Love Too," a board game that endorsed binge drinking and pill popping called Pass-Out, an unopened six-pack of Billy Beer. Even if it was all manufactured prior to 1989, it tested the limits of what belonged in Hall One. An antique mall, in its ideal state, was a sort of museum in which all the curios and artifacts were available for consumption, not just by the wallet but the mind and eyes, too, the perfect hybrid of gift shop and exhibit. Accordingly, a smart vendor selectively curated his or her allotted space. This booth presently inhabited by Seymour and Lee (it just didn't feel right, with Patricia so recently gone, to refer to it as *their* booth, as if they owned it, as if they belonged there) was meretricious, circus-colored. Surely the men meant no harm. They just hadn't yet been thoroughly familiarized with the mall's ethos. She'd just have to have a nice little nonconfrontational chat with them about it after the meeting.

Margaret turned away from booth #1-146, closed her eyes for a moment to clear the burned-in image of the big mess, and entered her dear #1-138. She felt as if she'd just emerged from the murky depths of a foreboding tar-colored body of water onto a sun-speckled white sand beach. Soft light and clean, delicious air seemed to flow outward from the yawning cavities of each piece of glassware surrounding her. She spun around, feeling almost girlish, picturing herself bathed in the kaleidoscope of colored light like that projected from a church's stained-glass windows. After all—no blasphemy intended, of course—there was something slightly solemn, holy even, about it, a sort of near-silent sound—a vibration or presence—that emanated from the glass; she'd always thought so, but never shared this thought with anyone, anyone but Patricia, who then took Margaret's hand in hers and whispered, her breath moist and particley from the crumbs of the Nilla wafers they'd just shared, "I know exactly what you mean. There's a word for it, hearing something just by looking at it." Margaret stopped spinning now and straightened her collar. The kiss—it had been meant only as a friendly gesture. That was the way they did it in Europe, wasn't it? It was true that there was no occasion for it. Margaret had never had many friends growing up, she hadn't been trained in how these sorts of relationships functioned. This is what she would say if Patricia finally answered the phone. Yes, she'd call again today, Margaret decided, after the meeting. She should be home by then. Margaret remembered that Patricia's Thursday yoga classes ended at six.

It was then, out of the corner of her eye, that she caught sight of a foreign body at rest in one of her sugar bowls. As the silhouette came into focus, she dropped her purse and pitched backward, tripped on a heel, and collapsed on the cold floor. Looking up at the doll's ominous brown face, its arms clutching the rim of the bowl, a tiny microphone in its tiny hand, she thought: This will not do. This will not do at all.

Anger lifted her off the floor and she grabbed the doll, careful not to disturb her bowl, and carried it, a plastic foot pinched loosely between two delicate fingers, down the aisles of Hall One. This was, in her opinion, grounds for eviction, and she was sure, if she reminded them of how loyal a renter she'd been these many years, Keith and Stacey would agree.

2

KEITH

Just last week Keith Stoller had had a very promising phone chat with an assistant producer on the new *Pickin' Fortunes* spinoff. The network was optimistic, she'd said. Ratings for all Mark-and-Grant-related programming were at a record-breaking high. And—she shouldn't be letting this out of the bag just yet but what the hell—Mark and Grant had an ulterior motive for their excursion across America and through its many inspiring small businesses. They were looking to expand their Antiquarian Pickporium retail franchise well beyond their flagship Nashville location. During the season finale, they would offer to purchase a stake in their favorite stops.

In Keith's wildest fantasies, the television exposure brought not riches or fame but merely relief. If he could get out without losing too much money, great. If Mark and Grant put him in the black enough to pay off the mortgage of his exceedingly overvalued Eastborough home, miraculous! No more scary Loan People calling at all hours and intimating threats. No longer would the house lie teetering on the precipice of foreclosure. And if there was enough left over to replenish the coffers of his daughter's college fund, well then, shit, maybe—just maybe—he would once again be able to sleep at night instead of lying awake inventorying his innumerable shortcomings.

For instance: everyone else on his block seemed always to know when the garbage pickup schedule had changed and only he ever dragged the bins to the curb a day early or a day late. Unlike Keith, these were decent, earnest folks who lived their lives without grousing internally about every perceived slight or inequity, who worked hard enough day-to-day that they never had time to ask themselves whether they loved or hated their jobs. They considered their children their greatest achievement and wouldn't hesitate to say as much if asked, and were moved to tears by television commercials for greeting card companies and cell phone plans. They understood the rules of every sport and could name their favorite books, movies, songs, etc., and explain with no small amount of passion why those were their favorites. Meanwhile, after nearly five decades on earth, Keith: had no hobbies or interests or friends; was in debt to such a degree that he worried even *thinking* of the amount he owed would trigger cardiac arrest; had lost track of how long it'd been since he and his wife had touched one another even platonically; had a beautiful grown-up daughter who hated his guts; was haunted by an unending sensation of dread, a feeling like knowing your shoes are untied and you will sooner or later fall flat on your face but you've forgotten how to tie a knot.

For although the "Peddlin' Pair" were due to arrive in just a few days—Monday at three o'clock, to be precise, as he'd written in the e-newsletter encouraging dealers and shoppers to show up in their telegenic best—the assistant producer had stopped returning Keith's calls. Finally, this morning, on his fifth attempt, someone at the production offices answered, an intern who would not tell Keith his name and refused to forward him to anyone important. "You say you're calling from Wichita?" he said as if the city were as remote as Narnia. "Hmm. I don't see it on the schedule, except—hold on a minute." After a wait of nearly ten minutes, he returned. "Yeah. There's a bit of a snag in the plan." The missing girl had made national news, he explained, and Mark and Grant were concerned about coming across as callous. "It wouldn't be a good look for them to go around appraising bottle cap collections with BTK Part Two stalking the streets."

"I'm sure that's an overreaction," Keith said. "The girl'll be found any minute now, camping in the backyard or something. I ran away as a kid once. My parents didn't even notice I was gone."

"We can only hope that things will work out."

"But you're coming, though, right? If not Monday, then another time?"

"Our schedule is tight. We're going to have to get back to you. Let us know what happens with the girl. Mark and Grant are praying for her," the intern said and hung up.

One little girl out of the six hundred thousand who lived here! Who knew what kinds of terrible things were happening in all the cities Mark and Grant toured, but they didn't cancel the whole show because of it. Okay, so a child in peril was unfortunate, but it would be worse to let one tragedy beget another—namely, the tragedy of the Stoller family's financial collapse. Without a Mark-and-Grant buyout, the Heart of America was doomed.

So when Veronica Samples, the midcentury modern maven of Hall Four, had met him at the doors during opening that morning and accosted him with a bouquet of neon flyers, he'd had more important things on his mind—more important to him personally, at least—than Lindy Bobo. "We need to take action before it's too late," she said as he struggled with the door's sticky lock. "Ninety-four percent of missing children are recovered within seventy-two hours. There's no time to waste. Things aren't just going to go back to normal on their own."

It struck him as the key finally clicked into place: She was right. Find Lindy and everything *would* go back to normal—including Mark and Grant's tour schedule. In fact, once he called up the producers and told them that he himself, proprietor of the Heart of America Antique Mall,

Kansas's largest year-round antiques market, had been the one to lead the search effort that found lost Lindy Bobo, there'd be no way they'd turn down such a compelling human-interest piece. Mark and Grant would *have* to reward Wichita's own hero with a stake in their lucrative Antiquarian Pickporium franchise. At once Keith became a willing conscript in Veronica's CHAANT (College Hill AMBER Alert Neighborhood Taskforce) group, offering to devote that afternoon's Dealer Association meeting to rallying volunteers.

He was back in the lounge stapling the very last of the two hundred packets he'd had copied at the nearby FedEx Office when Veronica came in and joined him at the table. "Just in time," he said. "I'm all finished."

"It's wonderful you've taken to the cause with such enthusiasm," Veronica said.

"No problemo." Keith surveyed the neatly stacked papers. Although it was menial, he could not remember the last time he'd felt such pride for a job well done.

Veronica adjusted her cat-eye frames. "It's just that . . ." She removed and unfolded a paper from her purse. "What I gave you before. It was missing a page. Would it be much trouble to ask you to run back to FedEx Office to make enough copies of this?" The page was titled "Abduction Glossary." "I'd do it myself but I'm expecting a really important call from Detective Skinner. My police contact."

"Of course. Anything I can do to help."

"That's such a relief." Veronica gently squeezed his wrist. It had been so long since Keith had been touched in any way by an adult woman that the innocuous gesture gave him an immediate erection. "Then you can remove the staples of the ones you've already done and put this as page four."

"Maybe to save time I could just put it at the bottom. A sort of postscript."

"No, that would be too confusing. Also, you'll have to renumber all of the pages. Actually, you should just scrap these and start over." Veronica stood and collected the completed packets in a bundle in her arms.

"I'll take these to the recycling. It wouldn't hurt to print off some more flyers, either. Oh, and maybe stop at the hardware store and buy some extra flashlights for tonight."

On his way out Keith stopped at the counter to borrow some cash from the till. Today he was in no mood to be humiliated by the pizza-faced FedEx Office employee respectfully informing him that yes, *all* of his credit cards seemed to be declined.

Ellie looked up from her textbook. "*You're* allowed to steal from the register but I'm not?"

"Legitimate business expense. I have to run some errands. Think you can steer the ship while I'm out?"

"No. You probably shouldn't trust me. I might find an antique gun and go on a killing spree."

"Don't joke about that, sweetheart."

"Fine. I'll just use it to blow my own brains out."

"I'll be back before closing. Love you."

"Who cares?"

Something changed between them after the business with the college money. It was Stacey's actions that screwed her, but Keith was the one Ellie regarded as the betrayer. He supposed he was just easier to hate. He recalled wistfully how they had once been such good friends who could stand to be in the same room together and enjoyed family activities like watching TV and making fun of Stacey's sibilant *s* when Stacey wasn't around. Ellie was so smart and such a unique person. Keith was terrified of her. He couldn't remember the last time the two of them really talked. Ellie invariably went straight to her room whenever she came home and only emerged for school and work.

No one had prepared him for how lonely middle age could be. It was why people had families, he supposed; they had to be your friend by default, they couldn't just break up with you or let the relationship fade with an unreturned phone call.

Recently, while snooping through Stacey's personal locker in the mall's back room, Keith had found a small black ledger, the pages filled with a simple chart listing every Heart of America employee and dealer, each with a cryptic caption:

Jimmy Daniels	Rookwood shape 962
Ronald Marsh	blue ovoid Teco
Margaret Byrd	Roseville Aztec shape 2
Ellie	Yagi Kazuo (?)

At first Keith thought it was a living will, though he was perplexed that she would distribute her collection among so many people who wouldn't want it. Not till he reached his own name did Keith crack the code: it was kind of inventory associating—based on head shape or body type or personality, who could say?—the people she knew with pieces from her collection.

Keith	Broken Cookie Jar

That she conceived of human beings this way should not have surprised him. She was herself an empty vessel. And yet, almost twenty years ago, when they first opened the Heart of America, he must have been in love with Stacey, really truly in love. He had to have been. Only that all-powerful delusion could have ever led him to his present ineluctable misery. They'd courted in antique shops, inexpensive dates driving to out-of-the-way historic downtowns, strolling the aisles on Saturday afternoons. Back then Keith didn't have to pretend to enjoy himself. Recently married, Stacey pregnant, they'd just closed on the exceedingly overvalued house in Eastborough, a modest one-story currently on its third mortgage with a finished basement, aboveground pool, and a two-car garage through whose disproportioned doors Keith's Bonneville could never fit, the least impressive in a neighborhood full of mansions and mini-mansions. Of course Stacey had chosen the house, for its proximity to good schools, for its safeness, for any number of reasons Keith hadn't paid attention to at the time, too in love was he to have an opinion of his own. Yes, it was true, and he was amazed to think of it now, that once he really did love Stacey. But what was love, anyway, especially at that impressionable age when Keith was just beginning to learn to be an adult, a lesson he didn't really comprehend until the birth of his daughter, or maybe in truth he'd never comprehended it, seeing as he had failed his daughter, he'd failed as a husband (although his failure was largely Stacey's fault, he thought), he was a loser, a crack-up, a creep. If not for Stacey's dream to open the mall, and the attendant and unpredictably astronomical expenses operating thereof, they would have paid off the house by now and had a chance—a slight one, at least—of a retirement plan better than his current one, i.e., keeping his fingers crossed for either a windfall or an early, painless death. Keith supposed he was more fortunate than many; few could pinpoint the single moment that ruined their life, but he could: the day he and Stacey signed the paperwork on the Heart of America.

3

RONALD

Although Ronald Marsh was an optimist by nature, even he had his un-happinesses. For the good of himself, his friends, and the friends he had yet to make, he kept them inside and private. The last thing he wanted to be thought of was as a lonely old widower.

He always made sure to sign up for walking duties on the first Thursday of every month, when Dealer Association meetings were scheduled. He loved the hustle and bustle of the mall when so many dealers were present, haggling with one another, loading their booths with newly acquired merchandise, comparing sales sheets, and just plain shooting the breeze. If he was said to collect anything other than the postcards arranged by subject matter in sharp-edged rows in the cabinets that lined his booth, it would be the small social exchanges he gathered while walking: reciprocated smiles, hearty hellos, chats about the weather or current events. Each, however brief or seemingly trivial, was an opportunity to partake in human connection. Ronald regarded small talk with uncommon reverence. Even a brief conversation between strangers before going their separate ways was, for its duration, a kind of friendship.

And today of all days Ronald needed to talk. He'd always fancied himself a particularly adept small talker, but what weighed presently on his mind was quite big. Ronald was clumsy and scatterbrained by nature, had a habit of knocking over juice glasses and stumbling into closed doors, leaving his wallet at the checkout stand and driving with the trunk open. With warmth, his dear Melinda, rest her soul, had referred to such incidents as Ronald's "oopsies." Ronald was currently in the midst of an oopsie he had no idea how to fix. To clear his mind, to gain the perspective he needed to shimmy himself out of this pickle, he would embrace routine. He would go about his duties as if it were any ordinary day. He'd figure it all out, he was sure. If he put his faith in himself, things would work out just fine. That he believed.

Yes, indeed. Ronald thrived on conversation. He was his best version of himself when engaged in the verbal patter that punctuated his lively existence. It was just the thing to put him back in his right mind. As a child he'd fantasized about being a TV talk show host, the kind who is so interesting and urbane that all his famous guests usually end up asking *him* the questions. Melinda had once pointed out that his love of postcards was not unrelated to his passion for chitchat, for what was a postcard but one half of a conversation, taken place over days or weeks or months, sometimes across continents or oceans, preserved by enthusiasts like Ronald. Some collectors preferred their pieces unused and like new, but not Ronald. For him the back held as much thrill as the front— what a wonder to eavesdrop on the handwritten voices of the past! Yet there was nothing that could compare to the spontaneous magic of being right in front of your fellow man. The finest breeze-shooters in the business could make an ordinary exchange of hellos look like an athletic feat, and soon enough Ronald would be partaking in a televised bull session of his very own. On Monday Mark and Grant from television's popular Home Channel were coming to film at the mall, and Ronald just knew he would impress them with his preternatural gift of gab.

He exercised it now as he stopped by Jake Backer's booth of sports memorabilia in Hall Two. Leaning against a bundle of game-used baseball bats stored in a tin trash can, he said, "Some game the other night, huh?"

"Oh yeah." Jake tapped the bill of his Kansas City Chiefs cap. "It's why I'm wearing my victory crown."

"Football is a fascinating game," continued Ronald. "May the best team win."

"Yeah," said Jake. "The best team won."

Jake turned his back to Ronald and began flipping through a box of trading cards. Satisfied, Ronald waved goodbye, although Jake couldn't have seen, and continued on. Yes, Ronald thought to himself, it had been a wonderful talk, a very successful talk, a charged sort of dialogue, few words exchanged but emotions running high—sports talk, manly talk. It was lucky Jake hadn't called his bluff. Ronald didn't follow sports and was only guessing that some sort of game had even occurred. But then again, it wasn't luck at all but really a display of Ronald's expert confabulation abilities in action. He was just such a likable and easygoing fellow that others couldn't help but relate to him. Today was already turning into a good one.

The way booth rental at Heart of America worked was you could get fifteen dollars off your rent for each four-hour shift of "walking"—that is, wandering the pathways of the mall while wearing an official Heart of America name badge, helping customers pick out items from the locked cases, carrying their intended purchases to the lobby storage racks for when they were ready to check out, and overall being a friendly representative of the business, as well as watching for shoplifters and tag switchers. Ronald had never witnessed any thievery himself, even though, funnily enough, a number of shoplifters had been captured on the mall's CCTV cameras during his walks. Keith and Stacey had shown him the tapes, gently reprimanded him for his lack of *presentness*—that was the way they put it. The way he would put it, proudly, is that he lacked cynicism. He wasn't out on the antique mall beat with a billy club and a gun in his holster, looking to crack skulls and finger some perps like the cops on prime-time television. He was there to be helpful, and just think how rude he'd come across if he started pointing suspiciously at every customer with bulging pockets or a purse that jingled a little too heavily. Besides, the accused had all seemed like good kids, kind ladies. Probably a few or even most had simply forgotten what they were carrying, had only accidentally walked to their cars and driven off without paying. (Heaven knew it was the sort of thing that could just as easily have happened to Ronald.) When he'd said as much to Keith and Stacey, they didn't get it. Keith kind of sneered and Stacey said she didn't share Ronald's idealism.

But Ronald had no ill feelings toward them. They were fine people and wise business owners, and he sympathized with the tough financial decisions they often had to make, even when they imposed a fifty percent maximum discount per month on booth rental for walking duties. Prior to this, Ronald had walked enough to cover expenses for six months. But nope, he didn't mind at all. He would walk for free if it came down to it, and he happened to be doing that now, as he'd already reached the limit for the month.

He made his way down Bicentennial Boardwalk, calling a jolly hello to Jimmy Daniels, who held the distinction of being Heart of America's most profitable dealer for many months running, with a diverse stock that changed entirely on a week-to-week basis. His picture had been pinned on the bulletin board in the lobby for so long the paper was curled and yellow. If only once Ronald's own picture got to adorn that tinfoil frame. But postcards were not where the money was, and he rarely sold anything more collectible or higher priced than the odds and ends from his ten-for-a-dollar bin.

"Ronald!" Jimmy said, pantomiming a fisherman's cast and reel.

Ronald eagerly took the bait. "Jimmy, my good man," he said. "I hate to tell tales out of school, but with the Home Channel's Mark and Grant show visiting our humble abode next week, I've a mind to—"

"Oh sure, man. Think of the exposure. You and me, buddy, we're gonna clean up," Jimmy said. "And there's no better way to celebrate making money than by spending a little. Have I got the find of the century for you." He moved some 1940s movie posters out of the way— "Hot sellers among aging cineasts and young hipsters alike"—shuffled some metal advertising signs—"Big moneymakers with young husbands, you know, decorating their man caves—I mark these up, like, six times what I pay and I couldn't hold on to them if I tried"—reached under a shelf holding a bundle of silver-and-turquoise Navajo jewelry—"Slightly imperfect, priced to sell"—until finally he found what he was looking for, a nondescript white box. "You're the postcard guy, right?"

"That I am," Ronald said with delight. His reputation preceded him.

"Well." Jimmy held the box out and then pulled it back. "You know what, on second thought, forget it. You don't want this. You're, like, *the* postcard guy. I'm sure this is just common scraps to you."

"I do have over ten thousand unique cards in my personal collection, but please, I'm always interested in anything deltiological."

Jimmy tucked the box under his arm. "Wow, man, wow. Over ten thousand. Wow. Then doubly forget it. This is useless to a master delti— what is it—*deltiologist* like yourself."

"No, no," Ronald said. "I insist. You never know what treasures you'll find in the unlikeliest of places. And it would haunt me personally if I never considered what you're offering."

Jimmy gazed over Ronald's head for a long, deeply quiet moment— quiet aside from oldies tunes that played on the mall's speaker system— and held the box gingerly in his hands like a sacred artifact. "Okay, Ron, okay. You've convinced me. But I'm gonna warn you that I'm a little weird about this." Ronald could barely concentrate on what Jimmy was saying. He couldn't take his eyes off that mysterious box. "This is totally ridiculous of me, I know, and a personal insult to you, but while I can tell you that this box is full of a wide assortment of vintage postcards"— he shook the box, the sound of accumulated paper rectangles so familiar to Ronald that it shuffled eternally in the deepest caverns of his ears—"I can't, for strange, personal reasons—*unreasonable* reasons, I readily admit—let you see the postcards inside."

"You're fooling me," Ronald said.

"I wish I was." Jimmy gave the box another maraca-shake. "I picked these up at a swap meet back in Nebraska. It was more of a gift, really.

My great-uncle—he's not really my uncle but we're so close I call him that—he's a big postcard collector since way back when, used to travel the country—a traveling salesman, vacuum cleaners, right? He'd pick up a few here, a few there. That's how he got started. He even has some of those, um, ah—you're the expert. Tell me, what are some of the rarest kinds of postcards?"

"Well, there are what you might call holy grails and one-of-a-kinds, like the hand-drawn postcard mailed by novelist Theodore Hook to himself with a penny black stamp in 1840, considered by expert delti-ologists to be the very first postcard ever. And there are too many prof-itable niches to name them all. Railway stations from before 1950 are quite valuable, for example. Halloween-themed cards, such as those by the artist Ellen Clapsaddle—"

"Exactly. Old Uncle had gallons of them. Anyway, the reason he gave me this gift—he said that if I was ever in any trouble, I wouldn't need to call him and ask for money. These would see me through. But he was a weird guy, insisted that they only be sold as a set and for the box to be opened only by the buyer. Said the right person would know to purchase them blindly. Like I said, he was a superstitious guy. You know that old-time spiritual bullshit. But I loved him, so I got to honor his request."

"Of course," Ronald said. "I understand. My wife, she recently passed, and—"

"So you want 'em or not? I hate to part with them, but I just don't have the room anymore, you know? If you don't take them, no hard feelings. I've already got an offer from another guy, a *serious* collector. What do you say?"

"Well, it *is* intriguing." Who could fathom what sorts of surprises the box contained?

"I'll do you a favor. Fifty bucks. That's like giving them away. The other guy offered me a hundred, but I like you. They're yours. I feel like they already belong to you."

"Okay." Ronald reached into his billfold and removed a crisp fifty-dollar bill. "I'll take them."

Jimmy clenched the bill in two fingers hesitantly. "Are you sure? I don't wanna mislead you. There's probably some junk in there, but I feel pretty confident that my uncle would leave some diamonds in with the rough."

Ronald nodded so vigorously it made him a little dizzy as Jimmy handed him the box. There was something mystical about it, he felt. He turned it over and over, listening to the satisfying *clomp*. Perhaps he should leave it as is and preserve the mystery. But he couldn't contain his curiosity. He tore open the lid and picked eagerly through the stack.

Something in Ronald's chest evaporated, and the sucking emptiness brought his ribs into his heart like needles. This fabled box contained nothing but countless identical sets of novelty cards in the "Men's Humor" category, photos of obese women in tiny bikinis with the caption "Glad you're not her!" The worst part was that Ronald had seen them all before; these had been his cards once, from his ten-for-a-dollar bins. They'd been included in a large lot he bought off a very elderly gentleman who couldn't be bothered to leave his nursing home to travel to shows anymore. When he'd needed to make room for some new inventory last month, Ronald tossed them in the mall's "free" box. Through some strange series of circumstances, they'd been returned to him.

"So how great are they?" Jimmy asked, grinning, seemingly so overjoyed for Ronald's luck that he was on the verge of laughter.

"Great," Ronald said and tried to smile. He slunk away as Jimmy said that it had been a pleasure doing business with him. Ronald wouldn't complain or ask for a refund. Jimmy had so much stuff coming in and out of his booth, he'd probably confused Ronald's cast-offs with the gift from his uncle. He didn't want to insult the man who was just trying to do him an honest favor. Anyway, if fifty dollars was the price for keeping Jimmy's friendship, that was just fine. A friend was priceless.

He wondered what to do with the cards. It seemed they were attached to him. Melinda had always teased him about the way he treated objects as if they had feelings. It was one of the reasons he had accumulated such a large and impressive collection. What had once been a couple of boxes in the basement had reproduced, multiplied, and spread throughout their home. Melinda couldn't even open the silverware drawer to get a fork without coming across a stack. She lived with him, she'd said, in a house of cards. It had been her idea for him to rent the space in the Heart of America as a way of paring down the collection or at least getting a portion out of the house. And, as always, she was right. He'd made so many friends here that had helped him through his wife's passing, he didn't know what he would have done without them.

His eyes downcast in thought, he nearly collided with Delores Kovacs carrying a case of Barbie dolls to her booth on Victoria Street.

"Pardon me, Delores," he said. Now, she was a real looker—not that Ronald was prone to looking with romantic fervor. Besides that his heart belonged forever to Melinda, she was far too young for him. Based on her collecting interests, Ronald guessed that Delores was in her late thirties or early forties, though it was hard to tell. There was an ageless glow about her, a silver-screen luster. She could be a movie star or model, not a hair or thread out of place, wrinkleless on both garment and skin.

Hugging the case tight to her chest, she looked at him with hard, glassy eyes. "Do you know what's in here? A 1964 swirl-ponytail Barbie in titian." Ronald followed her to her booth, a U-shape of bright pink shelves with teal trim on which was displayed an impressive collection of vintage Barbies. There were curly-banged Barbies in zebra-striped swimsuits; Barbies in high heels and bikinis; Barbies with sleek bubble cuts and deep red lips; blond, brunette, and redhead Barbies; Fashion Queen Barbies with interchangeable wigs, with sheared scalps like dear Melinda during her treatments; ditzy, sun-bronzed Malibu Barbies; thin-waisted, big-eyed Twist 'n Turn Barbies in colorful mod fashions; walking Barbies, talking Barbies, driving Barbies, toenail-painting Barbies; Barbies living the American dream in lush pink estates; Barbies down on their luck and trying to make ends meet, working the drive-through at McDonald's; and not just Barbie but her friends, family, pets, and associates, too: freckle-cheeked Midge; multiple Cousin Francies in varying hair colors and skin tones; Kens with clean-cut features and haggard, overworked ones, too; Alans and Rickys and Caseys and PJs; Barbie's pet dogs, cats, birds, hamsters, monkeys; there were even some off-brand Barbie wannabes mixed in: Barbara and Barb and Bar Bar and Barbé and Blarbie, on whose box Delores had affixed a label that read "Early black knockoff test-marketed in the South VERY RARE."

There were so many dolls that Ronald felt a certain kinship with Delores. Most dealers at the mall had their specific areas of expertise, had arrived at these areas through an initially casual interest that bloomed into an avocation and then maybe even into an obsession. But few had so comprehensive a collection as he and she. Others dabbled, spreading a wider net of interest. They liked different types of things, incongruous categories, pairing clocks and Christmas decorations, Disneyana and nineteenth century medical tools, for example. Not Delores and Ronald. They had honed their interests with laser precision. Yes, he and Delores were two of a kind. In their own way, they lived life to the fullest. Ronald had been attending an annual postcard show called Deltiomania for some years now, and it was true that he was in a sense a deltiomaniac. Collecting was addictive, like any vice, but he'd take his postcards over boozing or smoking.

"You have quite the collection," Ronald said. "Seeing all these dolls together, it really triggers the imagination. Like, for instance, what if Barbie were a real person? Think of the life she's lived, of all she's been through. Working a fast-food job one minute, and the next she's president."

"Barbie *is* a real person." Delores lunged for one of her dolls and began to comb its hair with her fingernails. "More real than a lot of people I know."

Ronald frowned. She must have been kidding, but it was a joke he didn't get. Ronald reassured himself that he was such an easygoing and well-liked fellow that his very presence solicited the kind of joshing of which he was now on the receiving end. One thing that differed greatly from generation to generation, he'd observed, was sense of humor;

modern comedy films and television programs frightened him with their vulgar mean-spiritedness, their dizzying camera movements, and bawdy dialogue; he preferred to watch the old movie channel or rent tapes of the classics at the library. There was no better movie, in his mind, than *Some Like It Hot*. Among Delores's many iterations of Barbie was one modeled on Marilyn Monroe in *The Seven Year Itch*. What an ideal topic of conversation! He racked his mind for an opener. He could simply come out with it and ask if she'd seen it. But that lacked a segue and maybe it came off as insulting if she had in fact seen the movie; of course she'd seen it, why would he even have to ask? No, that wouldn't work at all. He could start by complimenting the doll and, if only it would come to mind just now, he could charm her with some trivia about the film he'd learned from the tweed-jacketed man on the old movie channel's introduction segments. Then, once they got talking about *Some Like It Hot*, they could move on to the complete works of Billy Wilder, and who knew where they'd go from there—the possibilities were endless; pretty soon Stacey would be announcing over the intercom that the mall was closed and the Dealer Association meeting was about to begin and the two of them would be shocked at how much time had passed. It was a perfect plan. The only trouble was he couldn't think of what to say. Ronald, as outgoing as he was, sometimes had the tendency—especially since Melinda was no longer around to share his every thought with—to draw inward and become consumed with his own inner monologue, not realizing how much time had passed upon finally reemerging into what Melinda had called, teasingly, the waking world.

Quick, he told himself, keep the conversation alive. Say anything. You're losing momentum. Finally, Ronald coughed out, "Acute barbiturate poisoning!" recalling something the man on the old movie channel had said about Marilyn's tragic death. He had nothing to follow it, but that didn't matter. Delores either hadn't heard him or was pretending as much. With an unblinking eye, she inspected every last strand of hair on the doll. "I'll be seeing you at the meeting, then."

Unsettled, he sidled down the aisle. His exchange with Delores wasn't as satisfying as his last two, with Jake and Jimmy. Maybe he'd gone about it all wrong, but he couldn't figure how he'd flubbed up. He had really been feeling in tip-top shape and thought his opening bit, about what if Barbie were a real person, had been inspired, a little off-the-wall, maybe, but not off-putting. He was only kidding. He didn't think Delores would act so insulted. The trajectory he'd envisioned for the conversation got disrupted somehow—it was Delores; she was supposed to play along.

Oh well, he thought. Delores is one of God's unique ones, that's all. A little too shy for her own good. Yes, that was it. They can't all be like you, Ronald, old boy, a people person, born to talk, the life of a party no one else yet knew about.

Still, he couldn't shake this awful flustered feeling. If he ran into a customer who needed help, he would gladly assist him or her (unless he or she needed one of the cases opened—Keith and Stacey took away his keys privileges after the string of thefts that occurred under his watch), but he would not attempt another conversation. Now, if someone, anyone, approached *him* for a gab about today's edition of *Mary Worth*, say, or even deltiology, he was ready to return the kindness. Until then, the most anyone would get out of him was a simple hello. Continuing down the hall, he merely waved at Pete Deen, a quiet, chubby fellow who sold comic books and toys of all sorts, Pez dispensers, G.I. Joes, and Looney Tunes memorabilia. Pete glanced up from his hulking comic book price guide and muttered back, "Hey." But it was, Ronald thought, in a very friendly tone. His confidence increasing, he said, "Beautiful day today. Love those fall colors," to the gentleman around the corner who dealt in all kinds of vintage advertising including a treasure trove of material scavenged from the defunct Joyland Amusement Park; "Hidey ho, there, pal," to the wiry fellow in the next booth who focused on political memorabilia. But he didn't stop to chat, no. He didn't want anyone or anything to send him off his groove the way Delores nearly had. He was looking for someone who could always be counted on for a little small talk.

Instinctively, he worked his way to Hall Four, a section of the mall with wider aisles and more open space reserved for dealers of furniture and other large-volume goods. Feeling frisky now, he slowed his walk to an amble. He even began whistling. Whistling! He was becoming, no doubt, what many people affectionately referred to as a *real character*. Look at him, whistling and ambling his way to the floor space maintained by Veronica Samples, who specialized in midcentury modern furniture and who was, in her late twenties, the mall's youngest dealer by a wide margin.

Ronald had had his booth at Heart of America longer than anyone, save for Margaret Byrd, who'd been here since opening day, and it brought him great pleasure to serve as this youngster's mentor. He liked to think of her as a sort of surrogate daughter. Because of what one doctor had called—putting the prognosis from a series of complicated tests into layman's terms—a "biological fumble," he and Melinda had never had kids of their own.

Veronica touted her wares at all the seasonal flea markets and had a horde of loyal customers who followed her from one show to another hoping to snag her latest offerings. As Ronald approached, she was bent over a credenza, making room among piles of flea advertisements for a new flyer. Feeling a little goofy, Ronald crept up behind her and yelled, "Howdy!" Spooked, she yelped and spilled the fluorescent sheets all over the cement floor.

With her gaunt physique and hip clothing, Veronica was the sort of woman Ronald would call a *real classy lady*. "What in the shit are you doing?" she said. Before he could answer, she got on her knees to collect the papers. Ronald would have liked to help, but his old back wasn't what it used to be. Veronica's houndstooth skirt rumpled, and a tiny blue triangle of her undergarment showed beneath her pantyhose. Ronald sobered a little and cut his eyes modestly up at the ceiling. When he brought them back down a moment later he was startled to see that the papers she held in her hand were MISSING posters for Lindy Bobo, the little girl presently locked in a dog kennel in his basement.

Dread struck him like lighting, an electric jolt that entered his forehead, burned through his spine, and shot out of his quivering arms and legs. He'd had Lindy hardly more than a day and already there was, according to the information on the flyer, an entire task force dedicated not only to finding her but to turning any wrongdoers involved in her disappearance over to the authorities.

Veronica stood and smiled professionally. "I'm sorry about that, sir. You caught me off guard and I didn't get much sleep last night, as you can imagine. Before I ask if there's anything in particular you're looking for today, can I take a moment to tell you about our efforts toward the safe retrieval of Lindy Bobo?"

She was acting like she didn't recognize him. Was she only fooling around, or was it her subtle way of casting suspicion? He couldn't seem to move his body. It'd be rude to exit a conversation he'd only just initiated, but he wanted to run. He wanted, also, to confide in his trusted friend. Ronald had never been good at keeping secrets; Melinda could always tell when he had a good hand in gin rummy. He was no wrongdoer. It was all a misunderstanding, an oopsie. "Hello," he said again, Lindy's fluorescent face beaming at him. They stood for a moment in silence. "It's me," Ronald said uncertainly, as if he were trying to convince himself, "Ronald. I sell postcards in Hall Three."

She squinted through her stylish cat-eye frames, followed Ronald's line of sight to the flyers in her hand. "We'll be meeting in College Hill Park to organize a search party every night until little Lindy is found."

Ronald swallowed dryly. "That's just dandy. I'm sure she'll turn up real soon. Safe and sound."

"I share your optimism. I truly do. But we're on a ticking clock." Veronica disclosed some sobering statistics that Ronald couldn't follow for the deafening clatter inside his skull. He grasped only stray phrases: ". . . still a lot we don't know . . . within the first seventy-two hours . . . eighty percent of kidnappings committed by . . . to the harshest extent of the law."

Ronald smiled painfully. Drool glistened in the corners of his lips.

Today was just a day like any other, he reminded himself. "Oh my, I can't imagine something so nasty lurking around in our sleepy little neighborhood."

"Nasty things exist. I would know." Veronica's eyes moistened. Her lip quivered just a little. She composed herself, looked at Ronald as if she couldn't figure out why he was still here.

"Probably she got lost," Ronald offered. "She was at a friend's house and lost track of time. She's safe and sound but afraid to go home and get in trouble. You know what they say about the simplest explanation."

"Your hopefulness is appreciated." Veronica placed a few of the MISSING flyers in his trembling hand. The rest she set on the credenza. "You can leave these in your booth in Hall Three. Dissemination of information is the surest path to Lindy's recovery."

Of course, he was happy to spread the word about Lindy Bobo, Ronald tried to say. He opened his mouth. A barely audible squeak emerged, as if the tiniest white mouse had taken Ronald's throat for its new home. He twirled himself around, nearly tripping on his own foot, and hurried back into Hall Three.

At a trash can outside a restroom, he scanned his surroundings to make sure no one was watching and deposited the flyers under a layer of candy wrappers and soda cans. He wiped his empty hands on his shirt, as if there were blood on them.

He'd had high hopes for his walk when he started, but it had turned into one of those days. *One of those days*, Melinda used to say, *when he was talking louder than anyone but the world wouldn't listen*. He decided to head to the café and have a cup of coffee. There, if he was alone, he could pray to Melinda. She wouldn't talk back, but at least she would listen. Feeling her spirit with him, he would figure out what to do about Lindy.

4

SEYMOUR

It was called the Soul-Array Method, and Lee had forced Seymour to
perform it as they'd unpacked at the house. Oprah-approved and su-
perficially spiritual, it involved touching each possession and asking if it
"initiates a feeling of belonging," whatever that meant. With Seymour,
it was never a solitary object to which he was attached but the mass of
objects that formed the whole, a collection. Each thing, whether the
teddy bear you cuddled in your crib or a Fonzie doll bought on a whim
for a nickel at a garage sale, acquired under singular circumstances, became inextricable from personal history. Mass production didn't a thing
make; experience did. A collection was a record of a life lived, maybe
not well or happily but at least with attention and passion. It was au-
tobiography made tangible. Without his stuff, what did Seymour have
but the following dreadful statistics: forty-four years old, buried in debt,
currently residing in his boyfriend's childhood home in, of all places,
Wichita fucking Kansas.

But he could see the value of, in Soul-Array parlance, "exonerating
one's life-materials" now as he carried down the aisle labeled MEMORY
LANE yet another box filled to the brim with the detritus of a lifetime

of collecting: a set of complete Soupy Sales Society membership kits, a loose seventies-issue Stretch Armstrong, a Mattel Herman Munster talking hand puppet, various Keane-knockoff art prints, a couple generic tiki glasses, ceramic TV lamps, and novelty decks of cards. They were on the fourth carload with at least a couple more to go and their booth was already overflowing, but Seymour would defy physics to fit more of this stuff into their allotted space. It was mostly leftover stock from the short-lived vintage shop in Cambridge, a plentiful reminder of what had driven them to make the cross-country move *here*.

Only Lee's brown eyes and the dark, gel-stiff swoop of his hair showed behind a towering stack of boxes. "Is that the last of it?" he asked.

"Not even close," Seymour said.

Lee pulled the Stretch Armstrong out of the box and held its head daintily between two fingers. "The feel of this thing always grossed me out."

"I think there's something vaguely erotic about it."

"Well, keep it vague," Lee said and disappeared behind the boxes.

Seymour left to go lug some more boxes. He thought Lee laughed less in Kansas. Maybe it was something in the Great Plains air. Maybe it was that he rightfully blamed Seymour for the business going under. The problem had been that he knew how to accrue but not how to curate. He could barely tell what he himself actually liked anymore, let alone any potential customers, so he filled the shop with anything and everything but sold nothing. Lee loved being right, though it seemed to bring him smug satisfaction to never mention it, to act as if Seymour's failure was a burden they quietly shared. Sometimes, as he lay awake in the middle of the night or as they sat watching TV on opposite ends of the sofa, an insight would flash before Seymour's eyes before quickly fading: sooner or later, the accumulated weight of a decades-long relationship that, while not exactly tempestuous was at least periodically gusty, would be too much for either to bear and it would all come tumbling down like a precariously stacked pile of storage boxes.

He wondered if he'd be doing Lee a favor by leaving him preemptively. Lee was loyal to a fault. He couldn't dump Seymour no matter what Seymour did, even to save his own sanity. Any mercy killing would have to be on Seymour's hands. What was stopping him? The timing wasn't ideal. It would have been better if he'd ended it back East, but he'd had to go and let Lee delude him into thinking their relocation would be just fine. The Embarrassment, one of Seymour's favorite bands, had been from Wichita, Lee had argued, and the city had been home to one of the more famous serial killers of recent memory. There had to be an underground coolness to it.

But it hadn't taken long for Seymour to get to know this town, and the reality was one hundred percent surface: an endless backdrop of big box stores, anonymous apartment complexes, blandly familiar restaurant chains, and treeless plains of grass or cement. He missed Boston, with its openly rude citizens, always crowded sidewalks, a vibrant arts culture widely available for him to ignore as he spent yet another night at home listening to records and drinking gin.

The Embarrassment and BTK must have been aberrations, exceptions to prove the rule. Back in their eighties punk days, Lee routinely lied about his hometown, saying he was from Kansas City originally, as if anyone out East knew the difference. And Lee had never, in all their relationship, taken him back for a visit until last year, when Seymour finally met Lee's semi-estranged mother as she lay rigid in a casket. It was just their luck, or the old crone's final act in a life fueled (as Lee told it) by bitterness and passive aggression, that her death and the bequeathal of her home coincided with a historic low in the housing market.

The Heart of America billed itself as "the largest and friendliest antiques market in the Midwest," but no one here seemed all that friendly. In the lobby, the morose teenage clerk cowered behind an upright psychology textbook while an ignored customer wrestled with an unwieldy lamp. On the bulletin board the missing little girl asked

HAVE YOU SEEN ME?, but what really caught Seymour's eyes was the flyer beneath her:

RECORDS RECORDS RECORDS
EX-DJ'S COLLECTION
RARITIES APLENTY
PRICED TO SELL

He was tearing off an information tab when a heavy hand fell on his shoulder and gave a menacing squeeze. Bracing himself for his first Kansan queer-bashing, he turned around to be met by a guy as broad, soft, and tan as a hunk of cornbread. "Hey, brother. Didn't mean to creep up on you," he said. "I'm just so glad to meet ya. About time we pumped some new blood into the Heart. Saw your stuff earlier in Hall Three and I said, 'Who is the fucker with the killer record collection?' Said it to Keith, who told me to look out for you. Name's Jimmy Daniels," he said, sticking out his palm.

Seymour couldn't remember the last time he'd shaken someone's hand. It seemed an archaic gesture, but there was no way Jimmy was doing it ironically. If this was the friendliness the mall flaunted, Seymour could do without it. "Seymour."

"And here you are, admiring my graphic design." Jimmy referred to the flyer, which was adorned with 1950s sock-hop-themed clip art.

"You sell records?"

"I sell whatever comes my way. Last week it was spoons, souvenir spoons—and if you can believe it, I sold out in a day. Old ladies love that shit. This week it happens to be records. Next week it'll be, who knows, presidential locks of hair. I'll be seeing you Saturday at my place?"

"Your place?"

"The Heart of America is only one arm of my overall enterprise. I expect this collection to sell out so fast that it'd be a waste of my valuable time to set up here. Don't worry, I don't have bedbugs or anything."

"Good luck with the sale."

"You're not coming?"

"Tempting, but I'm not really in an acquisitions phase. At my age it's hard to find anything I don't already own. I keep thinking I've snagged a holy grail but then I come home, find its place on the shelf, and there's the copy I bought once upon a time and haven't listened to in forever." Seymour wasn't sure if he was sizing up his competition or sycophantically trying to prove his bona fides to a fellow collector.

"I hear that, man. I guess you tore that tab off as a keepsake, huh? Listen, I'm not into the hard sell. I don't even consider myself a seller. I'm a market in and of itself."

"Very ambitious."

"Yeah, so take this as a favor when I tell you this sale is one not to be missed. You're the record guy. Me, I don't know shit. I ain't hip, I'll tell ya that. You know what I listened to in the car on my way over here? Fucking ABBA."

"They're a great pop band."

"Damn right, but you get that I'm not part of your tribe. The guy I got this collection from—he was my uncle, actually, at least I called him that—he was one of you. Every collector's got a few of those things, those holiest of grails, they've never been able to find. So just for example tell me one of yours."

"Like I said, I've got pretty much everything I've ever wanted." Why was that so depressing to admit? Seymour wondered. His broke eighteen-year-old self could never in his wildest dreams have imagined one day owning the collection he currently had.

"Oh come on. I know guys like you. The collection's never complete."

"Well, off the top of my head, I'm always looking to upgrade some of my favorites. White labels, superior pressings. Wouldn't say no to the Velvets in mono, an OG Big Star—"

"I don't want to lead you on, buddy, but that sounds awful familiar. I could swear the guy I got this collection from said something about mono promos. And you said Big Star? Not familiar with that group myself, but I can see it in my mind, when I was sorting through this lot, that phrase was in there somewhere."

Seymour looked at the tear-off from the flyer. The address was not far from his own. This guy was obviously a liar, but he was also obviously someone who wouldn't know Big Star from Mr. Big, so it wasn't implausible that there might be treasures to uncover. "Thanks for the tip," Seymour said. "I got a lot more stuff to unload."

"Sure, man. I won't keep you." Jimmy removed from his sleeve like a magician a business card. JIMMY DANIELS, it read, PURVEYOR OF ALL THINGS, a simple caricature of a winking Mr. Moneybags alongside contact information including an AOL email address. Seymour stuck it in his shirt pocket along with the tear-off. "Mostly I buy whole estates, but you never know. Give me a call if you're looking to unload anything interesting."

"Will do."

"I'm not kidding about the hair, by the way. I know a guy, if you're interested."

Outside, the smell of exhaust and the unpleasant October humidity came as a relief from the stale air inside, the fluorescent lights and incessant piped-in oldies music not quite headache-inducing but suggestive of headaches. A man Seymour had earlier seen arguing with a customer over an alleged crease in a Beanie Baby tag sat at the picnic table smoking a cigarette with an unblinking, Buster Keaton–esque expression of abject despair. In lieu of *hello* he grunted, or maybe it was more of a whimper.

Is that what life in Wichita did to you? Seymour seemed to be noticing them more and more, sad-dad types standing befuddled on the street or in drugstore aisles patting the back pockets of their khakis to confirm that the inches-thick wallet was still there. Or maybe it wasn't Wichita that did this to them but just ordinary middle age. He shivered, and not from the chill of the air conditioner as he reentered the mall, another box wobbling in his weary arms. He had no kids, of course, but that didn't preclude him from becoming one of them.

Just because he and Lee shared debt didn't mean they had to share a life. All it'd take would be for him to open his mouth and say a few unpleasant words. No waiting for the right moment. No couching his terms in gentle euphemisms. Quick and straightforward was the only way to go. He dropped the box on the floor of their booth and looked Lee right in the face. A frayed red yarn, the vestige of a stuffed toy, stuck in his hair.

And like that, Seymour lost the nerve. What did he have to gain, anyway? He'd break up with Lee and then, what, move back East a newly single man and clutch to his faded youth with a weakening vise grip like his New England crowd, the guys who dressed in decades-old jeans and threadbare band T-shirts, who attended house shows religiously but spent the whole night complaining that the vox were buried? No, thanks.

Seymour plucked the yarn free, held it to his lips like an eyelash, and blew.

Lee drew the tear-off from Jimmy's flyer out of Seymour's shirt pocket. "What do we have here?" he said. "A sale? If I'm not mistaken, our objective is to downsize."

"Right you are, master, but it's something to do. Window-shopping."

"Maybe we need some kind of system. One thing bought for every five things sold."

"Oh god, if you're going to be mathematical about it, forget it." Lee had a system or formula or plan in place for everything. He'd calculated that with Wichita's low cost of living and the rent-free budget of living in the house his mother had left him, it would take about five years to pay off enough of their debt to "get back on track" and renovate the house—a dump with rotten floors, a broken water heater, and a code-violating electrical system that predated the invention of the three-prong plug—into salable condition. Only once they got their "finances in order" would they decide their next move. Seymour worried that their next move would be to *not* move. Lee wasn't treating their current situation as especially temporary, and Seymour knew from experience that it was easier to choose to stick with the misery you knew than to change course and risk ending up even more miserable. After all, their last major life decision—opening the store—hadn't exactly resulted in a bonanza.

Lee touched Seymour's elbow and feigned disgust. "Bony," he said. "Meatless." It was a thing they did, acting grossed out by the mere sight of each other, homing in on the perceived flaws that had haunted them since adolescence. Somehow, it was tender, this arcane language sprung from veteran coupledom.

"I've never seen such a thin man with such a fat face. So many chins," Seymour replied.

"Now, if your brittle bones can handle it without snapping, would you mind running home to get the stuff left in the garage and bringing it here before the meeting?"

"I live to serve," Seymour said.

Lee was insisting on attending the Dealer Association meeting. At a place like Heart, he'd said, dealers make more sales to each other than to anyone else. It wasn't for an hour or so yet, thank god. Enough time to do as told and then find a Heart-adjacent watering hole in which to condition his mind for the tedium to come.

Lee squeezed his wrist. "It's good to be back in business with you."

Seymour wished it were the truth.

5

ELLIE

"Are you even listening to me?" Margaret Byrd said to Ellie, who wasn't listening. On the antique mahogany bank's counter that served as the Heart of America's checkout station Margaret pounded like a gavel a doll resembling the nineties pop-rap icon MC Hammer. "Just wait till your parents hear about your attitude." She brandished the doll. "This, too. Unacceptable."

"Help yourself to a peppermint." Ellie slid a small sterling dish across the counter. "It's supposed to be calming."

Margaret huffed off to wait near the entrance. She looked like a petulant child who'd refused to share and been sentenced to a time-out in the corner. Ronald Marsh, that lonely old widower, ambled by and tipped an invisible hat to her. She ignored him, or tried to. A customer came through the lobby and nodded in his general direction, and at once he straightened the sulk out of his spine and began yammering. The customer smiled politely and tried to walk away but Ronald followed him down Fancy Street. He wouldn't be shaken that easily.

Ellie turned pages in her book, reading not a word. She was trying to blank out her mind so she wouldn't have to think about her miserable life, her mother's betrayal, her father's refusal to cosign on the private student loans she needed to attend a real school far, far from Wichita. "Your future self will thank me," Keith had said. Who cared about the future? In the future, she could be dead. It'd be easier if she *were* dead. If only she'd been lucky enough to have been abducted as a child like that Bobo brat, she could be rotting in a ditch right now instead of having to live at home, sentenced to work the register at Heart whenever she wasn't in classes with all the losers and hicks at the local community college while her few friends enjoyed life at coastal art schools where graduate instructors dealt weed on the side and you could major in astrology. All because Stacey blew her entire college fund on a pottery auction bender, resulting in a collection of such tremendous and esoteric value that it was impossible to find anyone else in the known world with both enough money and the incredible self-delusion to buy it.

She'd distracted herself from her misery for a short while by sleeping with her art history teacher. They were inexorably drawn to each other, he passably attractive though blowhardy, she the only student in his class whose brow wasn't furrowed, caveman-like, in a congenital stupor. He was an attentive but graceless lover offering her an orgasm ratio of one-to-three in his favor. She ended things after he gave her a B-plus on a short-answer exam, claiming she'd imprecisely used the term *art brut*. Complicating matters: for some reason Professor Douchebag had decided he was in love with her, and he'd been declaring his intentions by leaving his "outsider art" Troll figurines almost every day since their breakup in her "student cubby." (Why did they call it that when college was supposed to be for grown-ups?) The latest had been modified to resemble Kim Jong-il. His little dress-up dolls weren't real outsider art. Even she with her B-plus could see that. The Professor was an outsider only in the sense of being too stupid to be allowed to teach at a real school. He wasn't even really a professor, although he made his students call him that. "You're my muse," he'd said the other morning after cornering her in the parking lot. "Fuck off," she'd said.

This place was a graveyard. Ellie's parents had owned it since as long as she could remember and she'd worked here off and on since she was thirteen, but recent years had seen the Heart of America in decline. In some booths, the same merchandise had been sitting out for so long that it literally moldered. Except in Hall One, where the most steadfast and well-to-do dealers had always clustered, walking the aisles brought you past the empty spaces and dust impressions of once-reliable renters gone AWOL. Her parents had recently let go of all the full-time employees, forcing Ellie to fill in for an entire workforce, and cut the store's hours by a third. Ellie did not pay much attention to current events—Wichita was so culturally isolated from the rest of the world, it didn't seem like anything interesting on a national scale would ever penetrate it—but it probably had something to do with what was called the "financial crisis" by the pixie-haired cable news anchor Keith watched nightly and on whom he seemed to have a schoolboy crush. Either that or the customers had awoken one day to the epiphany that they'd been spending their hard-earned money on what was essentially garbage.

She'd never admit it to them, but when her parents used to bring her here as a kid, there'd been a magical quality to it, like the underground caverns in the *My Secret Princess* cartoons, full of hidden treasure and harboring its own population of misfits and eccentrics. But now during the slow hours it felt outright postapocalyptic, abandoned by all but the small cohort of plaintive losers who considered themselves Heart of America regulars. Even during her busy weekend shifts, Ellie's job consisted of watching a steady stream of browsers enter and exit without buying a thing. Mostly they came to loiter, to reminisce about the toys they'd had as kids and the tchotchkes that once rested on their grandparents' credenzas, to compare Heart's prices with the much lower ones glowing on their cell phone screens.

And yet, to hear Keith talk about it, the Heart of America was due not just for a reversal in fortunes but an explosion of wealth. The glut of TV shows about resalable family heirlooms and unexpectedly priceless junkyard oddities had burgeoned the public's interest in the antiques industry (not that that interest had ever manifested in sales), and through a mix of toxically masculine desperation and stupid (very stupid) luck, he had convinced the producers of *Pickin' Fortunes*, a Home Channel reality show about two sexless grifters who traveled the country defrauding old ladies of their priceless heirlooms, to send Mark and Grant to the Heart of America to film a segment for their new special about America's finest antique malls. Once it aired—according to Keith—the Stoller family would be "rolling in the dough" and Ellie wouldn't need any loans to go to whatever East Coast college she desired. For her part, Ellie did not quite follow how embarrassing themselves in front of the national audience of the perennial virgins and elderly shut-ins that comprised the Home Channel demographic would lead to anything other than, well, embarrassment.

Margaret Byrd, one of the plaintive losers, shrieked and came running back to the counter. Out of breath even though she'd crossed a distance of only some thirty feet, she gasped, "Him. He's the one," and pointed at the thin blond man standing in the threshold to Hall One.

Ellie recognized him as one of the mall's newer dealers. "I don't care," she said.

The man met them at the counter, dug his fingers into the candy dish. "Hello," he said to Ellie, then, "Margaret, so nice to see you. How's things at the Memory Lane/Treasure Way intersection? Business booming?" He picked the faded wrapper off a Tootsie Roll with his thumbnail and chewed it like bubble gum, brown dribble coating his teeth.

Margaret held the MC Hammer doll out like a gun. "You . . . you . . ." she stammered. "S-Seymour."

"That's my name." He put his elbows on the counter, one of them pinching Ellie's book closed, and waited with mock patience for Margaret to continue. Ellie tried to tug the book free. He flashed a cartoonish grin. As if she were amused.

He looked like the guy from the B-52s. A walking stereotype, the aging hipster whose every utterance and action was some sort of ironic statement that no one but he understood. Every bit of style, every personality trait and interest, every strand of hair on his precisely manicured head, had been borrowed or copied or stolen and then assembled, Frankenstein-like, into an approximation of a human being. The tongue-in-cheek gay guy—should she be impressed? He was acting, had been doing it so long he couldn't remember that there was a real person buried underneath all those layers of self-aware cliché.

"I found *this* in my sugar bowl. My Riverside Croesus," Margaret said, pointing the plastic feet at Seymour's temple.

"Oh, is that where that ended up? Must've been some party."

"This—this could have damaged a very valuable item. *This*"—she threw her hands up and slammed the doll on the counter—"is a very serious matter. Do you know who I am? I happen to be treasurer of the Heart of America Dealer Association, and more than that I am the mall's senior-most dealer." She gave Ellie a nod of affirmation, then picked the doll up and twisted her knotty fingers around MC Hammer's neck. "You'll be sorry."

Just then Pete Deen appeared out of Hall Two and made a beeline for Margaret. "Excuse me. Excuse me." He tapped her shoulder but she ignored him. "Excuse me," he said again, his potbelly quivering, the Stay Puft Marshmallow Man on his undersized T-shirt stretched and flattened into s'mores-ready form. He stroked MC Hammer's cheek. "Margaret, I never knew. How much? I must have it." He was already reaching for his wallet.

Margaret scowled and shook her head. "This is not the end of this. Your parents will hear about it." She threw the doll at Seymour, its arm catching on his collar, and walked off toward the lounge.

"I've got to have it," Deen said. "How much?"

Seymour licked the edge of his mustache. "I've got the box, too. Excellent condition, including all the accessories."

"The exclusive cassette?" He began to remove bills from his wallet, one by one.

When his hand practically shook under the weight of the cash, Seymour nodded and relinquished the doll. "The box is over in our booth, Hall One, one-forty-six."

Deen walked off mumbling happily to himself.

Seymour spread the cash on the counter like a deck of cards. "You hate your job," he said. It wasn't a question.

"Yeah," Ellie said.

"I remember being young and having a shitty job." He slid her a five-dollar bill. "A tip."

She balled the bill in her hand. She should be insulted—he was condescending to her—but for some reason she wasn't. And she wouldn't turn down the money even if she was insulted. Her parents paid minimum wage for this shit.

Seymour stared at the money crumpled in her open palm. He was thinking maybe he could have charmed her with just a couple ones. His gaze returned to her face. "I love your makeup," he said.

"Thanks," she said flatly. Strangers were always approaching her in random places—at bus stops, in restaurants, on the street, at work—and attempting to start little conversations with her, make pleasant small talk. If she were one of five people on a park bench, an inebriated homeless guy would choose her and only her to serenade with a ballad of expletives. She didn't think of herself as a friendly person, so she couldn't understand why everyone acted so friendly toward her. Stacey once said it was on account of her open face. "What am I," Ellie had said, "a sandwich?" Since then she'd taken to dressing in as off-putting a style as possible—combining, for example, a lime-green polyester sport coat from the Salvation Army with a neon-yellow pleated tennis skirt, zebra tights, and penny loafers—and covering herself with purposefully ugly layers of makeup: uneven streaks of blush across her pale cheeks, goopy dollar-store eye shadow, and dark brown lipstick. Seymour probably thought she was paying homage to some short-lived eighties fashion trend or aping the style of an obscure avant-garde German pop singer who had one hit before dying tragically young, when really she only meant to repel people like him. Cashier was one of the most open-faced jobs there was.

Seymour, one arm akimbo, had a look of expectation. He was waiting for her to pay him back a compliment. She was not very good at being nice or sincere. She tried to do both and the words fell out of her mouth like a brick. "I liked the way you shook down Deen for that shitty doll."

He brought his hand to his chest. "I want you to know that I'm not like the rest of these people. I'm not from here, and I was a young weirdo like you once. I grew up in Maryland and Massachusetts—and not so long ago. Wichita," he said, gagging. "The ugliest word in any language. *Witch-IT-Taw*. There's no way to say it without becoming slack-jawed."

Was she supposed to be impressed he was from the East Coast? Good for him, who cares? "If you hate it here so much, why don't you just leave?"

Seymour's smirk vanished and for a moment he looked panic-stricken. "Why don't you? For me it's temporary. Money to be made in this here Midwest. People see someone like me shilling any old garbage from the Goodwill and all of a sudden it's cute and camp and trendy and worth fifty times what we paid for it. I went to a liberal arts college. I liked to read Marx but in the same way I read poetry. In the real world, it's hard to feel bad about making money, especially if you grew up poor."

Despite herself, Ellie was starting to like him, or if not like, at least sympathize. She now saw the impetus behind his whole shtick and that they had something in common. Her makeup and his kitsch thing were force fields around the world's stupidity. Let people judge them and assume they know who they are. From their vantage point, separated always by at least one layer of irony, they wouldn't have to participate in the everyday social niceties that other people—stupid people, most people—engaged in as a method of deluding themselves into thinking they were good souls, contributors to society with rewarding and fulfilled lives. Nobody ever bought anything to make themselves happy. They bought things to fill, with a Rookwood vase or a Bakelite napkin ring or a complete set of *Star Wars* cards, an aching void in their curio cabinets, closets, hearts. "They call themselves collectors, but they've accumulated so much so mindlessly that whatever they collect doesn't even interest them anymore, if it ever did," she said. "Then they start to sell some of it, but they need to satisfy the compulsion to consume and gather and accrete, so they start buying things with the intent to sell them. Except most of them, they rarely ever turn a profit. So what are they doing with their lives?" It was more than Ellie had said to another human being in weeks, maybe months. She felt fatigued, thirsty.

"I'm calling you my friend now." He squinted at the name tag her parents made her wear. "Ellie."

She picked up her book and covered her face with it. "I'm not friendly," she said.

"Unfriendly people only get along with other unfriendly people."

The bells on the door jingled and Keith entered carrying a file box from FedEx Office in one hand while balancing a box of doughnuts in the other. It was custom for management to provide snacks on Dealer Association meeting days. All that fluffy sugar and fat cushioned the blow of being told you hadn't sold enough to make a profit that month, that you were in fact in the red and owed back-rent on your booth. The way he grunted as he heaved the FedEx Office box onto the counter made Ellie want to stab her eardrums with a ballpoint pen. He flipped the doughnut box open and pointed it at Seymour.

"I'll pass," Seymour said after a glance at the *Manager's Special* sticker.

Keith sat on his stool at the opposite end of the counter and took an indecent bite out of a stale cruller. He nearly choked struggling to swallow it all and had to wash it down by chugging coffee from a crusty old mug featuring the comic strip character Ziggy, a depressive endomorph. Ziggy reminded Ellie of Keith.

She put her book down on the counter and set her head against it. She had always gotten along with him better than with Stacey, but now she wouldn't deign to talk to him or even look his way. Stacey was too distracted to even notice Ellie was icing her out, so she had no choice but to direct her guilt-inducing ire at her father. If she kept it up for a few more months, there was half a hope that she could wear him down enough to agree to sign those loan forms in time for the start of spring semester.

"Ellie," her father said tentatively, in just the tone he'd used—four or five different times—to explain that the best thing for the whole family right now was for her to postpone her going-away plans and stick it out in Wichita. "Are you all right?"

No, she was not all right. Not as long as she was awake and conscious of what her life had become. She recalled a Health Channel special on the sex lives of Siamese twins. In it, sisters who shared half a skull held hands with their respective husbands, lumpy acne-scarred men who glared at the camera with pride and embarrassment while explaining the mechanics of conjoined intercourse. "When it's their turn," one sister said, "I just tune it all out, let my mind enter into a place of nothingness." Ellie lacked such a talent, but fortunately there were substances that could achieve similar ends, and she'd need them to get through this shift without smashing Margaret's precious "Riverside Croesus" to pieces and slitting her own wrist with the shards.

6

DELORES

Delores shook her head at Keith's offer of a doughnut, though she was tempted in particular by the one with pink frosting and teal sprinkles. It matched her outfit perfectly, a pink swoop dress under a teal cardigan and pink plastic poodle earrings, and so it seemed like it belonged to her, pink and teal her favorite color combination since the Christmas morning she'd received the original 1962 DreamHouse, with its glorious teal cardboard exterior and pink-accented furniture inside. The gift tag read *From: Santa* but really it was a hand-me-down, her mother's own from when she was a girl. Delores's friends, whose parents had been able to afford the then-current three-story iteration of the DreamHouse, had teased her, called her outdated version a "white-trash shoebox trailer." She'd cried. But then she and her mother looked up the value of the original DreamHouse in a collector's guide at the public library and Delores had the last laugh, for her mother took care of her things and taught Delores to do the same, so aged though the DreamHouse was, it retained its near-mint condition. And she still had that house today, along with every edition of the DreamHouse ever released, most in duplicates. One of each was just never enough, Delores thought. Ideally, she had to have three: one for her personal collection, one to sell, and—

though it was naughty, foolish even, to take them out of the box—one to play with.

But then again, she could always burn off the calories doing an extra walking shift today. "On second thought," she said, reaching for the doughnut that clearly was meant for her. She had to use one of the Lindy Bobo MISSING flyers from the counter as a napkin.

Keith smiled, revealing a slightly crooked canine tooth. The sight of people's teeth unnerved Delores, as did wrinkles, moles, under-eye bagginess, nose hair, uneven five o'clock shadows, bald spots—human faces and bodies in general, unless they had been maintained to utmost perfection. "I'm glad someone appreciates them," he said. "Post that flyer in your booth when you're done. We need all the help we can get."

She had finished only half before she was overcome with shame. The Barbies had been warning her to watch her figure. She wasn't exactly the Original Teenage Fashion Model™ at her age (though the Barbies assured her that with the right makeup and ensemble, she could easily pass for thirtysomething, and in the right light on a good hair day, maybe even late twentysomething). The Barbies would smell it on her breath, spot the crumbs on her dress. The Barbies knew better than her. She ought to listen to them. "I'm watching my figure," she said and discarded the remaining doughnut half on the counter. It was stale, anyway.

"No need to let it go to waste. We're all friends here." Keith shoved it into his mouth whole. Chewing patiently, he stared at Delores with dark eyes, pink frosting coating his mouth like lipstick. "I'm going to start setting up for the meeting as soon as Ellie gets back from break. Anything else?"

"I need to check my sales for the month." She drummed her painted fingernails on the counter as Keith dragged himself the few feet over to the sales computer. He typed in Delores's name and booth number and then swore for a minute or two as the Antiques SOS program repeatedly crashed.

When he finally got it working, he said, a lilt of surprise in his voice,

"Yes, actually. By god, you did make a profit." He slapped his knee as if giving himself a high five.

Affability did not wear well on Keith, and Delores was not laughing. She combed her hair with her fingers, a nervous tic for which the Barbies frequently scolded her. "Doesn't matter," she said. "Just tell me . . . what sold." This was bad. She wasn't ready for this.

Keith narrowed his eyes at the screen. "Says here it was"—he took a deep breath and read the words as if he were reciting letters off an optometrist's exam chart—"a 1966 A.G. ash-blond rare side-part variant low-color."

Delores bit her lip. Not her, not the side-part. She hadn't been ready to let her go yet. Sure, she had a duplicate in her personal collection at home, an exquisite never-opened new old stock piece she'd picked up at an out-of-business toy distributor's warehouse in Missouri, but though all of her dolls were her favorites, she was particularly attached to her side-parts, Japanese-manufactured variations with a superior brushed-to-the-left hairdo that was difficult for American manufacturers to achieve. The one sold was not in ideal condition—significant facial paint loss, nose and chin nips, pinpricks in the right leg, sold nude without the multistripe swimsuit, turquoise open-toed shoes, and matching ribbon headband—but nevertheless, Delores preferred to be on-site when a sale took place. Most often she preferred to sell and trade with her fellow collectors at the conventions and toy shows. And now without warning she was gone, her ash-blond side-part, without ever having had a chance to say goodbye.

Delores's breath went short, her stomach clenched. With numb hands, she wiped the sweat from her forehead, dabbed at the slickness with her fingers. Panic attacks were unbecoming, unladylike. The Barbies had told her so. She dug into her cardigan pocket and removed a key chain on which no keys were kept but instead a pair of Barbie doll legs (the bendable type) and a single crook-elbowed arm. She put the feet in her mouth, chewed on the sweet soft plastic, running the tip of her tongue along the ridges of the toes. She began to calm but not quickly enough, so she shoved the legs in deeper, chewed on the knees with her molars, the feet nestled not disagreeably in the sensitive gummy areas where her wisdom teeth had been.

"You know, it's always amazed me how much some people are willing to pay just for a little piece of plastic."

Delores was too red-hot with anger to be embarrassed. She pulled the legs out of her mouth, a strand of saliva settling on her chin. "And you're just a piece of flesh!" Delores noted the feeble comb-over on his down-turned head. She was breathing too heavily, too man-like, but she couldn't help it. Saliva dripped off her chin. With a vague sense of defiance she refused to wipe it clean.

"We'll get that check to you at the meeting. Congrats on the sale," Keith said.

Delores pocketed the feet. She couldn't stand for this. It was outrageous, him talking about ash-blond side-part that way. She ought to let him have it. She had never liked Keith, never liked, in fact, much of any man, save for Ken and Alan and Brad and the rest. But then she thought better of it. If ash-blond side-part were here, she'd remind Delores that those sorts of outbursts were unbecoming, that if she (ash-blond side-part) had behaved that way to her boyfriend, Ken never would have asked her to the prom, and then where would she be? Besides, Keith was pretending she was no longer there, evidently exhausted by their exchange, gazing into the open doughnut box trying to decide which to eat next. "Thank you," Delores decided to say, with as much poise as she could muster, and left it at that. The Barbies would be pleased.

When she returned to her booth, a pink oasis of cellophane and plastic among the drab, haphazard booths that surrounded it, Delores was once again dizzied by all the voices coming at her at once.

"These shoes don't match my hair, and my hair doesn't match my earrings, and my earrings . . ."

". . . me out of here. I want to play and . . ."

"Come on, Dolly, chew my feet. Wreck me. I don't wanna be mint condition no more. Pull my hair out. Pluck my head . . ."

". . . fries with that . . ."

". . . the real Barbie. The rest of you phonies can go . . ."

". . . your favorite, right, Dolly? Please, tell me I'm your favorite. You know I . . ."

". . . why I've been born if this is the life I've been burdened with. As Aeschylus wrote . . ."

". . . don't belong here, not a doll, not a doll, not a doll. You all are the crazy ones . . ."

". . . so come on and take it off, Barbies. Maybe all I've got is this bump, but I'm still all man, certainly more than this Blaine fairy over here . . ."

"Who you calling a fairy, you blimey little bugger? I oughta . . ."

"Math class is tough!"

". . . can't see. Where am I? What's happened to me? I remember Christmas, the pine smell of the tree . . ."

". . . itches. This price tag, worse than VD."

". . . so unbecoming, so unladylike . . ."

"Wanna have a pizza party?"

"I love shopping!"

". . . put on a few pounds, well then I'd just about die . . ."

"Dear diary, I did it. I killed . . ."

"Over here, Dolly. Listen to me when I talk to . . ."

"Oh, what a lonely way to start the summertime . . ."

". . . and then she said and I was like but he was like and I was all yeah but and she's like . . ."

". . . can't see . . . think I'm going blind! Who will love me now?"

". . . tips for healthy girls. Step one . . ."

"I'm talking to you, Dolly. Pay attention."

". . . one ever cares about Midge. Midge can't get a date on a Saturday night and meanwhile, Barbie . . . It's always Barbie, Barbie, Barbie . . ."

"Party dresses are fun!"

". . . on fire. Feel like I'm burning up . . ."

"Look at me, Dolly. Over here. Over *here*."

It always took a while for the noise to settle in her mind enough that Delores could concentrate on one at a time. A 1967 "sun-kissed" Twist 'n Turn Barbie, the first with real fabric eyelashes, called to her. She followed her voice, a pitch lower than most, sultry like a lifelong smoker, scanning the rows until she found her, between a Twist 'n Turn PJ and a nearly identical non-twisting 1967 standard. When Delores picked her up, her thumb and forefinger around her svelte waist, Barbie released a girlish sigh of pleasure. Delores understood; it was so nice to be touched once in a while—or at least it would have been. She began to comb Barbie's platinum-blond hair with her fingers.

Barbie scowled, only she couldn't rearrange her static features into a scowl. Rather, she made the sound of scowling. "I hope you've remembered to clean under your fingernails like I've told you, Dolly. Dirt streaks in the hair is not an appropriate look for a young woman like myself."

Delores examined her fingernails. "Of course," she whispered. She had learned as a child not to speak too loudly when talking with Barbie. "They're clean. I used a Q-tip like you taught me."

"Very well," Barbie said, allowing Delores to continue combing. Sharply she added, "Do I smell sweets on your breath?"

Delores reminded herself that Barbie was just looking out for her, the way she had since she was a child. After all, *someone* had to. Delores had no memory of her father, and according to her mother she was better off that way. Her mother worked three jobs and put herself through night school, was rarely home, and couldn't afford a babysitter. But she was never lonely, not with the Barbies around, along with all their boyfriends and little sisters and brothers and girlfriends and pets and cousins, with all their outfits and accessories and vehicles and DreamHouses.

"I had a doughnut. Only half of one," she whispered into Barbie's baleful, unblinking eyes. "And it was small. I'll walk it off. I'll skip dinner."

"I love you, Dolly. That's why you'll do what I say when I say you'll skip dinner *and* breakfast. And extra time on the treadmill tonight."

"Yes, Barbie. Thank you."

"And?"

Delores smiled, patted Barbie's head. "I love you."

"Your roots are starting to show."

Delores was about to ask Barbie what color to dye her hair next when Pete Deen, Dealer Association president and toy collector from booth #2-232, approached, his distinctive waddling walk—*thud-thud*—sending tiny vibrations through the floor that rattled the tiny plastic pieces set neatly upon Delores's shelves. Although he had a soft voice, he was such a loud and heavy-seeming person. His presence, frequently uninvited, carried with it a dank, almost subterranean quality; he was a dim, musty basement personified. He breathed heavily, a perspiration of accomplishment shining over his eyebrows.

"Hi," Pete said and nothing more. Just slow, labored breathing. Everything with him, the slightest gesture or movement or bit of speech, seemed to require an enormous effort. He held in his hand a Ken-sized doll with an African American skin tone, its gold box pinned in his armpit by his elbow. The first black male Barbie doll, Delores noted to herself, was Brad, introduced in 1970, friend of Ken and boyfriend of Christie. But this wasn't Brad. Nor was it Curtis or Steven or Jamal or Alan, all of whom Delores had plenty of, not even Blen, an early knockoff that only reached a select few southern markets before infringement lawsuits took it off the shelf entirely. For a moment Delores was only intrigued, but then unladylike anger coursed through her. Who was *he*, Pete Deen, with all his boys' toys, to have something Delores lacked? He wasn't even a true collector, she thought. A true collector focused on one type of thing and appreciated each piece as an individual, understood it—or *her*, as it were—down to every last detail and variation, could name her entire inventory and describe the condition of each item—or *girl*, as it were—from memory. Pete Deen, on the other hand, was an accumulator, a hoarder. So long as it could conceivably be classified a toy, he'd buy or sell it, whether it was old or new, valuable or worthless, boxed or unboxed, in mint or used condition, whether he really cared about it as a person or not. *Stuff* is what he called his inventory, as in, "You interested in any of my *stuff*?" "I can give you a good deal on that *stuff* over there." "I got some more *stuff* under that *stuff*." Stuff was all it was to him. Delores had once found a Color Magic Barbie sitting in his booth mislabeled as a Color Stylin' Barbie and had disliked him ever since. (She'd liberated the doll, and now she stood, leaning against her wire stand in Delores's second-to-bottom middle shelf, accurately labeled.)

"Hello," Delores said, trying to make out the face that was obscured by Pete's fat thumb, its nail ringed with dirt. She could barely hear her own voice over the chorus of cat-like hissing that surrounded her. She disliked Pete, but the Barbies hated him.

"So . . . um." Pete scratched his neck, searching for something more to say, an excuse to stand around and continue leering. "You heard about that missing girl?"

"We've all heard about it." Delores refused to look at him, gazing instead into Barbie's eyes. "That poor girl."

"Her name's Bobo," Pete said and chuckled. When Delores refused to join in, he explained, "Just like Bobo the Bear. From the Muppets?"

"I don't watch children's programming," Delores said. "It's a tragedy what's happened to that girl."

"It sure is," Pete said. He twirled his doll like a magic wand. Delores got a better look at his square-topped head, but she still didn't recognize him. "Just snagged it from the new guy. You wouldn't believe the deal I got." Delores said nothing, continued to comb Barbie's hair. "You know, I read on the internet that he has non-Hodgkin's lymphoma. When he dies, the values are gonna skyrocket. My contacts in Hollywood tell me they're working on a movie."

"What are you talking about? Contacts in Hollywood?"

"The internet," Pete said. He held up the box, pointed to the name "MC Hammer." He definitely was not part of the Barbie family, even if the doll was of comparable dimensions. "I thought he'd want to meet your Barbies." Pete forced a laugh, phlegmy and joyless, then blurted, without intonation, as if he'd been rehearsing it in his head for too long, "You look nice today, Delores. By the way."

Before Delores could reply, the Barbie in her hand said, "*Psst. Psst!* Dolly, listen up!*" Acting as if she were only scratching an itch, Delores lifted Barbie close to her ear. Barbie whispered, "Be nice to him, just this once."

Barbie had told her to do many strange things before, things that did not make sense until after the fact. But be nice? To Pete? This was confounding. She could scarcely stand to look at him. Those bad teeth, his grease-wet hair, a gut that wasn't just fat but misshapen and lumpy and pale, dark sacks under his eyes that were red and veiny from watching television all night, and that stale smell that always surrounded him. He was the opposite of Ken. The Barbies hated him, Delores knew it, but she knew better than to disobey. "Thank you," she said, her smile plastic enough for Barbie herself.

Pete smiled back, his yellow teeth framed by pale whitish lips and uneven stubble. Delores suppressed a shudder. He straightened his shoulders so that his *Ghostbusters* T-shirt rode up, exposing a slab of pockmarked belly. "So what are you doing Saturday night? I mean, do you have plans or anything?"

At this she unleashed a very unladylike noise—half whine, half bark, all shock, all disgust—expelling a moist lingering doughnut crumb onto the neck seam of Pete's T-shirt. He didn't even notice. Again, Delores lifted Barbie and held her close to her ear. *Be nice to him?* she wanted to say. *To him?* As if answering, Barbie whispered, "Dolly, he has her." Behind her, the other Barbies repeated as a chorus: "He has her! Her! Her! Her!"

Delores imagined the perspiration on her forehead bubbling and sizzling like oil in a skillet, but she did not wipe it away. She realized Pete had stopped talking and it was her turn to say something but she was paralyzed. Pete started up again: "Because I just got a great big package from one of my most reliable contacts. Guy used to work at Mattel in

63

the seventies. Met him at the PlastiCon in Seattle last year. Cost a pretty penny but I think it was worth it. And since you're the expert, I thought you could maybe help me appraise it. Supposed to be some limited runs and old prototypes and stuff in there."

At this the Barbies began a high plaintive keen, interspersed with gasps of, "Her! Her! Her!" One voice—it sounded like the 1961 Number 5 ponytail—rose above the din to proclaim: "This man has Skipper!"

All her life Delores had relied on the Barbies' intuition to build her collection. They shared a link, a sisterly bond, a higher consciousness, as if each was just one piece of a larger psychic whole. With their guidance, again and again Delores found herself in the right place at the right time, making the right deal from the right seller, and she'd come to acquire rarities—among them a freckleless Midge, a 1959 original with purple and gold wrist tag, and a brunette Miss Barbie—with preternatural ease. There was a plaque in her booth that read IF YOU DON'T SEE WHAT YOU'RE LOOKING FOR—ASK. I'VE PROBABLY GOT TWO OF IT IN STORAGE. But there was one whom Delores didn't even have one of, so rare that the collector's guides valued her at "priceless" and illustrated her entry with nothing but a big black question mark. Since learning of her at a convention in the nineties, Delores had spent a lot of time and money, with the Barbies' urging, to track down their long-lost sister. She'd even hired a private investigator to look into rumors that a disgruntled executive assistant at Mattel "liberated" her from the archives before disappearing herself in the late eighties. And now, if Barbie's hunch was true, Skipper was in Delores's grasp: Growing Up Skipper, model #7259-A, a rare prototype of the controversial 1975 Skipper, who, as the box put it, could "grow from a young girl to a teenager in seconds!" By rotating her left arm forward, that is, she grew small breasts. Growing Up Skipper in general—the ordinary model #7259—was much-sought-after but not uncommon; Delores had a dozen of them. What separated the prototype version from the rest, besides its extreme rarity, was the additional ability to menstruate, a twist of the wrist triggering an inner mechanism to drip ice-cold water into the accompanying undergarment accessory, spotting it red. According to legend, this feature was deemed either too expensive to manufacture or distasteful and was dropped before Growing Up Skipper went into full production. Many collectors believed she'd never existed at all, that she was nothing but a rumor or a joke, like Plastic Surgery Magic Barbie or Pride Parade Ken.

The thought was so beautiful and so impossible that at first Delores refused to believe it. In fact, she didn't allow herself to even acknowledge the thought's existence. It rested at the base of her spinal cord and subconsciously she fought to keep it there even as it forced its way up gradually like mercury in a thermometer and reached her conscious mind in a violent burst of realization. Now, faced with the reality that maybe, just maybe, she was in closer grasp of Growing Up Skipper than ever before, Delores didn't feel the excitement she would have expected. Instead, she was almost overcome with regret, as if she never actually wanted to find her and thus to reach the end of her collection. But this was chased by the stronger feeling that she sure as hell didn't want anyone else to have her, especially not Pete Deen.

"You know," Pete was saying, "when Mark and Grant from *Pickin' Fortunes* come to Heart you gotta have your best out, sure, but it helps, if you wanna be on TV as more than just a guy in the background, to have something special to show them. I don't know how much you've seen the show. Mark and Grant have very different tastes. Mark's more into . . ." Pete talked so fast that between sentences he gasped for air, his lips making disgusting fish-puckers. Sometimes he had to pause to use an inhaler he kept tied by a lanyard to the belt loop of his pants, picking up again precisely after the word where he'd left off.

Delores, of course, did not want to listen to it, and at the moment she couldn't care less about *Pickin' Fortunes*. All she wanted was that Skipper. They all—she and the Barbies—wanted that Skipper. She belonged to them, and Delores would do what was necessary to rescue her from Pete's greasy clutches. "Saturday," she said. "I'd love to."

Pete went into a minor, though ecstatic, asthmatic fit. "Great," he coughed, pausing to suck his inhaler. "I'll mix up a batch of my world-famous limoncello. And . . ." He seemed to be grasping at some romantic gesture. He held out the MC Hammer doll, its knuckle brushing Barbie's cheek. (She hissed.) "You can have this, if you want. For your collection."

"I don't collect outside of the Barbie family."

Pete held MC Hammer's head against his nipple as if it were suckling. "Oh," he said. "Okay."

Barbie squirmed in Delores's hand—or she made the sound of squirming. "Dolly, neither of us likes it, but sometimes a woman must do things she doesn't like to get what she wants. Understood?"

Delores shook her head. She didn't understand.

"Be kind," Barbie said. The Barbies on the shelves repeated: "Be kind! Be kind!" Except for one, who said, "Will we ever have enough clothes?"

"Never mind," Delores said. "I'll take it." She presented her palm dutifully, like a scorned child waiting to be whapped with a ruler.

The sound of a question fell out of Pete's mouth but no actual words followed.

"I didn't mean it before. I'd love your gift of the . . . *ehm* . . . MC Hammer." She reached out and plucked it from his loosened grip. It felt warm and slimy. She held it by the parachute fabric around his ankles. Making like she was stretching her arm, she passed MC Hammer's head before her ear for a second but heard nothing.

"Of course he doesn't talk, Dolly. He's just a doll."

Pete set the box on a container of loose accessories that Delores had yet to organize. "I'm already clocked in for walking duties. You could join me if you want."

Delores glanced at the Barbie in her hand. If she were capable of it she would have nodded her assent, Delores could see that in her eyes. "Yes, certainly," she said. The Dealer Association meeting started in a half hour. She could put up with Pete for that long, at least. Resignedly, she returned Barbie to her proper place and cleared space for MC Hammer on the shelf with her other early-nineties males, although he clearly didn't belong. Stepping back and seeing it on her formerly perfectly ordered display cut her breath short. Try as she could to ignore it, her eye was drawn to that sparkling purple jumpsuit, that self-satisfied grin. It would drive Delores mad.

She took the unwanted doll off the shelf and stuck it in her purse. "I will take it home to my personal collection," she said, planning to dispose of it the second Pete took his eyes off her.

7

LEE

Lee was in the Hall Three booth trying to decide whether this Suicide album belonged in the "Electronic Pioneers (~60s/early 70s)" section next to Silver Apples or before Television in the "First Wave Punk—NYC" section—the album came out in '77 but the band played its first shows as early as '71, nearly a half decade removed from punk's watershed year—when the countergirl Ellie emerged Spicoli-style from the restroom in a cloud of pot smoke. She slowed as she passed, staring at him with dilated pupils, her brow a question mark punctuating the *do I know you?* expression on her face.

But no, she didn't know him, not as anything but one of the new dealers. He had a familiar look, that was all—not a famous or handsome or notable one—just familiar. He seemed to fit in anywhere, even when he tried not to. Unfamiliar hands constantly grasped his shoulder. Wives marveled that he looked just like their husbands. At airports, strangers trusted him to watch their bags while they used the bathroom. He was distinct enough to attract attention, but somehow also bland enough to be as quickly forgotten, like a character actor cast in different roles in separate episodes of *Law & Order*.

Anyway, the girl was just stoned. Not as if she'd know him from his photo on the inner sleeve of the debut (and only) album by his punk band Tears in the Birthday Cake, which went out of print and into remainder bins almost immediately upon its limited 1987 release. And she was far too young to recognize him from his brief and embarrassing stint in the Sodashoppe Teens, a long-forgotten group of Bay City Rollers wannabes thrown together by producer Don "Lollipop" Llewellyn in the midseventies, just a bunch of dumb kids who'd responded to an ad in the back of an issue of *Teen World* and didn't look at the contract too closely, whose single "Handclaps in My Heart" scraped the bottom of the Top 100 in a handful of regional markets for a week or two. The band broke up after Llewellyn was arrested on child pornography charges, something related to a casting call for Sodashoppe Teenyboppers that the record company never authorized and the band knew nothing about. Today, they were trivia, only known—if at all—as an inauspicious early vehicle for thenseventeen-year-old bass player Mickey "Street" Gordy, the Teens' sole African American member, whom Robert Christgau once called "the Zelig of the American Avant-Garde," now known for a diverse and critically adored post-Sodashoppe oeuvre that held a towering influence on the post-punk, no wave, indie rock, anti-folk, and nu-funk movements. Meanwhile, no one remembered or cared about Lee's punk era, more than a decade spent in a series of bands that imploded after a handful of shows. Maybe everything would have been different if he'd moved to New York instead of Boston, but he'd wanted to keep his distance from Mickey, who Lee did not think had ever actually known his name.

So no, Lee wanted to say now that Ellie had drifted into his booth and began to finger listlessly through the crate labeled "Resort Lounge & Calypso." You don't know me, nothing to see here. Just a burnedout, bankrupt scenester, pushing sixty (Jesus!), who last night lay in his childhood bedroom pretending to sleep while his boyfriend jerked off to a Shaun Cassidy spread in an old issue of *Tiger Beat*.

Now here came Seymour out of the women's restroom in his own weed haze. "That rich Kansas farmland grows it strong, I guess," he said, offering Ellie a conspiratorial wink.

"I thought you were headed home," Lee said, annoyed that he didn't sound annoyed. There was still so much unpacking to do, and Seymour had always hated pot. He'd been weird since they'd moved—maybe since well before then, but it was especially noticeable lately.

"I'm in no state to drive. Ha, is that a pun? Is it ironic?"

"It's bullshit is what it is," Lee said under his breath. Now he'd have to go get the stuff from the garage himself—he needed it out yesterday, it was psychically oppressing him, all this junk left over from their shop—and risk being late for their first Dealer Association meeting.

Seymour turned to Ellie, who was staring at a Martin Denny album like it held the secrets of the universe. "Don't tell me you'd buy that just for the cover art."

"I own a record player," she said defensively.

"Oh god, I hope not some eighty-dollar Crosley from Urban Outfitters. Shit, I don't think Wichita even has an Urban Outfitters. Anyway, Arthur Lyman's better."

"You buy things for the cover art all the time." Lee was picking a fight, he couldn't help it. "You'll choose a breakfast cereal because the box color matches the kitchen."

"Quisp is really hard to find." Seymour eyed the Suicide record in Lee's hand. "File it with the early electronic."

Lee could think of nothing else to say, so he flipped past Silver Apples in the "Electronic Pioneers" crate and came upon the Sodashoppe Teens album, with its tawdry cover image of four clean-cut youths lying belly-down-feet-up on a purple heart-shaped shag rug and sipping milkshakes through curlicue plastic straws.

"Now, *that* is one I would buy just for the cover. Tambourine player's a real hunk." It was a prank Seymour had been playing for decades, hiding copies in Lee's personal stacks to interfere with his anally hyper-meticulous organization system. Artist and genre dividers were fine for those with small collections, but Lee would never be able to find anything without dividers dedicated to era and movement and sub-movement, e.g., "Xian Acid Folk 1966–69," "Private Press Folk Weirdos," and "Surf Rock Instro (Cosmic)." That was just common sense. ("You might as well front-load with ELP and Steely Dan," Seymour had said when they started to set up in Hall Three. "No one in Wichita could possibly have taste.")

"Ha ha," Lee said humorlessly. He replaced the Teens LP with Suicide and then tossed it into the dollar bin on the floor where it belonged.

"There *is* a Moog on one of those tracks."

Seymour didn't get the appeal of a private joke, of private *anything*. They'd just started doing business at the Heart of America. Lee would prefer to go at least a few weeks before word about his ignoble bubblegum pop past got out. "I think your parents were looking for you, Ellie."

She ignored him. So did Seymour.

"Hey, Ellie. Top five desert island LPs."

"Ugh. That's a lame guys' game." Ellie was still immersed in their booth's exotica department, gazing at cover after cover like they were Magic Eye posters.

"Okay, I'll go first." Seymour licked his lips. "This isn't in order." He took a deep breath. "Pre-ranking, here are the five. *Pet Sounds,* obviously. You gotta have *Pet Sounds. Golden Hits of the Shangri-Las.* Which one goes higher? Well, it's an issue of content versus form. We'll get to that later. Next up—in no particular order—*Mondo Deco* by the Quick. *Jonathan Richman and the Modern Lovers.* And finally, well, we can't forget Lou: *1969 Velvet Underground Live with Lou Reed.*"

"That's six, actually," Lee said. "The *1969 Live with Lou Reed* is a double LP."

"All right, *White Light/White Heat,* if you're going to be pedantic."

"You don't even have that on vinyl," Lee said.

"Sure we do."

"*I* do. I've owned that East Coast pressing since before I knew you."

"Pardon me for assuming we shared a love and a life. I'm only with you for your record collection, you know."

It was almost the truth, and in that moment they both knew it. Seymour changed the subject—or rather, changed interlocutors. "So, Ellie. Top five?"

"I don't wanna," she said. "It's his turn."

"Fine. Lee? Top five?"

"It's a lame guys' game," Lee said.

"So you're a lame guy." Again, it was almost the truth. "I know you too well to be impressed, but you've got a prime opportunity to blow a young and impressionable mind here. Compared to you, my tastes are tragically conventional."

Taste: Nothing mattered more to Seymour. Personality was a superfluous concept. Why get to know someone through conversation or confession or sex when you could just as easily scrutinize the spines on their shelves, the tags on their clothes, the pictures on their walls? If Seymour had a secret online dating profile, it wasn't for flings; it was to indulge his favorite hobby: judgment. (This was normal, right? To feel this way about your partner of twenty-some years? To so casually think things that you know, spoken aloud, would eviscerate him?)

Seymour went on: "All this categorization—art rock, math rock, proto-psych-punk-rock—but how to sum up my beloved's aesthetic, his most special of specialties? Is there even a word for it?"

"Headphones music," Lee murmured.

"Whatever that means," Ellie said.

Lee couldn't stop himself from expounding, even if the sound of his own voice sickened him. "In the milieu of Dead C or Cecil Taylor or early Amon Düül, whatever." For the past few years it had been what he focused his collection on: weird jazz, avant rock 'n' roll, mental asylum music, obscure noise, static dirges, art brut, field recordings of crazed inbred Appalachian folk dances, dance-funk remixes of primal scream therapy, *musique concrete*, monk chants played backward and layered over swirling psychedelic instrumentals, music to take drugs by, music for theorists and professors and aging rock journalists, music to be impressed by more than enjoyed. It was the music Lee was known for—more than the Sodashoppe Teens, more than Tears in the Birthday Cake. That is, this was the music he was known for as a collector, the dealers at the swap meets and conventions always setting aside their "oddball" stuff for him. He bought it all, practically sight unseen, no matter the cost. In a way, he was trying to keep up with Mickey Gordy. As if there were some sort of competition going between the two; Lee's entire career was Mickey's footnote.

In truth, it was music he wasn't sure he actually liked, but at least it demanded attention. The more abrasive, the better. The more obscure, the more worthwhile. Listening to it was edifying, productive. It increased his knowledge even when it didn't speak to his soul. Enjoyment was frivolous. Lee had so many records that he could listen to ten a day and die without having heard them all. Once upon a time his true love had been the two-and-a-half-minute pop song: verse chorus verse bridge chorus chorus fade-out. He had an unparalleled collection of sixties and seventies pop LPs and singles with special attention paid to the lesser-known also-rans of the British Invasion as well as American regional garage rock. But he couldn't bring himself to listen to it anymore. One night a couple years ago, alone in the basement record room of their house in Massachusetts, he got up to select an album and his heart began to pound, he felt like he couldn't breathe, his head spun. He thought, with a little bit of relief, he was dying. But it was just that he couldn't decide. There were too many options, he could only hear one thing at a time, how could he decide where to start? He ended up on the floor playing side A of *The Ventures Play Tel-Star, the Lonely Bull* over and over, trying not to have a panic attack. Since then, he'd taken up his regimen, plotting out in a leather-bound daily planner just what he would listen to each day. He had scheduled his listening sessions into the next year but always wrote in pencil so that he could make last-minute substitutions for intriguing recent acquisitions.

Seymour hooked his arm around him. "The first time I let him take me home, the sex was all right, but what I really wanted was to fiddle with his Sansui 9090."

Lee wondered if there was a phrase in French to describe the way the cheap weed scent made him nostalgic for the time in his life he'd been the most severely depressed.

Ellie had worked her way through the exotica crate and was re-admiring the Denny album that had first captured her attention. "How much?" she asked.

Lee was about to say that a green sticker meant five dollars, but Seymour cut in: "If you're going to stare at it like you're in love with it, just take it."

"Really?" Ellie tucked the record under her arm.

Seymour nodded.

"That was generous," Lee said, pleased to finally muster up some sarcasm. Since returning to his hometown, midwestern pleasantness had slipped onto him like a straitjacket. "We can definitely afford to just give stuff away."

"Who cares?" Seymour said. "It'll play fine but it's in crummy condition. Should've been in the dollar bin, anyway."

"The dollar bin still costs a dollar," Lee said in a melody of passive aggression he was mortified to recognize he'd inherited from his mother. An argument, a fight, or at least a bit of bickering was forthcoming, a welcome reprieve from the silent tension that had followed them from Boston to Wichita, though Lee wished he could reschedule it for a more private venue.

Ellie lingered, perhaps as drawn to histrionics as Seymour, perhaps simply too stoned to tell her feet to beat.

"Here, it's on me." Seymour produced a crumpled dollar bill and dropped it in Lee's shirt pocket. "But we should make it two for a dollar." He grabbed the Sodashoppe Teens album from out of the bin on the floor and presented it to Ellie. "Dealer recommends," he said and hummed a bit of the melody to "Handclaps in My Heart."

"Don't," Lee said.

Seymour pointed at the Teens' feather-banged visages. "You know who that is, don't you?"

Ellie narrowed her near-black eyes.

"Stop, Seymour. Not now." The last time Lee punched Seymour was in the mosh pit of a Hüsker Dü show in 1985; his restraint since then was perhaps overzealous.

"Well, don't you recognize him?"

Ellie shrugged.

"Kids these days"—Seymour gave Lee some side-eye—"need to familiarize themselves with the canon. See this guy right here? That's—"

"Seymour."

"This guy right here is actually—"

"Seymour!"

"Mickey Gordy," Seymour said. "This is where he got his start."

"Never heard of him," Ellie said.

"From the Spastics? Cultkill? Babylon Dreamers?"

Lee grabbed a bunch from the dollar bin and shuffled through until he found a copy of *Taboo*, a classic of easy listening Orientalism, the phony Polynesian birdcalls performed as virtuosically as the vibraphone. "Here." He put it in Ellie's hand, trading it for the Sodashoppe Teens, which he deposited in a box of broken stuff headed for disposal. "Arthur Lyman. Right up your alley."

Ellie studied the volcanic image on the cover for a long moment. "Forget it." She set both it and *Quiet Village* on top of a crate. "I only liked this for its look. The fact that you're trying to get rid of it makes me not want it anymore," she said.

It took Lee a moment to understand she was referring to the record, not Seymour.

8

KEITH

Meetings were held every first Thursday at six o'clock, closing hour, in the mall's café, which was not really a café but just a few plastic picnic tables and chairs set before a row of vending machines. Because Ellie had never returned from break and he'd been forced to balance the register himself, Keith was late. He planned to make it a quick one, for a change, forgo the usual rigmarole, spread the word about CHAANT and send everyone on their way to help find that poor kid.

Coming upon the café, he was surprised to find most of the seats filled. (Attendance had been commensurate with the mall's profit as of late.) Veronica, sitting by herself at a table in back, nodded at him appreciatively when he set down the box of updated information packets he'd paid the exorbitant extra fees to have FedEx Office collate and staple. Though it wasn't saying much, she was happier to see him than his own wife, Stacey, was, presently holding court over the dealers on a high stool in front. "Just a reminder to you all that meetings begin at six o'clock." Her voice was aimed at the assembled dealers, but her eyes were on Keith.

"It's six-oh-three," Keith said.

"Exactly," Stacey said. "We can't afford to lose a minute."

Although she only cared because she wanted to get the meeting over with by the end of an online auction for one of her bowls or pots or pans or etc., she was right, Keith thought sadly. Time moved so fast. Ellie was an adult now, he and Stacey would hit retirement age—though not retirement—before they knew it. There were TV shows he'd missed that he'd never catch up on, DVD box sets sitting on top of the entertainment center unwatched and never-to-be-watched.

He put the box of doughnuts—there were only a few left—on the front table and sat on the stool next to Ellie, who'd been tasked by Stacey with taking minutes. "You were supposed to help close out, sweetheart," he whispered to her. When she ignored him, he attempted a gesture of paternal affection, delicately touching her hair. She hadn't washed it recently and it was tousled and somewhat oily, not unappealingly so, a punk 'do, was what she'd called it in high school. When Keith had tried to compliment her the other day by telling her she was looking very punk, she'd scoffed and he'd felt as if his heart had been punched. Now his hand fell on her shoulder. She whapped his knuckles with the wooden clipboard.

"Now that everyone's accounted for, we can begin," Stacey said. "First order of—"

Margaret Byrd shot out of her seat. "Excuse me, but there's a matter of urgency and it behooves me to dispense with our usual process." The dealers rolled eyes, exchanged looks, murmured among themselves. Margaret made a motion to dispense with the usual process at almost every meeting. "Stacey, I am certain your husband has apprised you of the Hall One problem. Dealer Association bylaws state—"

"Sorry, Margaret, but we'll have to table it until the end of the meeting."

"This is serious! The new dealer—the pair of them—in booth one-dash-one-four-six. Patricia Blatt's booth, I might add."

"Her old booth," Keith said.

"They've been here barely a day and have already demonstrated flagrant disregard for mall policy." She scanned the seats for the offenders, at once pleased and disappointed they were absent.

"Margaret, *please*," Stacey said in the tone of disapprobation she usually reserved for Ellie. "There will be time for comments later." Margaret crossed her arms and sat on the edge of her plastic chair, as if the seat were covered with rain or dirt. "Keith has details to share about Monday's Mark and Grant taping. Keith?"

The dealers turned their attention to Keith. *This* was why they had bothered to show up, for once. They were as invested in appearing on the show as he was. "Yes, well. I've talked on the phone with the TV people, but that's the least of our worries right now. I'm sure you've heard about the tragedy that has struck our fair city. Veronica would like to tell us about what we can do to help."

Veronica shuffled her papers and stood, but no one could hear her over the sudden clamor:

"You talked to them on the phone?"

"Who?"

"Mark and Grant. You talked to Mark and Grant on the phone!"

"Keith, tell them to be quiet."

"Not exactly. What I—"

"I can't believe it! He was just talking to *the* Mark and Grant."

"Okay, but, I have to tell you—"

"Keith was about to give me the floor, and I—"

"I heard they were scouting for cohosts for a spinoff."

"I heard they're going to do a whole episode on us."

"Just tell them to make sure to stop by *my* booth. I got something that Grant's been looking for his whole life."

"Why should they film in *your* booth when my booth—"

Margaret let out an inhumanly loud whistle. The chatter abated. "If you won't let me speak now, at least let Keith get on with it." She held her palms out, as in, *After you.*

"Since you're all so curious, let's get this out of the way and then Veronica has something very important to discuss with us all. Now, about the Mark and Grant show." Certainly he could not tell them the hapless truth. Although he was painfully aware this disposition was what had brought him to his current state, he'd avoided confrontation all his life and wasn't about to change now. His throat thick with doughnut paste, Keith looked around for something to drink, but the coffee carafe was empty and the water cooler all the way across the room. He swallowed a droplet of saliva and inhaled through his nose. "Monday. Monday's the day, folks. It's going off without a hitch," he lied. "Be here bright and early to make your TV debut."

The dealers applauded.

Without taking her eyes off her watch, Stacey said, "We're running behind schedule, so I suggest we proceed." To her, the rising and setting of the sun, the rotation of the earth, the shifting of the tides, were all just ways of measuring the beginnings and ends of the online auctions on which she vaporized the last remaining dewdrops of financial liquidity they had left.

"The next order of business is this." Veronica Samples rose from her seat. Her cat-eye glasses slid down her nose as she waved a bundle of flyers. "The College Hill AMBER Alert Neighborhood Taskforce will be meeting nightly until Lindy Bobo is found. I know many of you live in the area. If you'd like to get involved, see the back of these flyers. And Keith has generously made copies of our information packet and child abduction manual." The dealers' response to her appeal was less than enthusiastic. As she passed the flyers around, most handed the stack to the person next to them without even taking one for themselves.

Keith leapt off his stool. "Come on, people! The Heart of America, all of us here, we're like a big family. And a family is like a community. For what is a community but a family of families? And what does a family do?" The inspiring words that fell out of his mouth were a surprise even to him. "They look out for the most vulnerable among us. So what do you say? I for one will be there every goddamn night until we find that little girl. Who will join me?" Unmoved, the dealers slumped in their chairs, their elbows on the table, twiddling thumbs or picking ears, eyes drooped as if meditating to the hum of the vending machines. "And I'll be giving a thirty percent discount on booth rental to anyone who joins us."

The offer was meant to rouse just a few more helping hands, but soon nearly everyone had taken a flyer and information packet. In his head Keith calculated the lost revenue, arriving at a figure that induced nausea.

"Very generous, Keith," Stacey said. Her tone even, he could not tell if she was angry or indifferent. She got up and left the café, headed toward the lobby where a computer and eBay awaited.

Veronica bowed her head in thanks. "That's the spirit. I just know that with your help, we'll find little Lindy. And if it matters, I'm told the family is offering a ten-thousand-dollar reward for information leading to her location or safe return."

Ten grand seemed a bit lowball, in Keith's estimation. Surely a child's life was worth at least twenty-five, fifty thousand. In the context of his own debt, a surplus ten thousand made as much difference as a lucky penny.

It was enough to motivate Ellie, however. She took an information packet and muttered, "Is it the same amount? Dead or alive?"

Veronica reddened. "As someone who has experienced firsthand—" She looked sadly down at Lindy Bobo's neon smiling face and became quiet. "When I was a little girl just like Lindy, my mother's boyfriend, he . . ." She buried her face in the flyers and wept quietly.

Nobody said anything as the sound of Veronica's weeping filled the room. Someone coughed. Finally, Veronica wiped her eyes and sat down. Ronald Marsh leaned over from his seat and patted her back. She flinched. He smiled and withdrew his hand.

"This is touching, and we all feel badly for that girl, but I believe it's *my* turn to speak." Margaret rose and looked over her shoulder conspiratorially. "Regarding the two *new* gentlemen. Seymour something-or-other. And his companion. You all should see it. This doll they're selling, this objectionable celebrity figure, and other things, too. There's plenty of room in the other halls for their chicanery. Hall One is special. And seeing as they have not even bothered to show up to their first association meeting, I make a motion to—" Margaret froze.

Two latecomers had turned up and were searching the café for open chairs.

"It's them!" Margaret said. "Showing up late. Not following the rules. This is exactly what I'm talking about."

Lee looked like he had stumbled into the middle of a stranger's party. "Sorry?"

"You will be," Margaret said and turned to Keith. "These men, Lee and Seymour"—she pointed at them with a crooked finger but mixed them up—"they tampered with *my* merchandise."

"Margaret," Keith said, "I'm sure it was just—"

"It was an attack on me personally."

"Margaret, dear, have we offended you?" Seymour's face was a mask of ironic mirth. Lee whispered something in his partner's ear, but Seymour just shrugged.

"You've offended the Heart of America," she said. "You could have damaged something. His—its—sharp edges against my fragile glass. This will not stand."

Lee's smile was as stiff as a mannequin's. "I think there's been a misunderstanding."

"Oh, I understand. And they know what they did. They know exactly what they did. In my booth, in my beautiful, fragile Riverside sugar bowl, they threw the offending item. It could have chipped. Who knows how such delicates react to that cheap plastic? Do they have any idea of its worth? Do they care?"

Keith supposed that as Heart of America co-owner it was his duty to defuse the situation, but just as he was going to try, Ronald stood and gave it his own best shot. "Now, now, fellows. There's no need for hurt feelings here. I'd hate to see this turn into a—" Someone threw a Nilla wafer and hit him square in the temple. Ronald smiled in good humor and sat down.

"Let's settle this now so we can all go back to being friends," Seymour said. "Just so we're clear, what do you mean by 'offending item'?"

Margaret held her handkerchief as if blocking out a sour smell. "You know as well as I. A toy manufactured long after December thirty-first, 1989. Some sort of doll."

"*What* sort of doll?"

"Not a baby doll but like Barbie and Ken." At this Delores Kovacs's head perked up. "An African American man. In a purple outfit, I think."

"Hmm. That could describe any number of dolls. Do you happen to know, Margaret, dear, what this certain doll was called? Does he have a name?"

"You know what I'm talking about."

"I surely don't."

"Very well. If you won't admit it. We all know it was . . ." Margaret closed her eyes. Keith wondered if she was about to faint. Would it raise their insurance rates if she croaked right on the spot? Finally, she regained composure and cleared her throat. She was about to utter the cursed word when—

"MC Hammer," Lee blurted as if confessing to a horrendous crime.

"An honest mistake," Seymour said. "One of us must have misplaced it in all the hubbub of moving in."

Finding his opening, Keith rose from his stool. "That settles that." The sooner this was over with, the sooner he could get out there and find that missing girl. "Meeting adjourned?"

"No," Margaret said. "That settles nothing. Keith, this is *your* mall and your problem. What are you going to do about these two?"

Seymour let out a long, exaggerated sigh. "Please, Margaret, you're only giving us a hard time because we're—"

"I assure you," Margaret said with an unexpected hint of apology. "This is not at all about that, but rather—"

"About what?" Seymour leaned in. "What do you mean?"

"Just because you're . . . it has nothing to do with . . ."

"With what?"

Margaret hummed nervously as she considered her words. "What you are." After a moment, she shrugged—an unnaturally casual gesture for her, it looked more like a spasm—and said, "Homosexuals." She cringed as if forced to utter an awful slur.

The dealers were getting restless, whispering among themselves and eyeing the exit. Throats were cleared, arms stretched, noses wiped, seats shifted, fingers drummed. The vending machines buzzed. Ronald stared forlornly at a Nilla morsel on his thumb as if it were a cancerous growth he had just noticed. Delores gnawed absently on the Barbie parts she kept on a key chain. Pete, mirroring her, gnawed on his inhaler's mouthpiece.

"New," Seymour said. "I was going to say you're just giving us a hard time because we're new."

"Well, I—" Margaret's old gray face was even grayer than it had been moments before. She flattened the wrinkle in her skirt and sat down. Quietly she said, "Yes, I suppose the meeting's adjourned."

As if on cue, the fluorescent lights overhead went out row by row, a wave of darkness surging toward the café. Stacey must have gotten tired of waiting and was initiating closing procedures.

"Another productive meeting, folks," Keith said bitterly. "I'll beg you to put your best faces forward for Mark and Grant on Monday. Until then, I hope to see you in the Lindy Bobo search party. I know I'll be there. Right, Veronica?"

But Veronica had already left, and soon the rest of the dealers—all but one—followed her through the darkness to the glowing exit that led to the lot behind the building.

9

RONALD

With the lights out, obscure sounds, unheard above daytime's fluorescent buzz, echoed through the halls: the squeaks, groans, and sighs of old screws loosening at a rate of micromillimeters per month, of wooden joints wearing, of plastic drying into brittleness, of paper yellowing, of tin and glass and brass and celluloid and silver and ceramic and cloth and stone all just being, the sound of settling, the sound of existence and therefore the sound of decay. And in the middle of it all was Ronald Marsh, who had, sometime during the meeting, around when the Nilla wafer hit his head, retreated inward to ponder his pickle: the matter of the child locked in a dog kennel in his basement. No, really, it couldn't be as bad as that sounded. It wasn't. But how to make that clear to the authorities, to the little girl's parents? She *liked* the kennel. It was a misunderstanding.

He recalled, as if through the haze of years and not minutes, the meeting's end. The dealers streamed past him to the exit, not one offering him so much as a goodbye. Pete Deen held Delores Kovacs by the hand (or, actually, clutched her extended pinkie finger) as he bade her adieu. It was so charming to see love bloom like this, especially between those two strange birds. Maybe they weren't the only birds pairing off, what with the way Jimmy Daniels cupped his hand over Margaret's shoulder and whispered in her ear; and of course let's not forget Keith and Stacey, the very model of a loving marriage long settled into, comfortable, comforting, but far from passionless. Ronald was happy for them but sad for himself, too. He was lonely. He missed Melinda. He missed the dramaless routine of his old life, when his most pressing concern was catching up on back issues of *Deltiology Quarterly*, not facing a minimum of twenty years in prison according to the figure Veronica Samples had cited.

When he found her in the yard and took her in he was only acting out of concern. He'd been in his office researching a batch of unsigned portraiture postcards for a pen pal to confirm that they were indeed, as he suspected, the work of Maud Humphrey. The small text of the guidebooks really did a number on these old eyes of his and it was when he went to the kitchen to get his reading glasses that he saw through the window a little body facedown amid the fallen leaves on the lawn. That gave him quite a startle! He rushed outside and scooped the poor thing up. The girl was breathing, her eyes open, not crying, but she wouldn't respond to anything Ronald said, so he carried her inside and down to the basement where Melinda kept the first-aid kit.

He set her on the couch and looked her over. She appeared uninjured, merely dirty from the lawn. "My name is Ronald," he said. "And who are you?"

But the girl just bit her lip and shook her head, a slight, mischievous smile on her face.

"Well, at least you're okay. Don't you want to talk to me?"

She shook her head again.

"Hmm. Now, this is a pickle. My Melinda used to babysit for the Willefords next door before they moved away. That little girl, I think her name was Dorothy, like in *Wizard of Oz*. She would never talk to me, either. She had the oddest habit. She'd chew up each chicken nugget till it was paste and spit it back onto the plate. One by one, just like that. Then she'd mix up all the chewed-up stuff and fork it down. What do you think of that?"

The girl shrugged. This was one of the toughest confabulation partners Ronald had ever faced, but luckily he had an ace up his sleeve. "How about we move this chat over to the studio?"

The studio was part of a project Ronald had begun a few weeks before Melinda's passing but had abandoned in his grief. He so relished the conversations he had about deltiology, with experts and novices alike, he'd decided it just wasn't fair to keep them all to himself. So he'd put together this little studio in a spare corner of the basement consisting of a video camera on a tripod pointed at a desk with a microphone just like the ones on TV and a couple of chairs, with bright lights hanging from the exposed pipes overhead. It was designed to be portable, the better to take along with him to conventions with the aim of conscripting his fellow dealers to appear on the show, which he'd named *Keeping Posted with Ronald Marsh*, and had planned to premiere on Wichita public access. However, he'd only ever managed to film one segment, in which he showed off his most favorite and rarest pieces to Melinda and spun humorous anecdotes about the trials and tribulations of acquiring such an impressive collection. It brought Ronald solace to know that the mellifluous sound of Melinda's laugh was forever preserved on tape.

Ronald set the girl in the chair beside the desk and took the host's seat. Upon seeing the camera's lens trained on her, she transformed in a way that only made sense the next day when he found out about her experience on the pageant circuit. She wiped the dirt from her cheeks and arms, tamed back her hair with her hands, and smiled unnaturally.

"That's the spirit," Ronald said. "Pretend we're on TV. My guest here tonight is, well, you might know her as a little girl from right here in the neighborhood. What did you say your name was?"

She leaned into the microphone. "Lindy."

"Lindy, I bet you've got a real kooky story about how you ended up in my yard. Why don't you tell me where you came from?"

Lindy licked her lips and grimaced at the camera. She looked Ronald up and down. After a moment, she finally spoke. "I—I wanted the Sanrio bedspread. Keroppi's my favorite."

Ronald scratched his head, pantomimed a shrug at the camera. "Are you talking English or are you talking rubbish?"

"Mom wouldn't buy it for me."

"I see." Ronald was not usually great with kids, but the studio atmosphere was just the ticket. After prodding Lindy through a professional-quality (if Ronald said so himself) series of Q&As, he finally pieced the story together.

On a shopping trip to Target, her mother had refused to buy her something she wanted, a bedding set featuring a cartoon frog named Keroppi. She loved Keroppi and his Sanrio friends so much she could not live without it. To teach her mother a lesson, she had run away. Her plan was to find her way back to Target herself and refuse to leave until someone there gave her the bedspread. But she'd quickly gotten lost on the way. And then she tripped on a branch and fell and—and that was when Ronald had found her.

"Aww, I'm so sorry to hear that, dear. I'm sure if your mother is watching our show tonight she's sorry, too. Now tell us how we can reach her?"

Lindy shook her head. She would not tell Ronald her last name or address, and she would not return home until she got the bedspread.

"Are you hungry?"

Lindy nodded.

"Will you tell me where your mommy and daddy live after we eat? No use in worrying them over a silly little thing like a bedspread."

Lindy shrugged.

He carried her back to the couch and turned on the TV, then went upstairs to cook a frozen dinner. When he brought it to her she was already asleep, curled up with her knees against her chin, breathing peacefully. He sat on the arm of the sofa picking at the gelatinous cheese casserole, wondering what to do, if he should wake her, what Melinda would say if she were here, until he, too, fell asleep.

He awoke the next morning covered in mottled cheese. The TV set was still on and the news reported the suspected abduction of pageant princess Lindy Bobo. An oopsie, he'd thought. Just a simple misunderstanding. He stood over Lindy, still asleep, wrapped in an afghan like a comfy kitten, the phone in hand, about to dial the police and explain away the whole silly thing. But he couldn't do it. Talking on the phone always made him nervous. He much preferred to look a person in the eye. Nonverbal communication was ninety percent of conversation— he'd read that somewhere. It would be much better to go to the police station himself. But he couldn't just take Lindy with him. Things might look a little funny that way. Ronald did not want to get in trouble. The station was just about a mile down Douglas Avenue. Lindy was fast asleep and looked like she wouldn't awake for hours yet. She'd be just fine if he stepped out for a short while.

In the car, it hit him. Hoo boy, was he in trouble. On the radio, the police announced they would "aggressively pursue" everyone who may have come into contact with Lindy in the past twenty-four hours. Ronald did not like the sound of that. He wished Melinda were here. She'd know what to do. What Ronald had done was turn the car around. What Ronald had done was go to Target and get that girl the bedspread she wanted, stopping at the McDonald's drive-through on the way.

When he got home, she was still asleep, thank goodness. He roused her, fed her, and gifted her the bedspread. Her eyes practically *glowed* when she saw it, it was just darling. Hugging the bedspread, she said, "Okay, you can take me home now."

"I'm sorry, dear, not just yet," he said gently and led her into the kennel he'd stuffed fat with pillows and blankets—it was like a playhouse, a fort, really—and locked her in.

Sure, it sounded bad when he imagined himself explaining it to an authority, but it was for her own good. He couldn't have Lindy running about while he was gone and risk getting hurt. In due time Ronald would figure things out, Lindy could go home without getting Ronald into trouble, and everything would go back to normal.

But he'd had Lindy for all night and all day now, and things just got less and less normal, and meanwhile Ronald got more and more pickled. There was no longer any use in pretending today was a day like any other, in acting as if Melinda would descend from the heavens and tell him exactly what he ought to do to un-oopsie his oopsie. He'd left Lindy alone too long already, and he had to get home ASAP.

On his way out, he caught sight of the doll, its arms hooked to the lip of the trash receptacle. It was the one Margaret had been carrying around earlier that day. Ronald thought he'd heard someone call him BC Hammer; perhaps he was a caveman character like Alley Oop. How'd it end up here? Margaret probably had set it down at some point and forgotten. A customer who didn't know better—or one, Ronald hesitated to think, who was just causing trouble for trouble's sake—discarded it instead of taking it to the lost-and-found. The funny thing was, this doll didn't seem to be in line with her usual interests, but perhaps she'd decided to branch out. Perhaps Delores had had an influence on her. With no small bit of envy, Ronald wished he could turn one of his fellow dealers on to the thrills and wonders of deltiology, though Lord and Melinda knew he'd tried plenty. Well, lucky for Margaret, Ronald would return it to her booth. And then—lickety-split—he'd rush home to Lindy and sort out this whole silly mess, even if it meant a tricky conversation with her parents. After all, he had nothing to worry about. He had only been acting out of concern. They'd see he'd only meant the best for the girl. Anyone at the Heart of America could vouch for him: Ronald was about the nicest guy anyone could ever meet.

He was also, he discovered when he pushed futilely against the unyielding exit door, locked in.

THE MOTIONS OF ATTAINMENT

10

MARGARET

There are dealers and there are hobbyists, Margaret Byrd thought as she unlocked the Heart of America's back door, a compote bowl tucked under her arm. Although Keith and Stacey or the girl were supposed to arrive one hour before opening, they rarely appeared even ten minutes before ten, and the girl especially was always late. Technically, Margaret was not supposed to have a key. She'd borrowed the spare set Keith kept with the half dollars and Canadian quarters in the cash register some time ago and had not found the occasion to return it. There are hobbyists and there are dabblers, she thought as she shouldered the door open and held the bowl now steady in both hands. There are dabblers and there are the ignorant. So why should she feel anything but pleased that she had, earlier this morning, having arrived at the rummage sale one hour prior to the start time posted in the *Eagle* classified, purchased from right out of the hand of the woman before she could set it on the rickety card table, for only four dollars, this Millersburg radium-green boutonniere compote bowl, which she now planned to sell in one of her own booths at a seventy-dollar markup? It wasn't Margaret's fault the woman hadn't the faintest clue of its actual value, and for all Margaret knew, she may have rescued it after an eternity packed away in a cardboard box marked "Grandma's things" abandoned in a cobwebbed corner of a dank basement crawl space, may have circumvented its sale to an unscrupulous teenager with intent to use it as an ashtray for his marijuana joints or a dippy housewife who'd fill it with Rolos. It was only fair that Margaret had gotten such a bargain.

In fact, the purchase had been positively moral. Patricia shared her distaste for *Pickin' Fortunes*, which Margaret had found enjoyable until a season-ending special, *Picking 101*, in which Mark and Grant lectured the viewer on what they so superciliously referred to as their "commandments of picking." "Thou shalt not fleece without due restraint," they'd said. Margaret did not consider herself a ruthless person, and certainly Patricia hadn't thought—*didn't think*—of her that way, either, but after the episode's end the two friends had a long, enchanting discussion about the ethics of dealing, reaching the conclusion that it simply wasn't right for anyone who'd spent years developing and honing a particular expertise to pay a single penny more than a given transaction required, that it was in everyone's best interest—and in the best interests of the industry toward whose preservation Margaret and Patricia worked so diligently—for bargains to be taken the utmost advantage of, even if that necessitated an imbalanced exchange. There was no such thing as a "rip-off," Margaret thought, only errors in judgment that occurred when less-than-knowledgeable buyers and sellers willfully, through impulse or ignorance, allowed themselves to be misled.

And who was to say there was anything wrong with being ruthless, necessarily—not that Margaret was at all ruthless. If anyone was ruthless it was that Jimmy Daniels, quite the flea market racketeer, the Heart of America's most reliably in-the-black dealer. Margaret had once—by pure casual accident, mind you, a mere absentminded glance—peeked on the screen of Keith's digital ledger and was scandalized by Jimmy's tremendous profits. One month was more than Margaret had made some years! She wasn't envious, of course. And she never particularly liked or disliked Jimmy one way or the other. Margaret was a specialist, her booths curated exhibits even more than displays of merchandise (she made an effort to place the price tags inconspicuously on the bottom of each piece so as not to spoil the overall effect), whereas Jimmy was not just a dealer but a salesman. His large booth on Bicentennial Boardwalk changed stock so frequently that it was hardly identifiable week to week: in would come an assortment of, say, vintage Wagenfeld table lamps bought at an estate auction (Jimmy claimed) of a foreclosed movie theater in Arkansas one day, only to be gone and replaced by, say, a deceased relative's (Jimmy claimed) snuff box collection the next time Margaret walked by.

So when Jimmy, after yesterday's humiliating Dealer Association meeting, stopped Margaret with a gentle tap on the shoulder, she was less than delighted.

"We should talk," he'd said, flashing unnaturally white teeth as he followed her out the door.

"Certainly not," Margaret said. Her hands had involuntarily balled into fists during the exchange with Seymour and she couldn't seem to unclench them to reach into her purse for her car keys. If only Patricia were here, she thought sadly. Her brain felt warm. Jimmy kept grinning like he hadn't heard her. Dealers continued to file out the door. Seymour and Lee, Margaret refused to acknowledge, were leaning against the side of their car, arguing about something. Their type, according to many true crime specials Margaret had accidentally watched on television, was given to tempestuous passions; maybe they'd murder each other that night. The thought calmed her. Her hands tingled and loosened.

"You'll like this," Jimmy said. "We should talk."

Margaret wondered if he had some glass he wanted to offer her a first look at. They'd done some dealing in the past, but although Jimmy played dumb, in truth he was a persnickety negotiator, hardly worth the hassle—unless he had stumbled onto something truly impressive. "Well, what is it?" she said in a tone she'd perfected at flea markets and estate sales over the years to exhibit absolutely no hint of interest. You could set a Matt Johnson lily pad pitcher in front of her, price it at twenty-five cents, and she wouldn't flinch, would talk you down to ten cents no-sales-tax.

"Come to my van." Jimmy looked over Margaret's shoulder at some lingering dealers. He went and stood by his beat-up brown Ford Transit with a vanity plate (JIMMY) and whistled like a cartoon character trying to play casual.

Margaret hesitated. Bad things, violent things, happened in strange men's vans. Jimmy was no stranger—she'd known him as long as he'd been at the Heart of America—but he was a *strange* man. He had always struck her as less than scrupulous; when he had promised to provide refreshments for the Fourth of July sales event, he'd brought a 128-count box of Moon Pies set to expire just two days hence. (They'd tasted fine, but still.) But what if whatever he was trying to sell her was actually worthwhile?

Jimmy unlocked the double back doors. "I don't want anyone to overhear," he said and climbed in. He held out a large, moist hand for Margaret. "You'll like this. It's about . . . well, it's about ownership."

The last word rang like a bell in her brain, compelling her, against better judgment, to accept Jimmy's palm and lift herself, careful not to catch her long skirt on the door latch. Unease struck upon the square echo of the closing doors. The van was distasteful in its enormity, the venetian blinds in the window crooked, the scent of tobacco dizzying, cardboard boxes and plastic tubs stacked haphazardly around them. She sat uncomfortably, her legs crossed in as ladylike a manner as she could manage, on an overturned milk crate, the ridges pinching the skin of her thighs. She kept one hand in her purse clutching a can of Mace (actually a deodorizer spray for shoes, but it was better than nothing).

Jimmy luxuriated in the tension of the moment. Finally, like a child tattling on a classmate, he said, "The mall is done for. By this time next year—kaput."

There'd been murmurings about the Heart of America's foreclosure or filing for bankruptcy or otherwise going out of business for so long now that Margaret had learned not to pay heed to unfounded speculation. "Oh, I'm sure," she said without meaning to say anything at all.

"It's for real this time." He told her about how his check had bounced a few months ago, how Keith had blamed it on a banking error, about how when his latest check was late Keith admitted that the books were telling a story that would lead gradually but surely to the mall's closing, that neither he nor Stacey wanted to do this anymore. (They had been drinking at the time, in the mall's back room, from a bottle of eggnog left over from last year's holiday event.) They were counting on the exposure from the Home Channel show to drum up public interest, but basically it was a lost cause. "In Keith's words: 'The Heart of America is fucked.'"

"Pardon your language."

"I'm just telling it like he told it to me."

It hurt that Margaret was hearing this now, and from Jimmy, of all people. It was just the thing she would ordinarily have shared with Patricia, in Patricia's car, with the air-conditioning going full-blast ("I'm hot-blooded," Patricia once said), spreading the potpourri scents of her air freshener.

"They're barely making enough to keep the lights on. If it weren't for me . . ." Jimmy leaned over the passenger-side seat and reached into the glove compartment. He removed and tore open a pouch of bubble gum candy, shoved a fistful of purple shreds into his mouth. The scent of artificial grape flavor was so pungent the air turned sticky. "Big League Chew," Jimmy said. "Heard the manufacturer was gonna discontinue it so I bought a few gross." He offered the pouch to Margaret. She shook her head *no* with as little movement as possible—a millimeter to the left, a millimeter to the right—for it scarcely merited a response. "You've seen how they've been lately. At the meeting tonight. Keith's delusional. They let go of the part-timers, put the girl on the register. You and I are the only ones still around who remember Heart's golden age. Used to be there was a vetting process for new dealers. Now any schlub—any two schlubs—can stumble in off the street and sell last week's newspaper in Hall One. Like the rules don't apply to them. It's worse than usual. Mismanagement, plain and simple."

Jimmy was right, but Margaret didn't see what it had to do with her insofar as requiring her to sit here when she should be at home, wrapped in the quilt Patricia had given her, watching television. "Well, if the time comes, I suppose I'd move my merchandise to another establishment, much as I'd hate to have to transport my—" The thought of all her beautiful, fragile glass clanking around the grimy interior of a U-Haul nearly brought her to tears. "My pieces," she choked.

"You don't get it, Margie, baby. Why rent the cow when you could sell the milk yourself?"

"Speak coherently."

"I'm saying: It doesn't matter whether it's the Stollers or some other big wheel. It's sunk cost to let some *owners*"—he spat the word like a slur—"take a cut of our hard-earned profits on every dang sale. Listen, I got a line on a place in Delano. It's not huge, but it's cozy. And between the two of us, it's more than enough space. Was planning to go in on it by myself, but it wouldn't hurt the fiscal side of things to partner up. When you stood up during the meeting, it strikes me: You gotta have some money stashed away, you're old enough. And this chick knows business. Plus, the lease is dirt-cheap. So what's the rub? There is none. No rub whatsoever."

"Please stop using that word: *rub*." Margaret couldn't say she'd never fantasized about a shop of her own, or even one she shared with a business partner, though of course it had always been Patricia she pictured at her side at the antique National cash register, not Jimmy Daniels. "I'm hardly stunned that a building in *Delano* is so affordable. I'm sure you'd get plenty of foot traffic from needle addicts and transients."

"Ever heard of revitalization, Margaret? We'd be in between a pizza parlor and high-end coffee place. And besides, it's an historical district. Old-time charm and whatnot. Not like the bunker we got here. I'm talking big storefront windows. Natural light out the ass. Think about looking in from the sidewalk and seeing your stuff just gleaming there. That's some classy shit."

"It's not for me to argue with your tactics, Jimmy. I credit you with knowing what you're doing. It's well established that this is your full-time career. Nevertheless, I remain unconvinced that our management styles would cohere."

"Exactly! Exactly, this is my full-time gig. I'm on the road four days a week minimum in the busy season. And for me, it's always the busy season. I'll practically be a silent partner." He helped himself to some more gum. "I'll even let you name the joint."

Jimmy Daniels was not entirely trustworthy. But after today's meeting, after the way that Seymour had humiliated her, now sitting here in Jimmy's filthy van, nearly choking on the tobacco and grease smell and Jimmy's grape-flavored breath, feeling Patricia's absence more than ever, hating suddenly Keith and Stacey and the whole of the Heart of America even while admitting she couldn't very well abandon it and start over at some other mall—not after all the years she'd put in—she was hopeless enough to be reckless and hopeful enough to already have a name in mind: Pretty Patty's Antiques Shoppe.

"I'm interested," Margaret said.

"Sweet deal," Jimmy said. "I'm a big-picture guy. I only see the big picture. You'd run the day-to-day. I trust your experience—no, I have faith in your expertise. Like I said, a silent partner." He mimed a zipper over his lips. "You'll see me when I drop my stuff off and that's about it. You don't even have to talk to me."

Well, *that* Margaret wouldn't argue with. "I'd have to view the location myself before I agree to anything. And I would insist on final say vis-à-vis décor and arrangement."

Jimmy spit the wad of gum into his hand and pitched it past Margaret at a window. There was a collection of seven or eight dry wads already stuck there, each a different color. "Deal?" He thrust his hand out for a shake, the same hand that had just held the gum. Margaret touched it gingerly with just her fingers, but Jimmy's hand cupped hers tight, the sticky candy residue connecting with the *smack* of a kiss.

That disgusting sound now echoed in her mind as Margaret, in the dim quiet of the empty mall, scanned her shelves for the most fitting spot for her latest acquisition. Some collectors called carnival glass "poor man's Tiffany," which Margaret thought crude. She personally had great affection for it. There was a humility to its luster, a playful insouciance that distinguished it from the haughtier Tiffany.

This time when she saw it, not lying inside any of her pieces, thank god, but sitting on the floor, its legs spread V-shaped and its square head leaning against the ridged rim of a fruit bowl, she felt no shock or surprise, no fear or offense, only rage, white-hot and pulsing through her veins, not directed at Seymour and Lee, or Keith and Stacey, or anyone but the dead-eyed doll itself. In that moment, it seemed all her troubles had started with this ill-shapen lump of brown plastic. It was MC Hammer that had caused her humiliation at the Dealers Association meeting, MC Hammer that had signaled Seymour and Lee's invasion of Hall One. She blamed MC Hammer even for driving Patricia away.

She picked it up, set the Millersburg in its place as if cleansing an unholy taint. She held the body in one hand and the head in the other and pulled with all her strength, relishing the sensation of the neck joint gradually loosening. Finally—a cork's *pop*—it gave, too suddenly, the smooth nub slipping from Margaret's hand and catapulting into a Beatty celery vase atop her booth's highest shelf. The vase teetered, spinning on its base like a toy top losing velocity. Margaret screamed, the high ceilings echoing with matching unease. Frozen, she braced herself for the shatter, an ugly, awful noise she'd experienced only once before, the time with Patricia.

"I know exactly what you mean," Patricia had said that day when Margaret described what she heard, how the glass had its own ethereal hum. Margaret then removed, with ginger fingers, the Royal Flemish biscuit jar from its place on the shelf and handed it to Patricia. "There's a word for it, hearing something just by looking at it." Patricia had learned about it on TV, a rarefied phenomenon exclusive to a small few with highly developed senses. She had it, too. "Synesthesia." Something about the way Patricia cradled the jar, like a newborn baby, her head tilted so that her ear just brushed the rim, the pucker of her lips as she pronounced the last syllable of *synesthesia*, made Margaret woozy. She hadn't been sure of what she was doing, but she knew it was all she had ever wanted to do, as she leaned forward and caught Patricia's lips in hers. And then: the jar in pieces, words said, Patricia's shadow trailing her under the fluorescent lights as she stalked down Memory Lane.

And now it was about to happen again. The bowl rattled, rattled, and then settled. No noise, nothing shattered. The near-silent harmony of the glass returned, and Margaret opened her eyes. The vase appeared undisturbed. The doll's head lay on the floor near Margaret's feet, its devilishly sloping forehead and toothy grin mocking her. She gave it a swift kick.

This chicanery had gone on quite long enough. She could not wait until she had taken proprietorship of Pretty Patty's Antiques Shoppe to rid herself of Seymour and Lee. Something would have to be done immediately. Still clutching the body of the doll, she stood at the edge of booth #1-146, nearly gagging at what appeared to be a fresh layer of sleaze. When had the men had time to deposit even more of this junk? It was as if it were multiplying of its own accord. There was plenty here that must be in violation of Dealer Association policies. For instance, Margaret could not recall having seen this despicable gelatinous-bodied toy figure labeled "Stretch Armstrong" (she pressed a pinkie to its latex skin, shivering in revulsion; if there were an opposite feeling to the near-frictionless pleasure of running one's hand across molded glass, this was it); this dusty container of "Cube Lube," an accessory for the Rubik's Cube toy Margaret recalled having been popular once upon a time; an automated model in the form of a red-nosed drunken bartender, which, at the press of a button, swigged from a bottle marked "XXX"; a framed and autographed poster of a buxom occultist named Elvira; imitation vomit in a cellophane package labeled "Gags and Giggles"; and most disturbingly, a porcelain ashtray in the shape of a woman's vulva.

It was perversion, pure and simple. They had *perverted* booth #1-146. If Patricia were here to see this—if only she were here to see this, she'd understand how out of control, how chaotic and sad, things had gotten since she'd gone. Margaret was hardly herself without Patricia around.

She missed her, but even more she missed the person she was when she was with her.

Their friendship had been so easy in the beginning. Margaret didn't see why she had to now make it so difficult owing to a trivial misunderstanding. Margaret was not a natural friend-maker. She always tried to be nice, but she suspected her intelligence and fine taste intimidated others. She wasn't going to dumb herself down and act like someone she wasn't for the sake of superficial companionship. Frankly, she was no good at pretending to be interested in things she was not. She valued integrity and sincerity and would rather be alone than engage with those she felt did not appreciate her for who she was. Before Patricia, Margaret had been solitary but not often lonely. Her collecting kept her busy and in touch—if not exactly friendly—with other collectors and sellers and buyers.

When Patricia moved into booth #1-146 about two years ago, Margaret had initially been disappointed with her stock's eclecticism. However, as she watched Patricia from behind her own shelves she began to admire the newcomer's uniformity of taste; she was not a collector like Margaret—she lacked the drive for completism—but nor was she a mere dabbler. Arranged with a sparseness that allowed each piece its own presence while exuding its *of-a-pieceness* with the booth at large, her merchandise included items as varied as a salvaged row of post office boxes with art deco lettering, a set of framed Charley Harper prints, a pair of hand-painted china dolls that were just darling, and an exquisite antique cuckoo clock whose unseen bird Margaret and Patricia would, in one of their silly moods, name Fritz, after one of Margaret's favorite twentieth century glass artists. Margaret ought to welcome her, she decided, before someone like Peter Deen came along and made a bad impression. But the longer she lingered, hiding and watching (not hiding, really, but standing just out of sight, and not watching, really, but glancing now and again), the harder she found it to step out and introduce herself.

It had been Patricia who first approached Margaret, of course. Margaret lost sight of her for a moment, and then a tap on her shoulder—

and there she was, encased in the reflections of Margaret's glass, a gray line of dust across her coral blouse.

"Hiya," she said. "We're neighbors, huh?"

"Hello," Margaret said. "I'm Margaret Byrd, the Heart of America's Dealer Association president—presidential candidate." This was during her last campaign, the one she'd only lost because, she suspected, Keith had forgotten to set out the ballots and ballot box in the back room until noon, despite the fact that association rules stipulated they be made available from opening till closing hours on election day. Who knew how many had been disenfranchised as a result? She handed Patricia the *Vote Byrd* sticker she'd had printed at FedEx Office.

Patricia stuck it to her sweater. "Well, you have my vote. I'm Patty."

Something in Margaret's chest cracked like an egg. Gelatinous warmth spilled out and spread into her veins. She felt suddenly rested but not calm, a first-day-of-school nervousness kicking about inside her.

When Margaret didn't say anything, Patricia stepped back and admired Margaret's glass. "Wow, they're so beautiful. This is really something, isn't it?"

"You're interested in glass?"

"I'm no expert."

It was an understatement. As Margaret guided her around the booth, pointing out some of her notable pieces, it became clear that Patricia couldn't tell a Tiffany from a Swanky Swig. Of her own merchandise Patricia also knew little. She'd been picking things up here and there at estate sales for years, whatever caught her eye or "had a niceness about it," but she was rarely compelled to research an item or seek out companion pieces. To her own surprise, Margaret was impressed with Patricia's casual attitude. It suited her earthy personality. She was the sincerest person Margaret had ever known.

It would be through her friendship with Patricia that Margaret would come to realize that she'd never actually had a real friend before, never in her life. She'd have felt foolish, infantile, if she wasn't merely blessed to have found Patricia; others probably learned it as children, that friendship wasn't a transaction, it wasn't something offered and received. It had nothing to do with shared interests or even compatible personalities. It was an act of opening up—your mind, your heart, yourself, whatever one called it. The only way to know yourself was to allow another person to know you, too. With Patricia, Margaret had felt more herself than she'd ever been.

As she gazed now at what #1-146 had become, every trace of her old friend eliminated, Margaret felt utterly alone. She clutched the decapitated MC Hammer and pictured the smug looks on Seymour and Lee's faces at the association meeting. They'd turned Patricia's booth into a garbage heap of doodads and gewgaws and thingamajigs, and what's more, couldn't bother to follow Hall One's most basic rule. And it wasn't just them. Keith and Stacey had failed to follow proper protocol for the Dealer Association, to respond to legitimate complaints in a timely manner or any manner at all, not to mention their failure to adequately screen the mall's dealer applications, which caused so many of these ethical oversights to begin with.

It was also against the rules to tamper with other dealers' merchandise, but was it ethical to let a transgression stand without retribution? She picked up the obscene ashtray, holding it squeamishly by its edges, putting the headless doll in its place. Who would own such a thing? Who would make it? What kind of person would put it on display at a family establishment like Heart, where children could see? It was in blatant violation of policy, but nothing would be done about it. If the ashtray required excision, she would have to be the one to do it.

Margaret hesitated. Never in her life had it ever occurred to her to break the rules, even the ones that were obviously wrong. What she would do was put it at the bottom of the lost-and-found bin, under the scarves and hats and umbrellas. That certainly wasn't quite in violation of policy. After all, the item could just as easily be lost as anything, and say Margaret absentmindedly picked the price tag off with her fingernail; in theory it would be lost, as no one could say for sure to whom it belonged. So in actuality, Margaret was doing the right thing in every way;

she was removing an offensive item from Hall One and also placing a lost item where it should be. It was as simple as—

A chalk-dry hand touched Margaret on the neck. She screamed. The ashtray fell to the floor and shattered. The sound of it, like the delayed echo of what nearly happened to her vase, terrified her even more than the unexpected touch.

"Oh dear," Ronald Marsh said. "That was an oopsie."

"One does not sneak up on a woman and lay hands on her like that, Ronald. It's inappropriate."

"Gee, I'm sorry, Margaret. I heard you yell and I wanted to check— I'm just so happy to find you. You see, I was locked in. I've been here all night and I've got to get home right away." He looked down at the broken pieces. "Too bad about that. I hope those boys won't be too upset about—"

"They won't be, because it wasn't theirs. It was one of mine, so there's no use telling them anything about it. Anyway, the emergency exits are there for a reason."

Ronald blinked. He scratched his head. He opened his mouth and inhaled wheezily, the slow churn of thought taxing his stamina. Finally, he said, "Oh jeez. The emergency exits—I didn't even think. I've gotta get home in a jiffy." He began to shuffle away, obviously dazed.

"And Ronald?" Margaret said. "You owe me fifty dollars for the ashtray."

11

RONALD

As Ronald rushed home from the Heart of America, he couldn't help but notice the telephone poles and yard signs that bore her beaming face. The thought hit him then, as if jolting awake with terrible dread: he had left an eight-year-old girl locked alone in a kennel in his basement all night, and that was very, very bad. This pickle had turned into a pretzel, and it was so mixed up and tied up and twisted, he just couldn't—for all his gift of gab—figure a way to explain it so that it didn't come off as fishy somehow. Not that there was anything fishy about it, no sir!

So he made a pit stop at McDonald's and Target to grab a few more things to make it up to Lindy for being away for so long, two Happy Meals and a bunch of toys including a Just Like Mom dress-up set, a Salon 4 Me home makeover kit, a *My Secret Princess* fairy princess wand, an entire box of Sparklevision trading cards, and the *My Secret Princess My Secret Adventure* home video. The Target employee was so helpful, pointing Ronald toward all the stuff kids today were into. He hoped Lindy wouldn't be sore at him.

There was no time to waste as he parked in the driveway of his modest ranch-style home, leapt out of the car, and climbed the steps to the front door. With his arms full with Lindy's food and presents, it took some maneuvering to get his house key from pocket to lock. When he finally did, the door opened barely a crack before Gable nosed his way out and into the yard.

"Dang you, Gable! You get back here this instant."

Gable was a rat terrier Melinda had picked out from the local shelter. Ronald had never been much of an animal lover. He was a people person, he'd told Melinda, leave the animals to the animal kingdom. But Melinda insisted, and as always he relented. He and the dog had never quite gotten along. He was Melinda's pet and never let Ronald forget it, showing his fangs when Ronald tried to get close to Melinda on the couch, accepting Ronald's half-hearted pets with raised hackles but collapsing on the floor in ecstasy at Melinda's slightest touch. He once bit Ronald on the nose, slinking up out of nowhere like a snake as he leaned to kiss Melinda good night. Worst of all, Gable couldn't be left unsupervised for a minute without tipping over the trash can or tearing up the furniture or making accidents on the carpet. He needed to be locked up whenever Ronald left the house, but given that his kennel was currently occupied, Ronald had been forced to let him run free.

"Gable! Gable! Come here, you mangy mutt! Get inside *now*!" Ronald couldn't call attention to himself having this mad dog on the loose. He tried to corner him by the bushes, but the dog was too quick and wily, slipped right between his legs and attacked a rubber ball one of the neighborhood kids had kicked into the yard.

The dog mystified Ronald—no, that wasn't it; the dog's relationship with Melinda mystified him. Gable was the one thing in their life that she hadn't shared with him. Once that dog was around, Ronald become outnumbered, like he was competing with Gable for Melinda's time and attention. When he'd griped about this, she'd simply stroked Gable's head and said, "He's my postcard collection." Ronald took to calling him just that: "Feed your postcard collection. He's clawing at his bowl again." "Why don't you take the old postcard collection out for a walk?" "Keep *your* postcard collection out of my postcard room. I don't need him pee-peeing on any of my rarities." The joke didn't last long, what with Melinda's passing. Neither she nor he had any family left, and although he'd invited them all, no one from the Heart of America came to the funeral. Not that he begrudged them, oh no, for the ceremony had been scheduled on a Dealer Association meeting day, and he knew how important that was. (He was sorry to miss it himself.) It was a lonely reception, just the priest and Ronald and Gable, and Ronald understood just how small and self-contained his life with Melinda really was. He sometimes walked Gable to the cemetery, where he'd always, despite Ronald's scolding, lift his leg and urinate on Melinda's tombstone. But the look on Gable's face was unlike other times he urinated, his mouth clamped shut in what seemed to Ronald a genuine frown. It was a gesture of mourning the way only a dog could express it, and it soon became a ritual, every walk reaching its climax with Gable's stream splashing against the marble of the tombstone and dripping into the same dirt upon which Ronald's teardrops fell.

"Oh my sweet goddamn," came a voice from behind. Ronald had been so ensconced in his own mind he didn't see Seymour, one of the new fellows, the blond one, wander up to the goofy little lawn ornament in the yard. It was a real kooky thing Melinda had purchased at the flea market, in the shape of a jockey riding a green Martian-looking giraffe. Seymour knelt and drew his hand along the seam in its neck. "Is it a Heatherstone? I've never seen any like it before." In his free hand he held a staple gun and a bundle of Lindy MISSING posters.

"Oh hello." Ronald racked his brain for a polite way to get Seymour out of his hair. He couldn't risk the man inviting himself in or snooping around the yard and getting a glance through the storm windows.

"Well, is it? A Heatherstone? I know he experimented with some Lewis Carroll–inspired molds in the seventies."

"A Heatherstone." Ronald scratched his chin. He had no idea what the man was talking about and wished he would go on his way littering the neighborhood with his needless posters.

Seymour stood and crept closer to the house. Ronald had kept the basement lights on—he didn't want to leave Lindy alone in the dark. From the right angle, if he knew what to look for, he might be able to see her in her cage, plain as day. "It's got a lot of the typical features. The contours that the knockoffs could never match. The almost Warhol-esque paint job. And the extra-thick seam. It's where the two halves of the mold met during production. A genius move, really: accentuate the artifice while the competitors fail at natur-o-realism." But before Seymour could take another step, Gable—bless that pooch!—emerged from the bushes and began to attack his shoes. Seymour looked down and said, "Don't do that. These are vintage Red Ball Jets. You have any idea how hard to find they are?"

The dog did not, but shamed, he slunk past Ronald up the porch steps and sat before the door waiting to be let in. Ronald had not seen him so obedient since Melinda.

The two men stood in silence. Ronald was afraid to speak lest he blurt something suspicious. Seymour checked his shoes for damage. What could Ronald say, how could he excuse himself without arousing suspicion?

Seymour looked up and blinked as if seeing Ronald for the first time. "You work at the Heart of America," he said.

"Yes, indeed. Booth three-oh-four-seven. You and your fellow took one-one-four-six, Patricia Blatt's old spot. Toys and knickknacks."

"*Knickknacks.* We wouldn't really use that word. What I would call them," Seymour said, "is *tragic treasures.*" He eyed the McDonald's boxes in Ronald's hands. "Wouldn't have pegged someone like you as a collector of premiums. You know, the market for Happy Meal prizes has gone to shit. Unless you've got, like, untouched display boxes from the nineties."

Ronald's arms were tired from holding the boxes and bags, and the Indian summer sun shone in his eyes with scorching intensity. Fall seemed to hit Wichita later and later each year, and it was not unusual for the temperature to hit highs in the eighties into October. He wiped the moisture off his brow and said, "For my appetite, the price of a Happy

Meal is just right. I've grown out of the toys, heh heh, but the stomach's never too old for a good old cheeseburger."

"Well, in that case, would you mind? Like I said, they're not worth anything, but if *you* don't want them, why let that plastic go to waste?" Seymour made to open a Happy Meal box, but Ronald pulled it away.

"I like to donate them to charity. Toys for Tots, you understand."

"How generous."

Ronald backed away, heading for the porch steps, ready to collapse, whether from the heat or the tension he was not sure. One of the plastic bags slipped off his shaking finger and spilled the sparkling *My Secret Princess* package onto the driveway. He scrambled, to the extent that his tired old body would allow, to pick it up. "Also for charity. Christmas is a ways away, I know, but it's never too early to start stocking up. I hate to be rude, good fellow, but I've got to be going. If you think that pooch is unruly now, just see how he is if I don't give him his lunch tout suite." All his pent-up nervous energy expelled him up the steps and to the front door. Suddenly exhausted, he had to steady himself against the wall to catch his breath.

"Hey! Wait a minute! You're not getting away that easy."

At this Gable's ears perked up and Ronald froze. How had Seymour figured it out? Had *My Secret Princess* given him away? In a way it was a relief to have been caught. No longer would he be burdened with the secrets he'd been keeping. He turned to face his accuser.

"Where'd you say you got this giraffe, pops?"

It took a long moment to sink in. Woozy with relief, Ronald sighed. He was getting away with it—not that there was anything to get away with. It was a simple misunderstanding, was all. "It belonged to my wife."

"So you don't know." Seymour combed his mustache with his fingers. "And I'm sure you wouldn't know a Heatherstone from a Duchamp."

"No sir, I sure wouldn't." Ronald gave Gable a little tap, sending him inside. "Now, if you'll excuse me—"

"Just one more thing." Seymour met him by the porch steps and slipped a bunch of flyers into one of his bags. The cheap photocopied halftone image turned Lindy's face cadaverous and ghostly. Veronica and her CHAANT crew didn't know what they were talking about. Lindy was fine. Lindy was *fine*. "Used to be I was handing out flyers to kick-ass punk shows. Now look at me. You know what? Take 'em all." He shoved the entire sheaf in. "I think I've done my duty for the day. If my man comes around looking for me, don't tell him I'm at the bar." He winked and waved goodbye, a little threateningly, with the staple gun still in hand. "Nice talking to you," he said in such a way as to indicate it hadn't been nice at all. But at least he finally left.

Ronald went inside and downstairs to the basement. His heart stopped when he saw the kennel door hanging open, blankets strewn across the floor, the room empty. "Oh dear. Oh gosh." He dropped the Happy Meal boxes and Target bags on the floor and began to pace about, calling Lindy's name. She was not under or behind the couch, in the storage closet, or the laundry room. Finally, he heard a shuffling from behind the curtains that led to his studio, and there he found her standing atop a stack of pillows on one of the guest chairs pushed up against the wall, reaching toward the window.

She screamed when Ronald grabbed her. "Now, now, my poor dear. There's no need to be afraid. Old Ronald made an oopsie leaving you alone for so long, and he sure is sorry."

Lindy tried to wiggle out of his grasp and speak through her tears. "Hungry" and "alone" were the only words he understood. He wiped her face with his sleeve. "Poor, poor dear. Don't worry, Ronald is never going to leave you again." At this she sobbed harder. He carried her through the curtains and placed her gingerly on the couch.

"I wanna go home," Lindy howled.

"Now, now," Ronald said, dabbing gently at her cheeks. "Everything's fine. You're fine."

Clearly Lindy was not fine, and it could possibly be misconstrued by an outside party that Ronald was—with no bad intentions or intentions at all—at fault for Lindy's being not-fine. But she was just hungry, was all. His Melinda used to get in such moods when he kept her too long past lunchtime at the library as he pored over the collectors' guides.

He went to retrieve the presents from Target—surely that would cheer her up. But he'd forgotten about the flyers Seymour had given him; they'd spilled out when he dropped the bag, twenty or so little Lindy zombie faces in goldenrod and salmon. Up until then he'd been able to keep it in check like a wild animal in a cage, but all at once the word sprang out of his subconscious and into his waking mind, unwelcome and, he swore in his heart, inaccurate: *kidnapper*.

12

ELLIE

Ellie sat at the sales computer scrolling through social media and dutifully clicking "like" on her friends' posts exhibiting the joys and rites of college life: photos snapped at free concerts of up-and-coming indie chanteuses Ellie was not hip enough to have ever heard of, statuses bemoaning the stresses of midterms illustrated with sororal study group photos, typo-ridden drunk posts hailing the most recent kegger as the "bset night evar." Ellie could relate to none of it. For her, college life consisted of splitting her time between till-running at the Heart of America, taking dumbass classes with the townies at the community college, and being semi-stalked by the Professor.

Yesterday, he'd waited for her at her cubby as usual, a cardboard file box in his arms. "Ellie! I'm so glad I've happened to run into you." The box was filled with more of his custom Troll dolls. At a glance Ellie recognized a Vladimir Putin, a Charlie Chaplin (or maybe Hitler?), an O. J. Simpson (complete with too-small gloves), and a Tammy Faye Bakker.

"I don't want your dolls," she'd said.

"Although doll art is a legitimate idiom, I'd classify my work more along the lines of—"

"Who cares? I dropped your class, so now you have no reason to talk to me." She motioned for him to step aside so she could get her back-pack from the cubby.

"And I'm heartened, finding you here, to see that our breakup hasn't soured you on higher education."

"*I* broke up with *you*."

"Yes, be that as it may. The work in this box, the product of a years-long process, is not for you, but—"

"Great, because I don't want it." She turned to leave, but he blocked her way.

"I have a favor to ask. A while ago you mentioned that Mark and Grant from the Home Channel were—"

"You want me to get your little craft projects on TV."

The Professor sighed. "If you had stayed in my class, surely you'd understand the distinction between 'craft' and 'art.'" He shoved the box into Ellie's chest. It was heavier than expected. "They're not insured yet, so be careful."

She'd thrown them all in the dumpster behind the cafeteria on her way to the parking lot, and presently the memory of the sight of them—the product of the Professor's years-long process—in a fetid pile of institutional food waste was all that kept her from descending into total despair as she "liked" a friend's new cover image depicting the cinematic skyline of a major metropolitan city. This same friend had not responded to any of Ellie's messages since June.

Keith had taken most of the day off to help the CHAANT crew work with police to broaden their search efforts. In all her life, Ellie had not known her father to have any hobbies—all he did was work, eat, watch TV, and sleep. This thing with Veronica Samples's task force was the closest he'd ever come, and who could guess what inspired it? Maybe he was really Lindy's abductor and he was sabotaging the search from the inside, he had a whole secret existence as a serial murderer, Wichita's heir apparent to the BTK. Nah, a psychopathic killer would have a rich inner life and a modicum of physical strength, the better to move corpses and evade law enforcement with, which Keith clearly lacked—and besides, even the phony gore in the horror movies Ellie watched on TV nauseated him. Or maybe it was pretext for an affair with Veronica or some other sad townie. Yuck. The thought of Keith being "romantic"—she pictured the way he'd devoured a cruller whole yesterday—made her gag.

Not that she'd blame him for straying. Stacey was hardly human, as silent and stiff as one of her pieces of pottery. They'd driven to work together that morning, had been sitting side by side at the counter since opening, without exchanging a single word. In point of fact, Ellie had intentionally not spoken directly to her mother in weeks. She hadn't noticed.

Probably Stacey had always been like this, and in fact, no matter how far back Ellie searched her memory, the obsession that culminated in the sapping of her college fund had always been there. Once Ellie had helped her father track down on the internet a piece Stacey had been pining after for months. It was to be a gift for her birthday, a Redware sgraffito plate, whatever that was. When she unwrapped the package, Stacey said thank you, tried to smile, but then her lip quivered and she sighed. It was not the real thing but a cheap reproduction. She fetched a price guide from her shelves and held up a page with a photo of the genuine artifact, which looked exactly like what Ellie and her father had bought. "The difference is obvious," she said and explained in a teacherly voice various methods for spotting fakes. Finally, she handed the gift back to Ellie, as if there were something *she* could do with it. She dropped the plate on the floor, ran to her room, and refused to open the locked door until her father negotiated to take her out for ice cream. Meanwhile, her mother sat in the dining room drinking wine from a box. When they got home, Stacey sighed and said, "I thought you were showing an interest in my interests," like Ellie had been the one to hurt *her*. She was only twelve at the time.

She had thought of this often in the past few months. Stacey had collected pottery for as long as Ellie could remember, but in the past few years it was all she lived for. It was clear her mother resented her.

That Ellie didn't give two shits about pottery, that Ellie was her own person with her own life and feelings, had wounded Stacey. But there was also the time this summer, a week or two after her parents had sat her down in the living room for a serious conversation about the state of her college fund, when Stacey roused Ellie awake in the middle of the night. It had started as a "small indiscretion," she'd explained in a tone of contrition Ellie had never before heard, and then *all* the money had "somehow gotten away after a while." For that moment she could admit Stacey surely never meant to hurt her, and Ellie could imagine the aloneness of devoting your life to a hobby no one in the world cared about. But the feeling wouldn't last. "You know I'm sorry," Stacey had said as she gazed down at Ellie in bed, and the more Ellie thought of it, the angrier she got. Stacey couldn't just concede that she had something to be sorry for, she had to say it like *that*, like it was a done deal. If all Stacey could do was put it in those words, then Ellie *didn't know* that her mother was sorry.

The mall was even more abandoned than usual. They hadn't seen a single customer all day, and the only dealer who'd even briefly passed through—unfortunately—was Margaret Byrd earlier that morning. Keith had done a good enough job promoting Mark and Grant's appearance that everyone was probably saving their visits for Monday. If Mark and Grant were even *really* coming. It was obvious something was up. Though Ellie tried to spend as little time as possible with her parents and did her best to ignore them when forced to share space, even she could see that Keith changed the subject whenever Stacey or one of the dealers asked for details about the filming, and he'd all but disappeared since joining the Lindy search last night. (Evidently he'd canvass to the ends of the earth to find some little brat he'd never met, but for his own daughter refused to offer a simple cosigner's signature.) He had to be avoiding some hard truth. TV People—people who actually appeared on TV, tan and handsome and charismatic, with animated eyebrows and bright voices, pearly Hollywood smiles and hairless necks—who could blame them if they decided to snub as unassuming a hellscape as Wichita, Kansas?

Between Keith and Stacey both, Ellie had lost the parent lottery. Fortunately, she had a plan to escape them, inspired by a half-remembered episode of *Encyclopedia Brown*. The first step was collecting her mother's Social Security number and easily forgeable signature on the fake Heart of America paperwork she'd created with the graphic design software at the school computer lab, which she would then transfer to a private loan cosigner's form. Unfortunately, the lack of customers today posed an obstacle. Stacey wasn't an idiot (in most ways) and Ellie's plan was not that clever. She'd been counting on a decent Saturday crowd to provide enough distraction so that Stacey wouldn't look or think too hard about the form Ellie would spring on her in the middle of a checkout rush.

Happily, however, Stacey provided her own distraction. She'd been watching the clock all day, intermittently popping into the back room to use the research computer to place last-minute eBay bids. Given that she was already deep in the hole for Ellie's college money, this was, of course, supremely fucked up. Perhaps if she wasn't inured to Stacey's idiocy, Ellie could muster up some rage. Instead she only lamented that Stacey couldn't have a healthier, more affordable addiction, like huffing gasoline.

"Mom? I'm done over here. You can use this computer if you want," Ellie said. She closed Facebook and opened eBay in a new tab. Stacey hesitated. "The computer in back has been freezing up."

If Stacey realized these were the first words Ellie had spoken to her in weeks, she didn't show it. "Thank you, dear." She took command of the keyboard and mouse and with a practiced tapping of her fingers logged in instantly, clicking through to an auction for something called a "1903 Van Briggle design #141 stoneware bowl," set to end in one minute's time.

With practiced casualness Ellie set the papers next to the mouse pad. "Mom?"

The red countdown clock glowed in the deep blacks of Stacey's dilated pupils. Her left-clicking finger twitched, and under her breath she whispered, "*Nope, not yet, too soon.*"

"Mom? Mom? Mom!"

"What, Ellie?"

"Um, Dad left some paperwork for you. The note said it's really important. Tax stuff or something."

"Sure, dear." The countdown clock was in the forties. Stacey paced nervously in place.

"Are you listening? Mom?"

"Yes, some paperwork. I'll get to it in a minute."

"Dad said it's really important and needs to be finished ASAP."

"In a minute, Ellie."

"Looks like he just needs your Social and signature. I can do the rest." Ellie took a pen from the cup on the counter and set it on the fake form. The fluorescents in the lobby were too bright, exposing the obvious seams in Ellie's handiwork, but now it was too late.

Stacey typed into the bid box a number greater than twice what Ellie got in her biweekly paycheck.

"Mom? It'll only take a second. Okay? Okay? Okay, Mom? Mom?"

"Okay!" Stacey grabbed the pen without taking her eyes off the screen. "It just so happens I have twenty-seven seconds to spare."

Ellie pointed. "Social Security there." Her heart throbbed. It was working. Her stupid scheme was actually working.

Stacey was on her fourth digit without having even glanced at the paper when the doors jingled and Keith sauntered in wearing a T-shirt with one of Lindy Bobo's pageant photos printed on it under the caption FIND HER!!!!

Stacey dropped the pen. It rolled off the counter and onto the floor. As Keith approached, she adjusted the computer monitor so that he couldn't see it. "Keith," she said, taking a quick glance up from the screen, "you're in early. I thought you weren't coming in till closing."

"It's almost five thirty," he said, "but I am going to have to skedaddle right after balancing the register. There's a Take Back the Night rally at College Hill Park."

Ellie forced another pen into Stacey's hand. She tried to position herself so that Keith couldn't see the form. "That's so interesting, Dad. Take back the night from who?"

Keith thought for a moment. "Well, take it back from Lindy, I guess. To find her."

Stacey clicked "confirm" on her bid with seven seconds to go. She was, at the moment, top bidder. Ellie touched her wrist to remind her to finish filling out the form, but she was frozen in concentration as the clock ticked down its final seconds.

"Dad, could you real quick get me a soda from the vending—"

"Shit!" Stacey said at the red *Sorry, you've been outbid* message. She cut her eyes at Keith. "Here, you do your own paperwork. I'm going home." She tossed Ellie's form at him and went to the back room.

"No, Mom, wait!"

Keith's brow furrowed as he examined the obvious fake. "Ellie," he said in a melody of disappointment. "I don't even have to tell you this is a bad idea. But that you've stooped to such dishonest—"

Stacey emerged from the back with purse draped over her arm. "By the way, Keith, the *Eagle* called to confirm the time of the filming on Monday. It's still on for three o'clock, right?"

Keith swallowed hard.

"Yeah, Dad. Three o'clock without a hitch. Right?"

"Mmmhmm." Keith crumpled the papers. "We'll have to discuss this later, Ellie. As punishment I'm going to leave closing procedures to you. Now that I think about it, Veronica could use an extra hand prepping for tonight. When you're done I want to see you at the park to help out with the search. Every action taken is a step toward recovering little Lindy." Unconsciously he patted his shirt.

"If I find her, I'm taking that reward money and you'll never see me again."

"Ten thousand dollars is not worth as much in the real world as you think. Trust me. Make sure you double-check the balance after you lock up."

That wouldn't be too hard, considering they had not made a single sale.

Ellie's parents left together. She couldn't remember the last time they stood or walked side by side. When she was sure they were gone, she locked the door, flipped the sign to CLOSED, and dimmed the lights. Fuck it, the Heart of America was closing early.

13

SEYMOUR

Wichita was not a city kind to pedestrians, its grid defined by commercial sprawl and characterless residential clusters stitched together by the crisscrossing of I-235 and Route 54, highways that took you nowhere interesting in any direction, not without at least a three- or four-hour drive past state lines. And no matter which way you went, it seemed to Seymour, the last things you'd see before the plains, the prairie, the flats, the empty heart of the country, were a Best Buy, a Dillons grocery store, a sad empty building with unblinking window-eyes where yet another doomed franchise met its bitter end. Even here in College Hill, one of the few areas one could call an actual, walkable neighborhood, no one expected to get anywhere without driving.

Wichitans, Seymour thought, those misguided people who had made the mistake of making the city their home, treated pedestrians with a regional brand of antipathy. The few times he'd gone for his nightly walk—and this was before the panic over little Lindy—cars would slow to a crawl, cast their brights as they followed him home, like they needed to reassure themselves he wasn't some thief or thug or monster, to make certain he belonged. If Seymour stopped or waved or acknowledged them in any way, they'd roll out of sight, circle the block, and return.

By now he had a hard time reminding himself there was anyone in the driver's seats. He was so unused to seeing a human being outside of his or her car that he tended to think of the vehicles as dumb, overprotective animals that didn't know any better than to trail him home and nip at his ankles.

So it made sense that when CHAANT, the College Hill AMBER Alert Neighborhood Taskforce (were you allowed to put an acronym within another acronym?) searched for lost Lindy Bobo, they searched by car, scouring the neighborhood with their windows down blasting Lionel Richie's "Dancing on the Ceiling," the little girl's favorite for competition dance routines, wagging high-powered flashlight beams across lawns. A mobile death disco, Seymour had called it when it began, and that got a chuckle even out of Lee, who was a tough audience these days.

What didn't make sense was that Lee had volunteered his and Seymour's time toward the search effort. "This isn't like back East," he'd said that morning when he'd tasked Seymour with posting MISSING flyers throughout the few blocks of the neighborhood that weren't yet plastered with them. "You have to actually talk to your neighbors here."

"Or they won't invite us to the cross burnings? They'd have to leave their cars first." When they'd announced to their friends their decision (though really it was much more Lee's than Seymour's, and it really wasn't much of a choice but a consequence, the end result of the shop's failure and their bankruptcy) to move here, at best they'd reacted with ironic delight, jokes about *American Gothic* and *The Wizard of Oz*. At worst, they'd acted as if Seymour and Lee had been sentenced to some sort of shameful exile. To them, Kansas was one vast sunflower field of pitchfork-wielding Westboro Baptists. In truth, Seymour felt more a victim of discrimination here as someone who preferred to walk or take public transportation than as a gay man. Which was not to say he and Lee didn't get ugly looks on occasion. But he soon realized that here everyone got that look, for just about any reason. He called it the Wichita Scowl. No one was openly hostile, just seething with unspoken judgment. Everyone in this town was so terrified of anything even vaguely unfamiliar to them that they all just went around scowling at one another like cavemen chasing their own shadows. It was one thing Seymour appreciated about Wichita. He'd always been the token misanthrope in his group of friends; here, everyone hated everyone else as much as he did.

So what was he doing at the tail end of Veronica Samples's mobile disco, holding their mint but unpackaged 1967 Bat Signal Flash-Gun out the car window? He guessed he owed it to Lee after how pissed he'd gotten about his little prank on Margaret Byrd, but that didn't mean Seymour was going to be nice about it. "I feel like I'm outside my body watching myself right now." He made a laser sound as he pointed the beam at a dog. It was the only flashlight they owned.

"This is what neighbors do for each other," Lee said, his knuckles white against the steering wheel. "At least this way we don't have to talk to anyone and we still get credit."

"I spent *all* morning on flyer duty. Isn't that credit enough?"

"You missed last night's meeting because you got loaded and passed out at eight o'clock. And then woke up at eleven today."

"That's when my morning begins," Seymour said. "And I bet it'll really endear us to the neighbors if we're the ones who drag Little Miss Prairie Princess's torn-up corpse out from under a dumpster." Lee ignored him, turned on the tape deck. The tinkling piano opening to "Endless Love" played. "Oh god, at least spare me the balladry," Seymour said, punching the eject button. A cacophony of asynchronous Richie croons blared from the cars in front of them. "Although Richie's early work with the Commodores is not so bad. MOR pop with funk overtones, occasionally inventive production." Seymour cringed as he spoke. It was a part of himself he couldn't turn off, the pedantic connoisseur that had to not just know everything but own it, too. How he had looked up to, as a burgeoning teenage collector, the cranky, bearded men who lorded over the record stores whose haphazardly stacked milk crates he spent every weekend digging through. These were men devoid of civility, whose every utterance was a reference to some obscure variant pressing—this *Rubber Soul* features an exclusive false start on "I'm Looking Through You," this *Headquarters* sleeve is the exceedingly rare version in which Davy, Michael, Micky, and Peter sport facial hair in the bottom right corner photograph, while in the common version they're clean-shaven. They were sleazeballs who worked on the side as exterminators or census takers so they could scout houses for unwanted collections, who had no time for anyone unappreciative of the wide-ranging influence of first-wave krautrock or the superiority of original mono mixes, whose stores kept no consistent hours, were only open when they felt like it, were often open even when the CLOSED sign hung in the door because they hadn't bothered to flip it, who accepted cash only, who never had correct change or any change at all, who would throw in this beat-up copy of *Trout Mask Replica* if you'd just let them keep the twenty. Seymour, now settling into middle age, had finally become one of them just as the breed achieved irrelevance; nowadays every asshole with a cell phone had instant access to hyperlinked repositories of the rarefied knowledge he'd spent his entire life accruing, and to corporate-owned algorithms giving recommendations not of what they should like but of what they knew they already liked.

Never again would he feel the thrill of discovery, that drunk, jittery feeling of being confronted with something totally new, like when he finally found a copy of *1/2 Gentlemen/Not Beasts* at an ex–college DJ's garage sale in Allston after only ever having read or heard about it for years, or when a friend gave him a scratchy cassette dub—maybe eight generations removed from the source—of the Shaggs' *Philosophy of the World*. He was the human embodiment of the *Trouser Press Guide*, with a massive collection, a vast network of fellow collectors, and an eBay account awarded a green star to signify over five thousand positively rated transactions. But nothing surprised him anymore. Nothing was new or unknown. He liked everything but enjoyed nothing.

Lee grabbed an old shoebox of mixtape relics from the backseat and steered with his knee as he sorted through them. It pained Seymour to see them now, the too-cute and half-clever titles he'd given them—*Fuck*

Songs: Pt. 69, Notes and Chords Mean Nothing to Me, Battle Hymns for Swingin' Bachelors—scrawled in his own scratchy hand, like looking at high school yearbook photos. He leaned out the window and shot the bat signal at a darkened window. The house lights turned on and a suspicious pair of eyes, glowing like a cat's, peered from behind the blinds. There it was again, the Wichita Scowl.

"What kind of kid listens to Lionel Richie anyway?" Lee shoved a tape into the deck: insistent yet inept drums, out-of-tune guitars. It was the Shaggs. Seymour had forgotten, it was Lee who'd given him the tape way back when, before they'd even started hooking up. They'd been in rival bands who frequently played together at house parties inevitably broken up by cops, crumbling unlicensed clubs with barely working electricity let alone functional plumbing, Lee playing saxophone in local favorite Tears in the Birthday Cake, a postmodern doo-wop band, Seymour playing tambourine, theremin, and a broken four-stringed guitar in Foxy Nazi, an almost universally reviled (Lee was their only fan) anti-funk group whose constantly changing member base spent more time mixing pill cocktails before each performance than practicing. For Seymour, this pre-show routine was not just to curb stage fright but also the anxiety of sharing a bill with Lee, who back then had an air of both guru and grizzled veteran. At least a decade older than Seymour or anyone else in his artsy-fartsy orbit, if the rumors were true he'd done time in pretty much every band that had ever broken big out of Boston since "college rock" had been a genre. Something about him was impossible to pin down; he wasn't punk or weirdo, he often came to shows dressed business casual because unlike most in the scene he had a straight day job (that he refused to talk about), but he wasn't totally square, either. Wholesome and seditious at once, Andy Taylor meets GG Allin. His mysterious past was subject to much speculation, and as far as Seymour knew, not even his bandmates had ever known about his stint as a would-be *Tiger Beat* centerfold; Lee only told Seymour about the Sodashoppe Teens after they'd been living together for a year, and it caused him more anguish, Seymour guessed, than coming out to his oppressively Christian family.

Lee drummed on the steering wheel, though it was impossible to match Helen Wiggin's manic arrhythmia. After such a long time together, it was hard for Seymour to remember there had ever been any mystery to him. "So what do you know about this show? The Mark and Grant show?"

Seymour soughed through his teeth. "*Pickin' Fortunes?* Guh. Just a tacky reality show for bored suburban housewives. Think I'll take a pass when they come to Heart."

"Since when have you had a problem with tacky?"

"Camp, kitsch, tasteless is one thing. Tacky is another. Can you imagine us on that Home Channel tripe? They'd edit us into a couple of *Queer Eye* queens or something. Oh, what the gang back home would say. I'll pass, thank you."

"Do you even talk to anyone 'back home'?" Lee stared straight ahead for a moment, as if he were concentrating on driving, then continued carefully, "I don't know. I think it could be good. Promotion-wise, I mean, for the eBay and Etsy accounts. 'As seen on TV,' or whatever. And don't act like you're not a natural performer. It could be fun."

"You kidding? Have you even seen two seconds of this show? My god, I think those Mark and Grant guys are centerfolds in the *Ladies' Home Journal* swimsuit issue. Having to live *here* is humiliation enough."

Lee could not hide the wound in his voice. "I'm just thinking of it from a business angle. It could be a lot of money just for putting our beautiful mugs on TV for thirty seconds."

Seymour didn't feel like talking about it right now, or ever. Maybe when he was younger he was attention-hungry enough to mince around for the Home Channel demographic, but the thought of a permanent broadcast record of his pathetic middle age made him physically ill. He squeezed Lee's knee. "So bony," he said, changing the subject. "Look at the way it sticks out. Freaky monster kneecaps."

"You're uglier," Lee said. "Forehead like Frankenstein. Rings around the eyes. Shady-looking, like a criminal."

"Tiny bird legs." Seymour tickled under Lee's knee. "Like in the Road Runner cartoon. Big stinking feet. Disgusting to look at. Just unnatural."

Lee held Seymour's hand. "Disturbed looks for a disturbed mind. The neighborhood task force ought to be searching your garage. Terrible things you've done to her."

"She's in pieces." Seymour said. "I was jealous of her beauty. I'm sewing her piece by piece onto my own body so that I may become one with her."

Lee simpered. "You're sick. You've got her tiny little-girl arms stitched to your nipples."

"Her face grafted to my neck."

"Eyeballs as earrings."

"Her belly button on my chin. It's an outie."

"Psycho," Lee said, pounding the brake. He'd nearly run into someone's bumper. The search was winding down. Flashlight beams died. Lionel Richie's croon faded. Cars were pulling out of the mobile disco and into driveways. Thank god, Seymour thought. Tonight was starting to feel surprisingly like a sex night, and anyway, there was an auction for the rare private press *J Ann C Trio at Tan-Tar-A* LP ending on eBay in a few minutes that he intended to snipe. Sure, in theory he was in the process of downsizing, but this record came along so rarely that whether he actually wanted it or not was irrelevant. He was acting automatically. He'd decided when the listing alert hit his in-box that it was his, and now he would go through the motions of attainment.

They neared their house, but Lee drove past.

"Where are you going?" This was a surprise. It'd been a long time since they'd last had car sex. It was unlike Lee of late, so paranoid about upsetting the scowling Wichitans' sense of neighborly decorum.

"To the meeting," Lee said as if he'd mentioned it long before and they'd both agreed on it.

"Meeting? Like the neighborhood watch meeting? Are you kidding?"

"It wouldn't be the worst thing in the world to make new friends."

"With these people it would be. Friends? We're too old to make new friends." Seymour held the flash-gun to his head.

"There'll be ice cream."

He pulled the trigger.

They ended up at College Hill Park after circling the perimeter searching for a legal parking space even though their own driveway was mere blocks away. The ice cream was the cheap kind grade-school kids had been getting as a snack since time immemorial, bland vanilla with chemically dense chocolate or strawberry swirls in little plastic cups with attached wooden spoons, distributed from a cooler with the words GO SHOCKS! painted on its side.

It depressed Seymour that he recognized so many faces after barely a week in Wichita. Let Lee do the mingling. He helped himself to a third cup while Lee introduced himself to people he'd introduced himself to previously but who pretended not to remember him for some weird, passive-aggressive reason. Keith Stoller, wearing a T-shirt with Lindy Bobo's face on it and standing around with a bunch of bored Heart of America dealers, waved Seymour into his circle. "Just to be clear," he said, his big red forehead furrowed apologetically, "the discount only applies to one of your booths."

Seymour was surprised to find Ellie standing beside him, flashlight in hand. "I wouldn't have guessed this was your scene."

"You know the kids these days. We're all about taking ecstasy and on-line bullying and volunteering for search parties," she said. "Especially if there's a cash reward."

Behind Ellie, Lee held court in his own circle. He called Seymour over with a tilt of his head and put his arm around his waist as he went on: ". . . lived in Boston but actually I grew up here in the little house on Waterman," Lee was saying to a disinterested couple who kept their small son harnessed in one of those dog leashes for children. He never failed to mention his childhood home when chatting with the neighbors. Someone asked Seymour if he, too, was from the area. Seymour bit into the wooden spoon and broke it in half. He was never good at this kind of thing—small talk, party chatter—not even at the house parties he'd played with Foxy Nazi. He could go on and on about mediocre Estonian post-punk bands for hours, but everyday pleasantries about the weather or current events clammed him up. In Boston, his friends had all been collectors like him, people whose personalities he didn't actually like but at least they shared his arcane interests; they were friends by default, as no one else could understand or even stand to listen to them prattle on to each other about variations of Quisp cereal boxes or argue over which issues of *Playboy* contained Kurtzman and Elder's *Little Annie Fanny* serial. ". . . And we just thought it was time to move back home."

Seymour smiled mirthlessly. Lee gave him that disapproving look like he knew Seymour was going to say something inappropriate, something honest.

Lucky for him, Veronica Samples, self-appointed leader of CHAANT, spoke up. "Okay, everyone." She waved her hands over her head like a schoolteacher trying to capture the attention of an unruly class. The men and women of the task force, wooden spoons in their mouths, gathered around. They were serious, earnest people who could live their lives not making a difference to anyone or anything so long as they participated in something seemingly important at least once in a while, when there was nothing good on TV. Seymour hung back. He felt like he was watching some cultic religious ceremony. Veronica baptized each congregant with a stack of flyers. "I'm glad we're all having a good time, and thank you, Lydia, for the ice cream. But I can tell you all there's one person who's not having a good time tonight." She held up a flyer, stuck her finger on Lindy Bobo's button nose. "Think about her tomorrow as you post these around your place of work or worship, anywhere we haven't covered yet. It's time—past time—to move the search outward!" She spoke with unnecessary emphasis, pausing as if waiting for some sort of applause.

Keith offered a hoarse cheer, more suitable for a homecoming game than a neighborhood canvass possibly for the slaughtered remains of a would-be JonBenét. "Forget tomorrow! We're not going home till we find her. Right, folks? I mean, come on, this is some serious shit."

Veronica nodded. "Thank you, Keith. This *is* serious. Something you may not know about me," Veronica was saying, "is that I've been in Lindy's place. I know what it's like"—she wiped a burgeoning tear—"to be little and scared and alone, to be someplace strange and to wonder if I'm ever coming home." It was something everyone knew about her by now. In each of the few interactions Seymour had had with her, she never neglected to mention that she'd been nabbed by one of her mother's ex-boyfriends when she was twelve. Seymour had looked up newspaper articles about it online. She was missing for all of eight hours. The police found her and the guy at an indoor Putt-Putt place at the local mall. She'd effectively gotten the day off from school and the guy told the cops, "I've been a father figure to her for the past six months. Why does breaking up with a lady mean you break up with her daughter, too?" This city was full of lonely people incapable of rationally dealing with being alone with themselves. Maybe Seymour was one of them. He shuddered.

The crowd, humbled by Veronica, gazed down at Lindy's photocopied yellow face in one hand while with the other they licked the last bit of syrup from their ice-cream lids. Except for Keith, who applauded and said, "Hell, yeah! Let's get out there and find this fucking kid!"

"Your enthusiasm is wonderful," Veronica said, "but please, Keith, there are children here."

The group returned to mingling but with graver purpose. No more polite chatter about TV shows or day jobs or home improvement projects. The subject was Lindy Bobo and nothing else. Lee turned to Seymour, waving the flyers like a fan. "Have you left any of these at the bookstore? Or by the high school?" he said. "There's a lot of foot traffic there." He was deliberately speaking too loudly, wanting to be heard, wanting the approbation of the task force, of Veronica.

"Yeah, well, all the flyers in the world aren't going to bring a corpse back to life." Seymour also spoke too loudly.

At once the Wichita Scowl, an especially virulent strain, surrounded him. There was even a bit of it on Lee's reddened face. Veronica had her arms crossed, her whole body somehow a scowl, her cat-eyes arched devilishly.

"You make that kind of remark when morale is so important to our efforts. A girl was kidnapped. A little girl. You're right. She could be dead. She could be abused, tortured. She could be raped. The College Hill AMBER Alert Neighborhood Taskforce doesn't require your participation. But if you do participate, at least take it seriously."

Seymour's smirk was gone. For once he had no rejoinder. It all became even more awkward when Veronica's anger dropped with such suddenness that her glasses slid down the tip of her nose and she began to cry. Shoulders stooped, she was a shuddering little girl again. The task force gathered around, Lee included, and mumbled words of hope and consolation, turning their heads back to offer Seymour brief but penetrating glares. And it used to be so charming when Seymour said distasteful things at large gatherings.

It was time to exit. "My joke was better," Ellie whispered as he passed by. Feeling the task force's resentment hot on his back, he resisted the urge to turn around and gauge the damage on Lee's unhappy face, to attempt an expression of contrition. Apologies sounded the least sincere when Seymour really meant them.

Lee had the house keys, so he'd have to hide till the meeting ended and Lee went home. And it would be easier if he waited till after Lee was asleep or was pretending to be. Seymour had left his wallet in the car, too, so it wasn't even an option to go the few blocks to the old-man dive bar across the street from the grocery store. Anyway, he didn't want to get hassled for walking around at night as usual. Following the park's dog-walking path, he crossed a concrete bridge overlooking a small ravine littered with soda bottles, cigarette butts, and potato chip bags. Someone had scratched the words THE CLASH and IGGY into the parapet, surely the hippest person to ever live in this neighborhood. Hell, maybe it was Lee's work.

Seymour wondered what it must have been like to grow up here. He imagined Wichita in the sixties as, illogically, quite like the Old West:

Lee riding to school on a covered wagon, racing the tumbleweeds down the cacti-strewn roads. But the reality, he knew, was as banal as to be expected. Breakfast at the diner every Sunday after mass—Lee had mentioned this to Seymour once and it made him immeasurably sad. He was sort of relieved that Lee's parents had disowned him since before they met, just because he never had to go through that awkward meet-the-parents ritual, never had to do the home-for-the-holidays thing. In photographs, they looked like stern types who'd cross to the other side of the street rather than face Seymour in his punk look: all Mohawk and torn clothing with extra zippers, a leather jacket stencil-painted with dirty words.

He shouldn't be so judgmental. It wasn't as if his own childhood in suburban Baltimore was so glamorous or bohemian. When he thought of it, he mostly pictured his after-school ceremony: the key under the mat and the empty house, the TV on (cartoons and syndicated sitcom reruns), a bowl of mac and cheese atop a Donald Duck lunch tray, a Little Debbie Cosmic Brownie unwrapped and set on a plate for no good reason other than to fool himself into thinking it was homemade. He wondered where that Donald Duck tray was now.

Seymour was used to being alone, had learned to embrace it. He could see now that even back in their band days, when Lee would get hopped up on amphetamines and slam dance till he passed out or break so many noise ordinances at a Tears show that a high-level police officer threatened to have him formally banned from the city of Boston, it was just about fitting in with Seymour's crowd. The unspoken thing that all their fights lately had been about was this: it was Seymour's turn, finally, to fit in with Lee's crowd.

14

LEE

The CHAANT meeting had concluded and everyone had gone home except for Lee, not eager to reconvene with Seymour for yet another round of argument or, more likely, silent, simmering resentment. Instead, he sat in his car looking out over the shabby little park that had seemed to him as a child boundlessly verdant, half listening to this ancient mixtape while enumerating the many ways in which his life was not so bad. For instance, he did not have any disfiguring injuries. Nor was he physically handicapped. He was not the victim of any apparent discrimination. He had not been imprisoned for crimes he did not commit. He had not been born in one of those unfortunate countries on TV populated by sad children with sallow eyes and distended bellies, his mother an AIDS-afflicted peasant, his father a savage warlord-rapist. He did not have Alzheimer's. What did he have to be depressed about? Aside from the fact he was broke, a failed musician and business owner, in a loveless relationship, living in the crusty house his estranged mother had passive-aggressively left him in her will, sleeping each night in his childhood bedroom (it would've been creepy to move into his parents' room), the forty years since he'd first left home having taken him on a circuitous path to nowhere, and he'd just spent his Friday night beating the bushes with a motley assortment of neighborhood lookie-loos and weirdos, as if the girl would be found if only they searched hard enough, like a lost contact or dropped dime.

Seymour had been right to be pessimistic, but he should have kept his mouth shut. (Had he ever in his life had a thought he chose *not* to express aloud?) Lee was not even pissed, just embarrassed for the both of them. As the CHAANT meeting broke up, Veronica had gone from person to person giving light hugs or placing her hand on a shoulder or arm and saying with excruciating sincerity, "Thank you for your help." Considering what Seymour said, Lee had not expected to get his turn, but nevertheless Veronica embraced him with both arms, whispered in his ear, "Thank you for your help," and after a moment added, just as sweetly, "Please don't come to any CHAANT meeting ever again."

Seymour would be glad to hear this. Lee had been naïve to get the both of them involved to begin with. Seymour was right; they were too old for new friends. Hell, Lee was too old for *old* friends—his few friends from childhood and high school had been smart enough to get out of Wichita and stay out. How pathetic: AARP-eligible and he remained haunted by the teenage feeling of not fitting in. But he had not volunteered their time to CHAANT to make friends. No, his true motivation was much more pathetic.

There nested in Lee's mind something tiny and fragile, so buried under layers of guilt and shame and self-loathing that ordinarily it could only be retrieved with the greatest of effort or inebriation: hope. TV crews would be arriving at the Heart of America in two days. At first he'd not seen any reason to show up for the filming; the thought of his pallid, moist, thumb-shaped face broadcast on television, even for a second, even in the background, sickened him. But like most people, he had caught an episode of *Pickin' Fortunes* now and again, and he'd noticed that besides the obviously big-ticket items, the things that got the best segments were those that were intertwined with the seller's personal history. Even he had to admit his past as an also-ran pop idol and first-wave punk musician might make an excellent centerpiece for Mark and Grant's show. Hell, maybe they'd even license a track or two from the Tears in the Birthday Cake album to be played during his segment. Against his will—intellectually he knew how far-fetched it all was—a fantasy had grown in his mind of a career resurgence, a much-belated fame and fortune that would, among other pleasures, allow him to leave this life and move far, far away from Wichita. (Whether Seymour came with him in this fantasy depended upon his mood.) This was why he was so intent on playing nice with everyone at Heart, including Veronica; as a brand-new and unproven dealer, the surefire way to some screen time was through ingratiation. Now, because of Seymour, he'd made enemies of Veronica and Margaret Byrd both, two of the Heart of America's most powerful tenants.

On the bright side, as far as Lee knew, he did not currently have stomach cancer, multiple sclerosis, or a warrant out for his arrest, but in his present mood none of that offered much consolation. Striving for positivity, he reminded himself that no matter what happened, he'd always have his kick-ass record collection.

Late last night he lay in bed, Seymour snoring next to him, in that uncomfortable liminal state between sleep and wakefulness, until a niggling thought agitated him into full, panicked consciousness: What *were* his top five desert island LPs? It had been a recurring topic of conversation over the course of his and Seymour's relationship, but besides earlier that day when he was trying to show off to that teenage hipster, Lee could not presently remember the last time Seymour had asked. In that lonely midnight moment, nothing seemed more urgent, so Lee crawled out of bed, sneaked upstairs to the record room that once served as his mother's "sewing room," and surveyed the collection.

He started by flipping through the stack of recently played albums leaning against the right-side speaker. He'd been working through the grip he'd picked up from his last big trade with one of the oldest dealers in New England just before the move to Wichita. Plenty of quality stuff, rare and much-sought-after among Lee's community of collectors—early Jandek, the Legendary Pink Dots, Moondog, etc.—but none of it top five material. On the arm of the beat-up pea-green easy chair Seymour insisted was worth the effort of hauling cross-country "for sentimental reasons" lay the leather-bound daily planner in which Lee scheduled his listening sessions. On page after page he'd noted everything he listened to and intended to listen to, cold hard proof of both his refined taste and enviable collection. But again, none of it felt top-five-worthy, and, worse, it struck him how joyless something as elemental to his identity as listening to music had become. He might as well have kept a diary of his bowel movements.

Lee then found himself scanning the IKEA Kallax shelving units that lined the walls for the still-familiar spines of albums he couldn't remember the last time he'd listened to—none of the weird stuff, the avant-garde, or obscure, but rather simple pop music. This was what he'd grown up on, and deep in his soul, this was what he really liked: re-petitive, earwormy, likable, obvious. What was wrong with that? Like so many others, his interest in music had begun with the Beatles. As a teen-ager in the seventies, when his friends were listening to Yes and Rush and ELP, he hunted for the hard-to-find variant mixes, the B-sides, the fan club exclusive Christmas singles, the bootlegs and foreign releases with alternate takes. So he tossed aside his planner, removed the Throbbing Gristle LP from the turntable, and put on one of his all-time favorites, a strong contender for the number one slot on his desert island list: not the Beatles but the Kinks, their 1968 LP *The Kinks Are the Village Green Preservation Society*, a concept album with songs linked by themes of nos-talgia, memory, and pastoralism, as tuneful as their better-known early hits but with a gentle melodicism unmatched, in Lee's opinion, even by the Fab Four themselves. As the first notes of the title song swelled, he began to cry—not a few sentimental tears; he bawled so fiercely he had to turn the volume up. It'd been so long since he'd allowed himself to listen to any pop music at all, it was as if he were hearing the album for the first time—no, not the first time but more like the fourth or fifth or eighth. The best listen was the first only in the tidy narrative of memory; in reality, that sweet zone was between the second and twentieth spin when you had just enough of the melodies committed to mind that the listening was effortless; you fell into the music as seamlessly as warm bathwater, forgetting yourself for those few transcendent songs before the A-side ended. In subsequent listens, it would all become so familiar, so known-by-heart, so burdened by past experience that it was no longer the music itself but rather an accumulation of all the play-throughs of the past. It was when an album crossed this threshold that Lee would begin obsessing over the disc's flaws: pops, skips, crackles, and scratches he hadn't noticed while still in the early thrall. He'd obsessively clean his disc on his expensive vacuum-powered record washer, scour the crates of other dealers at shows and on the internet with the aim of upgrading to the mintest condition available, accruing many different editions in the process. He would still enjoy albums after exiting the sweet zone but never in the same way.

But now if *Village Green* could sound fresh to him after all these years, who knew? It was possible he could reenter the sweet zone of anything, maybe even as foundational a song as "I Want to Hold Your Hand." Lee was not young. The best days of his life were far behind him. If his only ambition was to avoid major tragedies such as disfiguring injuries and debilitating destitution while taking solace in his record collection, he supposed he could live with that. He would listen only to pop music from now on, he decided, whether as sophisticated as *Pet Sounds* or as vapid as Ohio Express—or, hell, even the Sodashoppe Teens.

Now, thinking of all that awaited him in the record room, the manifold favorites he'd neglected for far too long, Lee pulled the car out of park and turned up the volume on the stereo. He sang along to "The Screw," an unreleased Phil Spector piss-take, and was pleased with the sound of his voice. He'd only ever sung backup in any of the bands in which he'd played—he was no natural front man like Seymour—but like the heartland cliché that he was, his earliest performing experience had been in his church's children's choir.

Pulling into the driveway, he was relieved to find all the lights off in the house. Seymour was either still out or asleep, thank god. Lee hadn't shared a word with him today about his dramatic break from his usual diet of "headphones music." He would just be disappointed in him, and it would only exacerbate the tension in their relationship. Seymour could only love someone he admired, and he could only admire someone with taste even more obscure than his own.

However he felt about Seymour, Lee couldn't deny that he made a damn good mixtape. He hit the eject button, intending to finish listening to it inside, but all of a sudden he couldn't move. Something caught his ear and wouldn't let go, the tail end of a song he couldn't place. He stared at the tape in his hand—he couldn't understand how it continued to play even after he'd removed it from the deck—before realizing the console had switched to radio output. Normally they kept it tuned to NPR (there were no good stations in Wichita), but whatever this was, it was good, really good, incredible even: chiming Big Star–esque guitars playing a progression indebted to fifties doo-wop and yet somehow new; subtle string accompaniment in the vein of *Forever Changes*; elaborate but not show-offy vocal arrangements; a chorus that was catchy in an unobvious way; simple but eloquent love song lyrics; and the crucial element that to Lee always signified a great song, a bridge that was even catchier than the chorus. It was all captured in analog-warm production, eschewing the antiseptic compression of most modern-day tunes, so true to that 1960s AM chamber-pop sound that Lee wondered if some previously unreleased gem had been discovered in the Buddah Records vaults.

As recently as yesterday, before the rediscovery of the *Village Green* sweet zone, before the leaf-turning embrace of his true musical love, he would not have allowed himself to admit how much he liked this song, but now he wanted nothing more than to hear it again and again. As the coda faded out, the dulcet voice of Terry Gross informed Lee that he was listening to *Fresh Air*. "My guest today is—"

The gaseous heat of misery filled Lee's stomach, rising up his spine and simmering beneath his forehead. He held the steering wheel with a throttling grip and tried to scream, but the sound wouldn't come.

Today's guest was Mickey Gordy. The song was from his new album,

Popular Music, a collection, according to Terry, that "explores, deconstructs, *re*constructs, criticizes, and celebrates the tropes and permutations of the twentieth century pop song, a surprising project from the auteur behind works including the experimental ballet adaptation of Phillip K. Dick's *Ubik*, 'Drone: a piece for forty-nine guitars and one broken washing machine,' and the artsy jam-funk band Barthes, among many others. Many of your fans would say this was—"

"As likely as a Sodashoppe Teens reunion," Mickey cut in. "Look, from the start I've been interested in exploring music in all its forms. I've collaborated with Glenn Branca. I've had a chart-topping dance-pop album. There's nothing in my career I'm ashamed of, but that one comes close." He and Terry shared a laugh. "I've never said I had so much integrity that there were things I didn't do just for the money, especially when I was starting out. To be frank, it was miserable. The music was awful. The Osmonds rocked harder than us! And the people—delusional kids who thought they were the next Lennon/McCartney. Hell, we weren't even the 1910 Fruitgum Company. But you know what? This might surprise you, but I *like* the 1910 Fruitgum Company!"

He went on to talk about the insatiable nature of his creative drive. It was a compulsion. He'd written whole albums in his head while riding the subway. He couldn't not make music. If he stopped making music, he said, it meant only one thing—he was dead. This was the way most artists talked, like they just *had* to do it. But quitting had been easy for Lee. After the self-released Tears in the Birthday Cake album failed to land a record deal, he'd put away his sax and began a long stint of uninteresting day jobs that somehow accidentally culminated in a respectable career in "human resource management" that ended the ill-fated day Seymour convinced him of the money and freedom that awaited them as small business owners.

"I've never really considered myself a musician. I'm more of a music fan. I keep up with the new stuff, but what lights my fire is discovering those neglected gems. Not to be elitist, but I'm a vinylhead, a crate-digger, and as I was throwing this platter together, what inspired me the most was the classics—for instance, the three Bs: the Beach Boys, the Beatles, and Big Star—but also a lot of barely heard stuff, eighties college rock, private-press garage loners, anything with photocopied sleeves, real art brut stuff, if you know what I mean, bands even I have barely ever heard of, like . . ."

Crate-digger? Bullshit! The fat cat bastard probably had his assistants trawling Fee-Bay for him. It wasn't enough that his music career had to overshadow Lee's, now Mickey Gordy was acting like he'd out-collected him.

Before Terry could cue another selection from *Popular Music*, he punched the radio off, scraping his knuckle on the hard plastic edge of the knob. He could not pretend that the song he'd just heard was not excellent. It was easy with the other stuff, Mickey's weird arty noise projects he didn't understand. But this was different. Tears in the Birthday Cake was the only one of his post-Sodashoppe bands that ever caught any real heat, regularly selling out shows at the Rat and garnering ecstatic write-ups in the local press. This was near the sound Lee had been going for with their album, but he'd lacked both the budget and the talent to pull it off. Mickey Gordy had beaten him at his own game, and worst of all, Mickey Gordy probably didn't even know there was a game or that Lee had ever been a player.

He went inside. The TV in the living room was still on but the room empty, Seymour out at a bar or asleep in the dim bedroom, it hardly mattered. They'd gotten into the habit of never acknowledging each other's comings and goings. A picture of Lindy Bobo, hair curled to maximum voluminosity, shone on-screen. The local news anchor noted the picture, from last year's Little Miss Midwestern Belle Pageant, would be posted on a billboard along Route 54 and printed in the local newspaper every day until the lost girl, age seven, was found. Then they cut to footage of Lindy's family, her mother and grandmother, sitting on a beige couch in a beige room before a coffee table strewn with MISSING flyers, while her little brother, oblivious, pushed an empty Saltines box like a Tonka truck along the carpet around their feet. "We just want her back. We want our little Lindy back," Mother Bobo said, her voice cracking. The camera pulled in on her pleading face and the reporter's voice asked, "Where *is* she? *Where* is she? Where is *she*?"

Damned if Lee knew—or would be any help finding out. He turned off the TV and went up to the record room. The Kinks album rested on the turntable, the stylus cued to "Picture Book," but he didn't feel like playing it anymore. Last night he'd opened the gatefold door of *Village Green* and reentered its sweet zone for the first time in decades, but thanks to Terry fucking Gross it'd closed to him once again.

Scrutinizing a collection meticulously cataloged by micro-genre and date of release, he saw only a wasted life, the ruins of ambition. He turned to the shelves and began pulling every Gordy-related release he could think of. He owned pretty much everything the man had ever done, though he almost never listened to it. He'd been compiling them since the first Barthes album, released less than six months after the Sodashoppe Teens crashed and burned, as if through them he could make sense of his own failures, could pinpoint just what it was that Mickey Gordy had that he lacked. When it failed to reveal anything, he took his first steps into his weird-stuff phase. Now he could see he'd devoted all these fruitless years to the study of music he would never understand and—he could finally admit it—actively disliked.

Leaned against the wall, the stack of Gordy records stretched nearly a yard. In front was a later period Barthes album, the cover an image of Mickey and his bandmates sipping through straws from a bottle of Thunderbird fortified wine, a parody of the Sodashoppe Teens' cover. The album even included a scathingly ironic cover of the Teens' "Handclaps in My Heart," which consisted of Mickey barking Iggy Pop–like over a deluge of feedback and drum-chaos. Then Lee pulled the two releases that comprised his own piddling oeuvre. Quantity was not quality, but even so, Lee's legacy had amounted to, what, a couple millimeters, a half inch if he included his duplicate copies? And half of it was Mickey's, too—the Sodashoppe Teens belonged to both of them, even if neither of them wanted it.

The front door creaked open. It was interesting how, if you spent enough time with someone, you knew who they were just by the sound of them entering a room. Seymour always paused after passing through a threshold, like a sitcom character waiting for applause from a studio audience.

Lee locked the door and made a bed for himself on the easy chair.

SATURDAY

LOST AND FOUND

15

RONALD

"Gable!" Ronald called. "Gable! You get your buns over here!" The dog poked his snout in the crack under the door to the basement and tapped his nails on the floor, his signal that he wanted in. What was with that mutt? Probably he smelled the fast food. Or he smelled Lindy. He looked up at Ronald with suspicion in his eyes—no, stop it, that was silly, Gable was just an animal.

One that was not used to discipline. "You keep away from there, pooch!" Gable licked his rear and trotted to the kitchen where his food bowl was kept. For his part, Ronald had been avoiding Lindy since he caught her out of the kennel yesterday. He delivered meals to her promptly every few hours but that was it. Neither of them felt much like talking.

Ronald took the plate of reheated pizza out of the microwave, crept down the basement steps, unlocked the door, and shut it firmly behind him.

Lindy was asleep in the kennel, curled up in her cartoon bedspread. The door was now reinforced with a padlock, but that was for her own safety. He couldn't have her falling down trying to escape out the window again. She could hurt herself. And the sheets he'd taped up to block the windows were to keep the light from getting in her eyes. He set the pizza on the floor within her reach and watched the small up-and-down motion of her breath. Good, he thought. She was not dead.

There was no reason she would be. Ronald took extra-special care of her. But what if she did die, in some random and unpreventable way, through no fault of his own? Suddenly his hands were numb. He rubbed his eyes. He wasn't seeing right, like he was looking at Lindy from the bottom of a well. He struggled to breathe. He was dying, or they both were, there was some kind of gas leak or carbon monoxide poisoning or something—if Melinda were still around, she would know. He tried to rouse Lindy, to shout—he wouldn't touch her—but he couldn't seem to find his voice.

By the time he climbed the stairs and made it out the basement door, he was gasping for air like a swimmer emerged. He went to his office, where he kept his most prized postcards. The smell of paper and Mylar and postmark ink calmed him. This was his sanctuary, his collection organized in the drawers of the custom oak units lining the walls, his rarest and most favorite pieces mounted and framed. Above his desk was an arrangement of early twentieth century exaggerated fruit and vegetable postcards, illustrations and doctored photographs of giant-sized celery, carrots, apples, potatoes, cucumbers, and tomatoes, big enough to fill semi-trucks and flatcars. These were the first type he'd collected. As a young man, he'd stumbled across one in a pile of old recipe books at a yard sale in Hutchinson. It was, he'd found after some research at the library, one of A. S. Johnson Jr.'s earliest works: *Onion Harvest from Waupun, Wis.*, dated 1909, depicting a family of farmers carting a white onion the size of a wrecking ball.

It'd been a couple long days since he'd last been in here, as busy as he was with Lindy. There was something else. This room, it was too quiet. When he prayed, he couldn't find Melinda in the silence. In her absence, his conscience nipped at him like Gable at his ankles. Part of him didn't want to let Lindy go. He was a lonely old man. He liked having someone else around. It had seemed fated when he found her in his yard and when he learned her name was Lindy—short for *Me-*

linda! A miraculous coincidence, a cure for soul-sickness. How could it be wrong?

But it was. Any fool could see that, and Ronald must be the biggest fool of them all. Again, his chest tightened, his breath shortened, his vision darkened. What he felt before, maybe it really was a gas leak. He could escape and survive, but for Lindy it was already too late. How simple it would be if she did die, if they both died.

No—Ronald was not that kind of person. He was a good man who'd gotten himself in a pickle then a pretzel and now a whole darned twisty noodle, who had made a terrible mistake. A sense of doom seized him as he lay awake at night and when he walked Gable past Lindy asking HAVE YOU SEEN ME? on telephone pole after telephone pole. Melinda would say the only right thing to do would be to let Lindy go. But that didn't have to mean dire consequences for Ronald, did it? Surely Lindy's family cared more about having her back than exacting vengeance on him— once again the word *kidnapper*, joined by *abductor* and *criminal* and *bad guy*, flashed in Ronald's mind before he dismissed them—a *temporary caretaker*, and they would see that their precious Lindy was unharmed. Perhaps they'd even find that her brief time away had done her good—a sort of surprise vacation, it was.

According to the flyers, there was a cash reward for any person who helped to recover Lindy safe and sound. Ronald didn't care about the money, but even a numbskull like him could imagine the press coverage that such a heroic act would garner. The TV people would be arriving in two days and *that* would be quite the icebreaker with Mark and Grant. It wouldn't even be a fib, since Ronald *had* after all been the one to find her.

But would Lindy stay mum? Ronald could only hope. It was up to him to explain it to her in terms she would understand. Then, when the time was right—late tonight when the CHAANT folks had gone home—he'd call the police and tell them the story of how he'd found her. Not the *whole* story but, so to speak, the edited-for-TV version. Of course they'd understand. He was just a harmless old man. He'd never even gotten a speeding ticket. And if Lindy let slip anything about the kennel—well, she was just a little girl, easily confused.

Yes, indeed. That was just the ticket. A calm came over him, his breathing slowed, and warmth flowed to his cheeks as if Melinda had blown a kiss from heaven. Things were going to work out fine.

16

DELORES

"You're a grown-up now, Dolly," the Barbies had said while Delores dressed for her—not date, it wasn't a date. "We might not always be here to keep you ladylike."

"I love you," Delores had said, fiddling with the straps of the blue corduroy jumper dress she slipped over a simple white blouse and black pantyhose. "I need you."

"Tonight you fly solo."

And here she was, solo, at Pete Deen's doorstep, a nondescript brown house just a few blocks from her own. She'd driven, though it would have been faster to walk, since she'd been stuck at a stop sign for nearly ten minutes waiting for the CHAANT caravan to pass. She pressed the doorbell. It made an unmelodious buzzing noise, insect-like and ominous. A nagging feeling of lightness had been haunting her since she first stepped outside. The Barbies were not with her. Her pockets empty, they hadn't even allowed Delores her key chain. "Pacifiers are for babies," the brunette Dramatic New Living Barbie had said. "Even my little twin siblings Tutti and Todd wouldn't be caught drooling on such a thing."

Inside, Delores could hear Pete barreling down the stairs to the foyer. The door did not open, however. He was probably leering at her through the peephole, planning all the "moves" he was going to make on her. Delores wanted to run, but she reminded herself why she was there. If Growing Up Skipper 7259-A was going to be rescued, it would all be worth it. Inside, a woman's muffled voice said something Delores couldn't make out. In response Pete screamed, "Stay in your room, Ma! You promised, goddamn it."

Finally the door swung open, unleashing a dense cloud of men's cologne, the scent of wet leather with the sharpness of rubbing alcohol. Delores preferred subtlety. She swore that the plastic of a Ken or Blaine smelled different than Barbie and the other girls, a hint of pinecone and tobacco.

"Delores, hi, hello, how are you?" Pete spoke fast, like it was all one word. He wore a button-down bowling shirt with a line of neon flames along each side, his inhaler on a lanyard around his neck, light gray cargo shorts, and sandals with white socks pulled nearly up to his knees.

"Fine." Delores combed her hair with her fingernails. Without Barbie, she didn't know what to do with her hands. She stopped when she saw Pete was mirroring her, running his own fat fingertips through his sticky red hair. She invited herself in, wanting to get this over with as quickly as possible.

Inside, the house was not what she had expected. In fact, as far as she could see it was neat and clutter-free, with a bright, clean citrus scent that offered welcome relief from Pete's cologne. The living room held a couch and easy chair upholstered in a matching floral pattern, a glass-top coffee table, candles and small potted plants on the mantelpiece, framed black-and-white family photographs on the wall.

"The toys are upstairs," Pete said, almost like an apology. "But first." He led her to a seat on the couch, not touching but hovering his hands just barely over her shoulders, his palms radiating warmth, not the pleasant kind. Pete had stacked pillows and folded blankets on one end of the couch so they'd have to sit near each other. "Make yourself comfortable. I'll be right back."

Delores moved the pillows onto the center cushion, fashioning a plush barrier between her seat and Pete's, but then changed her mind. If Barbie were here, she'd remind her she was to obtain Skipper via any means necessary, even if it meant violating the usual rules for retaining your feminine dignity while socializing with boys. Delores sometimes thought she would, under the right circumstances, kill for the Growing Up Skipper prototype, so she supposed she could stand to bump elbows with Pete Deen.

Pete returned carrying a vintage Mickey Mouse Club TV tray on which were set a pitcher filled with what looked like lemonade, two jelly glasses, and a plate of Hostess CupCakes and Twinkies. He put the tray on the table and poured Delores a glass. She mumbled thank you (*Enunciate!* the Barbies would have commanded) and sipped. The combination of the artificial sweetness and the bitter burn of the alcohol was nauseating.

"My homemade limoncello." Pete reached into his shirt pocket and removed an empty Country Time packet. "The secret ingredient," he whispered. There were chocolate crumbs on his chin and numerous small cuts on his freshly shaven cheeks.

Delores pretended to take another sip but did not let the liquid touch her lip.

Pete bit into a Twinkie and stared at the cream filling as if he were surprised to find it there.

"Don't you want one? I put them in the microwave for a few seconds."

Delores searched for something to say. "That's innovative."

"That way they're kind of warm. I had deep-fried ones at the Sedgwick County Fair once."

Footsteps from upstairs. An older woman's voice called down, "Pete, the VCR won't work."

"Quiet, Ma. I told you to stay in your room." He shrugged at Delores.

"I am in my room. The VCR won't turn on."

"We don't have a VCR anymore. It's a DVD player. DVD!"

"You know what I mean. How do I play my movie?"

Delores took slow, deep breaths and imagined herself encased in the cardboard and plastic of a Barbie doll box. She could make it through this. If it led to Skipper, she could make it through anything. She would not let doubt enter her mind. Barbie could not be wrong. If she said Skipper was here, she was.

"Just press the button on the remote, Ma."

"Button?"

"The play button. A green triangle."

"The green button? Pete, what green button?"

"On the other remote. The play button, Ma! It's the same as the old VCR."

"I don't know what you're talking about. There are a lot of buttons. What button?"

"The button! The fucking button, for fuck's sake! THE FUCKING FUCK BUTTON!" He went clomping up the stairs. A door opened and shut. The tones of an argument could be heard but the words were indecipherable. Delores gazed at the front door. Now was probably her last opportunity for escape.

Pete returned a few minutes later, out of breath, the strain of the stairs too much for him. He sat so close to Delores their legs were touching and sucked on his inhaler. "You know, I've had girlfriends before," he said. He took a sip from his glass but most of the liquid dribbled down his chin.

A grandfather clock chimed from somewhere deep within the house. "Oh shoot, it's time." Pete grabbed the remote and turned on the cable box, settling on the game show channel.

They watched *Match Game* and *The Gong Show* and *The Joker's Wild* and *The Newlywed Game* and *The $20,000 Pyramid*. The seventies-era sets, all rust and orange and wood paneling, were framed ideally by Pete's blandly manicured home, tidy but as the night wore on increasingly suffocating, the air stiff as if Scotchgarded. Pete laughed wildly at tired innuendos spewed by baggy-eyed celebrities. Delores did not much care for Pete's brand of nostalgia. The toys he collected were playthings to him, a means of reenacting a childhood that couldn't have possibly been as happy as he remembered. Barbie was different, aspirational: an exemplar of poise and sophistication, a model of idealized adulthood, not a relic of childhood fantasy. It was not that Barbie wasn't a toy—of course she was—it was that she was more than that, she was a person—a person Delores hadn't been apart from in many, many years. She almost teared up, dabbed at her eyes while Pete slapped his knee in response to some idiotic Charo bon mot.

This had gone on long enough. If Delores wanted Skipper, she'd have to be proactive. *Hollywood Squares* over, she grabbed the remote and turned off the television. She took a cupcake from the tray and offered it to Pete. "You want?" When he reached for it, she pulled it away. Taking Pete's outstretched hand, she brought the cupcake flirtatiously to his lips, holding it by the tips of her fingernails so as to avoid direct contact. Pete sucked it down, his eyebrows arched in a grotesque façade of seduction. She was glad the Barbies weren't here to see this.

Delores wiped her hand on the couch cushion. "Show me your room. Show me your toys."

"My collection?" Pete smiled. "My *real* collection and not just the junk I sell at the Heart? You'll flip your lid." In his stocking feet like a child, he led Delores up the stairs, past a door behind which his mother snored over the looping sound bites of a DVD menu, to the end of the hall and up another staircase to his attic bedroom.

"There's a lot more in the basement," Pete said. "This is just where I keep the essentials." Toys of all kinds filled the room, which was narrowly navigable owing to impregnable layers of boxes and display shelves. Model airplanes and spaceships hung from the ceiling. Meticulously painted model kits of sci-fi and horror creatures were displayed on a bookshelf by Pete's bed. Some of what he kept up here was apparently so precious he stored it in a specially lit glass case, such as a set of shampoo bottles shaped like the Universal Studios monsters and an original *Star Trek* phaser replica, but some of it was treated carelessly, like the mass of loose action figures on the floor tangled up like a rat king. This was not a safe place for any Barbie, let alone Growing Up Skipper.

There were no chairs, no place to sit but the bed, so there she sat, on the very edge, pulling her skirt over her knees. "You said something about a shipment? From a man you met at PlastiCon."

Pete ran his hands through his hair, then examined his fingertips, greasy with pomade. "Let me give you a tour." He pointed at a comic book titled *Cyberspasm*. "See that? It's being adapted into a major motion picture. Right now it's worth about fifteen dollars. A year from now it'll be one-fifty, easy. And that"—he referred to a boxed Castle Grayskull—"three hundred. I'm sure you've seen the previews for the new cartoon. After the debut? Three *thousand*." He went on like this for a while, divulging intel from his "contacts in Hollywood."

"About the Mattel shipment," Delores said.

Crouching, Pete inspected a paint job on a gila monster model kit. "I'll tell you something I learned." Pete was whispering now, as if about to impart sacred knowledge. "Besides the Hollywood stuff, there's really only three types of stuff you'll ever make any money off: stuff that's really old, like a hundred or eighty years or whatever; stuff that's in brand-new perfect condition; and stuff that's about twenty years old. See, this is when people have kids of their own and they start to get nostalgic for their childhood, the stuff Mom gave to Goodwill." He snapped his fingers, but they were too damp with pomade to make a sound. "Gold mine."

"You wanted me to appraise some dolls?"

He sprang up, dug around in the flotsam, and emerged with a box about the size and dimensions of three 1990 DreamHouses. "Wonder what's inside." Delores about fainted when he rattled the box, stamped with a bright red FRAGILE. He plopped it on the floor beside Delores's feet. "Now, where did I put that box cutter—no, wait, ha ha, I'll open it with this cool sword I got for my birthday. Do you know that kiosk at the mall?" Pete began once again to rustle around.

Delores pointed her ear toward the box. Was something murmuring from within? It was hard to tell with all the noise Pete was making. "Dang it, I know I put it right here, but where is it? Ma!" he yelled down the stairs. "Ma! Have you seen my sword?"

"It's dangerous!" she yelled back. "I don't want you playing with that thing."

"Goddamn it, Ma! I told you to stay out of my room!" Delores couldn't wait any longer. She stuck her diamond-hard fingernail into the seam of the packing tape and sliced it open. "Oh," Pete said, "you got it already." He sounded a little disappointed.

Delores tried to soften her expression. "I'd love for you to show me what he's sent you. I can help appraise any Mattel fashion dolls."

"Yeah, okay." Pete knelt and lifted the box flaps. "Oh wow! Holy jeez!" Delores could not see what was inside, Pete's enormous quaking back blocking her view.

"Oh lord, what is it?" She pushed him out of the way.

"*Battlestar Galactica!* The original, complete and in brand-new condition." He held a couple of boxes displaying robots and spaceships. The package was full of them. Delores was not interested in science fiction toys, save for Astronaut Barbie, especially the 1965 edition. "Oh man! The Cylon Raider! Colonial Landram! Mark and Grant are gonna love this." Somehow the Barbies had been wrong, but Delores felt like she was the one who had failed them. Whatever preternatural intuition they had about these things must have been thrown off by Delores's petulance. She'd known better than to eat that doughnut! When she got home, she'd face the Barbies and vow to be better. Hopelessly she eyed the door. It seemed an improbably long trek down the stairs and to the exit. "I've got some episodes recorded we can watch later. Can you believe they're actually coming to the Heart of America on Monday?"

Yes, the TV show filming, Delores thought sadly. Keith Stoller had let slip that the producers had already expressed interest in filming a special segment about her. Evidently her reputation preceded her. It would not be the first time she was subject to media coverage. Her collection

LUKE GEDDES

was so revered in some circles that she'd been featured in venues such as *American Dolls Quarterly* and *Collectors' Monthly*. She'd even once been quoted in a *USA Today* article on a proposed Barbie redesign. They'd referred to her as a foremost expert on the brand. But that was a lie. She was nothing without the Growing Up Skipper prototype to complete her collection.

She stood to make a brisk exit when she heard a sound from within the package, the whisper of a whisper.

She shoved Pete out of the way and dug in, flinging *Battlestar Galactica* toys at him as she made her way to the bottom. He cheered as he caught each one. "Yeah! It's like Christmas!" Finally, all that remained was a plain white unlabeled box. She lifted the lid and the revelation of what was inside knocked her back onto the bed.

"Well, hello, Dolly. Took you long enough."

It was her: 7259-A, the ultra-rare Growing Up Skipper prototype with additional menstruation feature. Delores twisted her trigger arm and wrist, some internal mechanism clicked, and all at once Skipper grew in height, her breasts expanded, and—yes, it was true, a flip of her checkered skirt proved it—a droplet of water leaked out from Skipper's refillable torso, initiating the color-change spot in her undergarment accessory. After all this time, Delores had her, she finally had her! She couldn't wait to display her (under lock and key, of course) at the next convention. She had done it. She had completed her collection. She had achieved perfection.

Pete finished sorting through the *Battlestar Galactica* junk and joined Delores on the bed, his leg touching hers.

All that was left was the matter of getting Skipper away from Pete. "Peter, Pete, Petey. I'm so impressed with your collection."

"Yeah."

"I don't suppose you really want this Skipper."

Pete grabbed Delores's wrist and studied the doll, eyeing the stained underwear. "Gross! Hmm. Not really, I guess."

Delores bit her lip. "I'd give you a fair price. Really I would."

Pete blushed. "Oh, Delores, I couldn't sell anything to you. We're friends." He sucked on his inhaler but the way he pressed it to his lips was almost like a kiss.

"Then, you mean you'd—"

The metallic groan of Pete's fly zipper echoed, and in an instant, without the click of an unseen internal mechanism, his erect penis appeared like a red rubber doll between his thighs.

Delores looked to Skipper, who shrugged without moving. So long as she did not have to offer Pete the privacy of her own body (in truth, she hated that thing itself, so complicated and busy was all that stuff compared to the smooth perfect blankness between Barbie's legs), she could distance her mind from the actions she was about to perform. She turned Skipper's head so she would not see and looked with dread at her own trembling palm. But before she could touch him, Skipper said, in the tone of a wink, "A girl does what she has to, Dolly, but a woman does only what she wants."

At once Delores understood perfectly. She said to Pete, "I have a surprise for you."

"Oh boy, a surprise!"

"But I'm shy. Close your eyes. It'll be worth it."

Pete took one last proud look at his throbbing member and closed his eyes.

"No peeking. Or else no surprise." Off the floor she picked up a HOT WHEELS CONVENTION 1998 sweatshirt and tied it as a blindfold around his face.

He leaned back on his elbows. "Okay, I'm ready for my surprise."

"It's going to take me a while to get ready. Count to thirty. Slowly."

Pete had not quite made it to twenty by the time Delores burst through Pete's front door, Skipper in hand. She'd have escaped even quicker if she had not stopped to knock on Pete's mother's bedroom door to tell her that Pete needed to talk to her about something *right* away.

She buckled Skipper into the passenger seat and climbed in beside her.

"I see my sisters have taught you a thing or two about a woman's resourcefulness. I sure have missed my family."

"We've missed you, too."

Skipper did not talk much after that but in the middle of the short drive home she shrieked. Delores pulled over to the curb and asked if she was feeling well.

"The man in that house. I don't like him."

"Of course not. Pete and his boys' toys, but we got him—"

"No! Not that man."

"K-Ken?"

"I mean the man in *that* house." They were parked on Belmont Street. Skipper directed her voice at the dingy ranch house with the weird lawn ornament and pathetic decayed wreath on the door. "He's hiding something. He's bad. Bad for pretty girls. Beautiful girls like us look out for our own."

"You think I'm beautiful?"

"Not you, Dolly. Do you remember when you first met my sister?"

"Of course. On my sixth birthday. I can still picture the wrapping paper—"

"Uncharge your batteries, Dolly. I wasn't asking for a soliloquy. Do you know *why* Barbie chose you? Don't answer. You were in trouble. Such an unhappy child."

"It's unbecoming to frown."

"Yes. It's a shame for pretty little girls to be in trouble. But I have a plan, Dolly. Are you going to be a good girl and do exactly what I say?"

17

SEYMOUR

A miasma of B.O. filled Jimmy Daniels's basement as the horde of collectors swept frenziedly through the record crates set up in rows too narrow for some of the portlier among them to comfortably fit, marking their territory with outspread elbows and surreptitiously released farts. They were nearly identical in their wrinkled and untucked button-ups, their baggy pants, their unkempt or grease-slicked hair. Though Seymour had always idolized the monomaniacal, socially guileless types that surrounded him, with their near-autistic focus and endless depth of trivial expertise, he'd also prided himself on being better than them; he had a multitude of interests apart from vinyl, a robust sex life (up until recently, at least), a wardrobe that consisted of more than just a couple faded checked oxfords, a few pairs of khaki chinos, and a tweed jacket for special occasions.

But that wasn't true. He had lied to Ellie about not being one of them. He had lied to himself. He was as bad as these guys or any collector scum, even Pete Deen or Margaret. Worse, actually, because he had the unfortunate self-awareness to realize how pointless it was and he still couldn't stop himself: terminally unimpressed, incapable of having a conversation that didn't involve such scintillating topics as the minute differences in mixes across international pressings or impassioned defenses of 1970s Doug Yule–era Velvet Underground bootlegs. When he was a kid, he'd had such an easy time talking to anyone and everyone, was on a first-name basis with all the homeless people in his neighborhood. He'd long forsaken his natural curiosity. He had too much information in his head already, and none of it was interesting.

In his career, Seymour had gotten used to the particular melancholy of estate sales; seeing a person's or a family's entire material life price-tagged and on display was worse than a funeral. And he'd had countless awkward and soul-deadening encounters buying stuff off craigslist from lonely spinsters, teenage drug addicts, poor single mothers in desperate need of rent money. But this was depressing in a new way.

He could guess exactly how Jimmy had ended up with this collection. He'd seen it before. In Seymour's crowd they called it the Purge, an existential sickness hitting in late middle age that drove collectors to a complete and total divestment. Of all the guys he knew who'd done it, there were none for whom it wasn't their greatest-ever regret. One sad sack seen regularly at shows around Boston used to tell anyone willing to listen about the collection he'd once had that he was now trying to rebuild piece by piece. A long while back, this guy had been evicted from his apartment after a bad divorce and a job loss and had to move into a buddy's studio where there was no room for his vinyl. He didn't have any friends or family who could offer storage space, so he carried them—"four thousand and thirty-eight total, including about sixty minty Blue Notes, a bunch of Sun 78s"—to the dumpster behind his apartment building and trashed them all. "I could have sold them," he'd said, "but I just couldn't stand the thought of someone else having them." Not a day went by, the guy said, that he didn't think about it. "The ones that nag me the most are the ones I can't remember. How can I replace them if I don't know I used to have them?"

As Seymour browsed among the vultures, he struggled to think of a single record on his personal checklist. Not that it stopped him from building a to-buy stack heavy enough to strain his arms. The guys flanking him side-eyed each LP he pulled with envy and judgment, and he soon found himself participant in the inane patter of the connoisseur. So far he had selected: Small Faces' *Ogdens' Nut Gone Flake* (Guy: "Let me know if you change your mind on that. I've got the stereo already but not the mono." Seymour: "Mono's much better, I heard."), The Raspberries' *Fresh* (Guy: "Carmen's one of the rare few who transcend their influences. He's a better songwriter than McCartney, in my opinion." Seymour: "I agree, but only because McCartney's overrated."), the Beach Boys' *Love You* (Guy: "One of my favorites." Seymour: "Gloriously stupid lyrics." Guy: "I don't know, I think they really work in their own way. For the Beach Boys especially. You don't have to be Dylan to be profound and—" Seymour: "No, I totally agree. I know it's a crime but I've never been that big on Dylan. I can dig him up through *Highway 61 Revisited* or *Blonde on Blonde* but after . . ."), the Osmonds' *The Plan* (Seymour: "Um, no comment." Guy: "Actually, it's better than its novelty reputation. 'Let Me In' and 'Goin' Home' are really decent cuts."), The Scruffs' *Wanna Meet the Scruffs?* (Seymour: "Been looking for that one for a while." Guy: "It's a fair price, especially for a target purchase."), *Shangri-Las-65!* (Guy: "Almost grabbed that one myself, but the B-side's got a nasty crack." Seymour: "Doesn't bother me. I've already got two copies of this in better condition. But I never *not* buy the Shangri-Las when the price is right. My all-time favorite but also the single most important group of the 1960s. I love the Beatles, but fuck the Beatles."), Tommy James & the Shondells' *It's Only Love* (Guy: "Not their best." Seymour: "I'm a completist."), Shoes' *Present Tense* (Guy: "Excellent choice, sir."), and Roger McGuinn's self-titled (Guy: "Love the Byrds." Seymour: "I go back-and-forth on 'em.").

When he'd had enough, Seymour took refuge at a card table near the door. He separated his finds into Yes, No, and Maybe piles while stragglers barreled through with the emotionless determination of Black Friday spree-shoppers and suicide bombers. No point in getting *that* excited. Ultimately he found the selection rather pedestrian—no mono Velvets, no OG *#1 Record*, as Jimmy had teased. With each pass-through, his Yes and Maybe piles shrank, and his No pile grew. He was having a hard time convincing himself there was anything here he actually needed or wanted to own.

Finally, it all ended up in the No pile. What was wrong with him? There was some great stuff here. He remembered the ruthless macho hunter instinct that used to overcome him when he entered a sale like this. There was no greater feeling than finding that one thing that for months or years or your entire life you'd been searching for and paying next to nothing for it—that is, other than finding that thing you never knew existed, the thing you never could have thought to look for, the electric jolt of discovery like a drug or orgasm—creating a new, bigger hunger even as it satisfied an old one.

He could pinpoint the portion of his life in which he'd been happiest with sober accuracy. It was when he and Lee spent a few months traveling cross-country, stopping at every flea market, antique mall, barn sale, and swap meet they passed. The idea was to build up stock for Tragic Treasures, the little vintage shop they opened in Cambridge that hemorrhaged money for a year before they jumped ship and washed up in Wichita.

He could see why Lee found him so irritating lately. He didn't know who he was anymore. Seymour's personality was a collection of quirks and affectations, defined more by the clothes and furniture and assorted junk he owned than attitude or disposition. His was more a commentary on what a personality was than a personality itself. He didn't hate himself. He hated his stuff. He was starting to question his trenchant belief that you are what you like. What were you if you didn't like what you liked anymore?

Probably most people felt this way. Probably most people acted in accordance with the personality they'd decided on, or that had been decided for them, when they were much younger, even if inside they felt fundamentally alienated from who that self was. Seymour didn't want to think about it anymore. He abandoned his pile and left no opportunity to regret it; collectors had descended upon it by the time he took one step away.

Upstairs, Jimmy stood guard over a money box while a young woman—his wife, his girlfriend, his daughter, who knew?—handled all the transactions. Seymour had to admit it was a good strategy; the overwhelmingly hetero male clientele was less likely to attempt haggling when faced with an attractive woman.

"Seymour, my man," Jimmy said, eying his empty hands. "I'm offended. My wares aren't good enough for ya?"

"Looks like you'll do just fine without me."

"I'm not in it for the money. It's the personal connection I make with each of my buyers."

"Consider the connection made. No charge," Seymour said. "Turns out I'm not really in an acquisitions phase."

"You said that before." Jimmy narrowed his eyes. "But I get it, you're on a budget."

"What gives you that idea?"

"I overheard you and your guy the other day," Jimmy said. "I used to have a wife like yours. Spouse, I mean. Whatever you call him. Used to have a spouse who didn't understand the value of spending money to make money, let alone spending money to get stuff. I said, Hey, if you're such a minimalist, I'll do you a favor and make sure you get nothing in the divorce. That was three wives ago now." He nodded at the woman presently accepting a wad of cash from the heavy breather who'd accosted Seymour with his opinion on the Osmonds. "No hard feelings. I'll let you know the next time I hit the motherlode. It'll be a while. Lots like these don't come along every day."

"I don't plan to stick around much longer." The words emerged without thought or foresight, but now, hearing them, more as listener than speaker, Seymour understood them to be completely true.

"Well, in that case," Jimmy said. Repeating the gesture from the day they'd met, he produced a business card from his sleeve. "Moving's a bitch, ain't it? Especially for guys with fine tastes like you and me. When the time comes, I'd be happy to lighten the load in your U-Haul. Ask around, I pay fair prices, all things considered."

Seymour went straight from Jimmy's to the sad bar across the street from the grocery store whose décor could most charitably be described as *retirement community for leather-skinned Parrothead burnout trash* and brooded on a stool upholstered with duct tape among a surprisingly robust crowd of career alcoholics and grunting enthusiasts of loudly branded sports apparel.

What was wrong with him? Nothing these days, as the Soul-Array Method put it, initiated "a feeling of belonging," nothing in his old collection, not any new acquisition. It used to be the glow of a choice find like a mono *Ogdens' Nut Gone Flake* would last weeks. What could it mean now that regret struck preemptively, before point of purchase? In a strange way, it was almost a relief. Getting what you wanted only reminded you of all that you didn't yet have. But then again, so did *not* getting what you wanted.

He struggled to recall the last time he felt true desire, the last object which upon a glance he *wanted* not because it fit with his collection or because he could resell it for a profit but because he just had to fucking have it. All he came up with was Ronald Marsh's lawn ornament. Even if Seymour's hunch that it was a rare limited-run piece was correct, Heatherstone blow molds weren't worth much on the market. There weren't enough dedicated collectors to drive up values. And it wasn't in his usual wheelhouse; lawn ornaments were so Kitsch 101, a suburban housewife's idea of "character." That Ronald's wife had picked it out only proved it. But there was something special about it. Like the later work of Sid and Marty Krofft, it embodied both the whimsy and horror of the American early seventies, the love generation's sellout counter-cultural hangover. It was no coincidence that this period coincided with Seymour's own coming of age; deep down he was just another loser nostalgic for the trinkets of his misbegotten youth.

Two faces have I, he thought. The phrase was familiar but he couldn't place it. Song lyrics, maybe. There were too many songs in this world already. He resented anyone with the audacity to start a band. There was too much everything.

He swigged his drink, a sugary old-fashioned. A man at the end of the bar who exuded a lifetime of loneliness was trying to pick up women on their way out of the restroom by offering candy from a jumbo-sized bag. Surprisingly few declined but all walked briskly away after selecting a Saf-T-Pop or Tootsie Roll. There was so much sadness in this world, Seymour thought; there were discontinued candy bars, sweet morsels redolent of childhood, that no online petition would ever bring back.

That relaxed drunk feeling began to set in, like the first tenuous bubbles on the surface of near-boiling water, making him thoughtful but not yet gregarious. The muted television on the wall played endless local news coverage of the Lindy Bobo case, the closed captions frequently reminding the viewer that there had been no significant developments in the case. Below it, at a claw machine next to an internet jukebox, one man manipulated the joystick while another looked in from the side giving directions: "North. A little more—stop. Now west about three clicks. Give it a moment to steady itself—now." The crane dropped, the prongs of the claw closed on a teddy bear with the Wichita Wild logo sewn on its chest, but its limp grip did not even ruffle it. Undeterred, the men pounded more quarters into the coin slot.

Seymour thought of the low-rent carnival he and Lee had stumbled upon in the parking lot of the Towne West Square shopping mall when they'd first arrived in Wichita. They'd gone to pick up a few things for the house and here was this scene out of a Diane Arbus photograph: a rickety Ferris wheel, its joints squealing with every strained rotation; an out-of-order SPOOK HOUSE with a surprisingly ornate painted marquee, an art brut tribute to Hieronymus Bosch; a carousel spinning to the tune of Meat Loaf's "You Took the Words Right Out of My Mouth" ridden only by a girl in a plastic princess crown, screaming in inscrutable terror; and a row of precariously tented games of chance and skill. Seymour dragged Lee away from the car to get a closer look, thinking for a moment that there could be something fun, in an ironic sort of way, about living in Kansas, an undiscovered or at least underexplored grotesquerie; he had already been planning a road trip to visit the farmhouse from *In Cold Blood*. They came upon a game simply labeled RAT WHEEL. When Seymour asked how to play, an unsmiling woman with bruise-colored eyes and tobacco-stained teeth told him to pay ten dollars and pick one of about a dozen different-colored holes along the rim of a tabletop roulette-style wheel. Seymour handed her a bill from Lee's wallet and picked blue. It was not until the woman reached under the table and brought up a large, quivering rat that Seymour discerned the bite marks on her wrist. She placed it in a container in the middle of the wheel and spun. The wheel settled, the woman released the container's door mechanism, and the terrified rat scurried into the nearest hole: yellow. "You lose," the woman said. Normally Seymour loved this kind of thing—bizarre, horrifying, and hilarious at once—but now it only made him sad. Maybe if he didn't have to live here, maybe if he and Lee were just passing through on one of their road trips, he'd have been able to enjoy it. But they weren't just passing through, much as Seymour tried to convince himself otherwise. As they walked back to the car, Seymour attempted to diffuse the tension by saying with a sigh, "That poor rat." But it had gotten to him, to the both of them, he didn't know why. It was a bummer—simple as that.

Seymour hadn't exchanged a word with Lee all day. After waiting out the CHAANT meeting and walking home last night, he found Lee had locked himself in the record room. He was still in there when Seymour woke up around noon, refusing to answer when Seymour knocked or called his name. At first he figured Lee was still stewing about his innocent gaffe with Veronica and her task forcers, but when he put his ear to the door, he knew it was much worse than that. Lee was listening to the first side of *The Kinks Are the Village Green Preservation Society* on repeat, which meant he was going through another bout of what Seymour had taken to calling over the years, with decreasing affection, his vapors. Something would set Lee off—hearing a certain song on the radio, coming across an old photo on Facebook, finding his first gray hair—and he'd sulk around for days, agonizing over the career in music that never was. At the end of each bout, Lee indulged in selective amnesia and acted as if it had never happened before. The last time it struck, back in Boston, Seymour had had to chase the garbage man down and dig Lee's saxophone out of the back of the truck. For better or worse, what drew him out of the pits of depression then was the idea to open Tragic Treasures.

It hit Seymour with the last gulp of his drink. "Two Faces Have I" was an old Lou Christie song, one Lee's band used to cover, a cacophonous post-punk version. Seymour was lonely for Lee, would have been even if Lee were sitting next to him at the bar. People changed so slowly—or refused to change—that it was surprisingly easy to stay with someone you no longer even liked. He wasn't sure if this was how he felt about Lee or how Lee felt about him. He was drunk.

Then he was feeding the jukebox a five-dollar bill, searching for the song. *No Results Found.* They didn't have it or maybe he spelled it wrong. He searched again and again as if it would appear if he kept trying, then gave up and returned to his seat. He removed Jimmy's card and set it on the bar top. How much would he pay him for his whole collection, for everything he owned? he wondered.

Seymour signaled to order another drink, but the bartender ignored him, the bar suddenly unnervingly quiet. The men at the claw machine, now down to their last credit, were the focus of all eyes. "It's more about timing than position," said one to the other. "We got this." Seymour was capable of expounding on the metaphor of the claw machine as it pertained to man's eternal hunt, be it for a cheap stuffed toy, rare records, or life-sustaining meat. But he said nothing.

The men finally got hold of the teddy bear. They held their breath and stood dead-still as the claw journeyed tenuously to the prize slot. When it opened, they screamed. One man held the bear in the air while the man who had been guiding him gave him a hug. The entire bar, save Seymour, broke into applause. The men slapped high five and rejoined groups seated at separate tables. They were strangers, drawn together by the pursuit of a cute little toy. It was a beautiful moment, genuine and unironic. Seymour's face felt heavy; he was giving them the Wichita Scowl.

•

And then, an indeterminate amount of time and drinks later, Seymour was dodging the CHAANT procession's headlights as he crept up the street to Ronald's house. Of all the offenses Wichita had committed, perhaps the worst was that he now had the lyrics to "Dancing on the Ceiling" memorized. He was relatively sure he'd think this was a good idea even were he sober, as sure that Lee would not agree. The idea, generated in the haze of his fourth strong drink, being to steal Ronald's Heatherstone. The geriatric idiot didn't deserve it. What did he know of its delicious camp value? He was terminally earnest. And Seymour, despite the awful onset of middle age, still had punk blood throbbing anarchically through his veins. This would prove it, that he wasn't just some old fart who used to be cool. He'd be punk till the day he died.

But there beyond the silhouette of the jockey and giraffe, a shadowy figure knelt in the dirt, fiddling with the storm window. Obscured by darkness, the object in its hand was surely some deadly burgling device, a gun or crowbar. Great, Seymour thought, peeking over the hedge that bordered Ronald's yard. Now he was going to have to be a Samaritan or else risk having the poor guy's murder on his conscience. He mulled his options: Run home and call the police or try to take on the perpetrator himself. The latter was the more glamorous option, and if he died in the midst of the struggle, it would be a very punk death. Or would it? On the one hand, violence was definitely punk. On the other, protecting private property was not.

The figure stood and whispered to an unseen accomplice, "I told you, it's not working. It doesn't open from the outside . . . Yes, I *know*. There aren't any rocks heavy enough. And now I've broken a nail. Maybe we should try—" The figure headed straight for Seymour. "You!" it shrieked, the aural equivalent of the Wichita Scowl.

Before Seymour could react, a lagging CHAANT car blaring "Hello" turned the corner, its headlights illuminating—why, it was that batty broad from Heart, Delores Kovacs! And that was no gun but just one of her dolls. Together they ducked behind the hedge and waited for it to pass.

Delores held the doll to her ear like a telephone. "What're you doing here?"

"Oh, just out for an evening walk," he said. He could not have picked a more suspicious answer. It didn't help that his breath reeked of whiskey. "I don't want to intrude on you calling on your friend Ronald Marsh, so—"

"Ronald Marsh? The man who lives here?" Delores's forehead seemed to throb with thought as she stared into the unblinking eyes of her doll.

"Um, yes. Anyway, I think I'll be— Oh neat. Growing Up Skipper." He reached out, but Delores pulled it away and held it to her breast like a swaddled baby.

She smiled, though Seymour could tell she was trying not to. "Not just any Growing Up Skipper." She lifted the skirt and triggered the breast-growing mechanism. A red stain appeared on the doll's undergarment.

"I thought it was just a rumor!"

Seymour spoke too loudly. Inside the house a dog began to bark, and a light flickered on. Delores skulked back over to the storm window. On instinct Seymour followed. She crouched and put her ear against the glass, Skipper's, too. The shades were drawn so you couldn't see inside. Delores rapped her fist on the window. A wordless cry from deep within sounded back. A small voice, but not small like Ronald's. A child's voice.

Seymour's run-in with the old man the day before—the toys, the Happy Meals—it all made sense now. "Do you have a cell phone? We can call—"

Delores grabbed Seymour's wrist imploringly, her nails sharp but her fingertips pleasantly warm. "There's no time! Who knows what he's doing to her down there?"

"Even if you got this window open, the only one of us who could fit is Skipper."

Delores pressed Skipper's head to her lips like a thoughtful finger. "We must get inside."

Seymour followed her up the porch steps. She shook the knob—locked—and put Skipper against her lips again. She was breathing heavily—or whispering. To Seymour she said, "Do something! Before it's too late!"

This was going to make a good story. It was a shame he had no friends anymore to tell it to. Already Seymour was watching himself from a distance, narrating his actions. Whatever happened, he was sure Lee would find a way to make himself embarrassed about it. Nervously Delores chewed the doll's plastic foot. She was crazy, that thing had to be priceless. "Kick down the door if you have to."

It seemed like a great idea. Instantly he felt useful, tough, hetero-normatively masculine. A rush of endorphins or lingering whiskey sent him into action. He gave the door a few hard kicks—Red Ball Jets be damned—but it repelled any force he drove at it.

From deep within the recesses of his mind a bit of wisdom from a spy novel he'd once read sprang forth. The trick to kicking a door down, the buff pulp hero had explained to his buxom companion, was to hit precisely below the knob where the lock was.

All right, Seymour would try it that way. He steadied himself on the railing and aimed below the knob. This time the door shook, something seemed to give, but still it would not open. Delores raised the Skipper doll encouragingly. Seymour's leg would be sore in the morning. He braced himself for another kick.

18

RONALD

My gosh, Ronald thought. They were going to batter the door down. Who "they" were he did not know, and it didn't matter. They were determined, and Ronald was in trouble. Gable let loose the howl he used on mail carriers and garbagemen. In a frenzy he ran circles around Ronald, who leaned into his knees and practiced the breathing exercises from *Dr. Oz* Melinda had taught him. He was known to become, as Melinda put it, easily flustered.

Meanwhile, Lindy was working herself into a fit. "Who's there?" she screamed. He wanted to tell both Gable and her—gently—to just button their lips for a moment. He needed quiet to think this through. He *was* going to do the right thing, if only he could think of what it was.

A hinge flew loose and rattled on the floor. They were coming in, Ronald couldn't stop them. He'd have to hide Lindy. Yes, that's what he'd have to do. If she could keep quiet until they were alone again, he'd repay her with all the sweets and toys she wanted before he set her free. Yes, indeed. He raced to the landing at the top of the basement stairs, Gable trailing him. All he needed was a suitable hiding place—the crawl space, of course! Lindy's kennel could just about fit. Gable bit his ankle and Ronald tried to shake loose, taking his hand off the railing to feign giving the dog a smack. Lindy was still screaming. "Please, dear. Be quiet," Ronald said. Gable snarled and weaved about Ronald's legs, taking quick little nips. "Darn it, Gable, I'll—" The wood-splintering crack of the door bursting open shot terror into Ronald's heart. Everything went quiet and he heard Melinda's voice as quiet as a whisper: *It's over.* He hardly flinched as he tripped over Gable's sinewy body and landed with a thud on his back.

Though the circumstances could have been better, he couldn't help but feel pleased that his dear friends from the Heart of America had come to visit him. "Delores! Seymour! How unexpected." The two looked like trick-or-treaters, Seymour with an unctuous grin and Delores clutching her dolly. "I'm afraid the time is a teeny bit inconvenient."

Lindy shrieked, "I'm down here!" and Gable helpfully pointed his snout in the direction of the stairs. Who did that mutt think he was, Lassie?

Ronald sat up. "I'm sure you're wondering what the commotion is. I can assure you it's all—"

Delores toppled him. The face of the doll appeared an angel welcoming him to heaven as the hammy fist that held it collided again and again with his chin. Sometime during the unrelenting stream of blows, the angel's face was cast in a sinister red light and Ronald began to think she was not an angel at all and was instead beckoning him to the other place. It was then he understood the ringing in his ears to be the wailing of police sirens.

19

LEE

It had been a strange night already before the call. Through the locked record room door, Lee had heard Seymour leave for Jimmy's sale in the early afternoon and he still hadn't returned. Probably on another bender—he'd always been a drinker, but since the move he was loaded more often than not. "I can't help if there's nowhere to go and nothing else to do in this town. I'm not going to stay shut up in this hole like you," he'd said when Lee gently remarked that at least he could save some money by drinking at home.

It was true that a surfeit of free time could be a burden. Without a store to run or a job to report to—or, Lee thought sadly, Seymour to talk to—days in Wichita stretched interminably. To distract himself from the crushing depression of his wasted life he began a listless project of re-cataloging his doo-wop 45s by geographical origin rather than re-lease date. Hours later, when he was almost finished, an insistent knock drew him to the front door. He assumed Seymour had locked himself out again or was too drunk to work the knob, but awaiting him on the porch were two CHAANT members whose names Lee could not remember.

"We got 'im, Veronica," said the woman into a walkie-talkie. "See you soon." Lee recognized her as the one who'd brought the ice cream to the last meeting.

The man—her husband, Lee guessed—gazed over Lee's shoulder. "Have you talked to him yet? Do you know when the police will be done with him?"

"Who?" Lee said, his throat dry. It was the first word he'd spoken aloud all day.

"Seymour!" the two said in unison.

"He's . . . what?" Was Seymour in trouble? Was Lee? The crazed, cultish look in their eyes was not reassuring. Perhaps Veronica had dispatched her lackeys to capture and punish CHAANT's excommunicated.

"Of course. Tell him to catch up later." They each grabbed Lee by a shoulder and pulled him onto the porch. Lee acquiesced as they led him to their car, still running and playing Lionel Richie at such volume they didn't hear when Lee asked where the hell they were taking him. He got into the backseat and when the doors automatically locked he wondered if he was under citizen's arrest.

They drove two blocks and parked in front of Veronica Samples's powder-blue A-frame. The party-like atmosphere, discernible through the wide-open front door and the Lionel Richie tunes blasting from inside the house, helped to dispel his dread.

Inside, absent were the sad, perfunctory ice-cream cups, the polite chatter, the serious frowns. Instead, the task forcers reclined on Veronica's Eames-era furniture holding low-end craft beer bottles, gesturing animatedly, laughing, and even—Lee searched for the word—*whooping*? *Whooping it up?* Where was Veronica to put the damper on it all, to remind everyone of poor defenseless Lindy, to paint the grisly picture of the worst-case scenario even as she stoked the coals of hope for a safe recovery?

The occasion was obvious. Lindy had been found. Alive and well enough. But that didn't explain why Lee had been dragged here. Neighbors with whom he'd barely exchanged a few words clapped him on the back, put their hands out for shakes and high fives, pinched him ten-derly on the shoulder. People he was sure did not know his name (Lee didn't know theirs) said, "Lee's here," said, "The man of the hour!" said, "How you doin', Lee, buddy?" as if he'd arrived at his own surprise party.

A group was gathered around the television watching the local news. Lee couldn't quite make out the words over the chatter. Veronica emerged from the huddle and sought Lee with open arms. Her soft cheek brushing his, leaving, he was sure, makeup residue, she said, "It must be so exciting!"

Why the hell was she acting this way? Lee pushed his way through the crowd to get a look at the television. On-screen, Seymour was being interviewed under the glow of a streetlight by a bottle-blond reporter with bleached teeth and a tan like a carrot:

"And do you have anything you'd like to say to Lindy? Or perhaps some words of hope for the community after this harrowing ordeal?"

Seymour thought for a moment before his eyes lit up. "To the peo-ple of Wichita, I say: Get out of your car once in a while. It's no crime to go on a harmless little walk, and yet the people around here act like—"

"And what a fateful walk it was. Tell us again about the daring rescue. How did you know where to find Lindy?"

"Well, I just happened to be around. Right place, right time." Sey-mour pointed off-screen. "She's the one who, let's say, *neutralized* the threat."

The camera swung and the reporter pivoted to—why, it was that batty Barbie lady from Heart! "And you, Delores Kovacs, recount the events from your perspective."

Delores stared unblinkingly into the Barbie doll she held with both hands, her makeup taking on a clownish mien under the lights. She nodded at it, faced the camera, leaned into the microphone, and said, "No comment," before wheeling around and staggering off into the darkness.

"Overwhelmed with emotion, obviously," said the reporter.

The camera panned back to Seymour. "*I* kicked the door down. You should have seen it. Like a Bruce Lee movie."

"And when you saw what was going on, you called the police?"

"What? No! They were already on their way. Some friendly neighborhood narc called the fuzz on *me*. 'A suspicious person appearing to case the neighborhood.' It's called taking a stroll, people!"

They kept repeating the same clips—the interview with Seymour, footage shot at a respectful distance of Lindy being reunited with her grateful family in the back of what the reporter called a "crisis van," a creepy still image of the suspect's basement where Lindy was held captive—so it didn't take long to piece the story together. The culprit was a man named Ronald Marsh, that pathetic old guy from the Heart of America. The same awkward photo they used for the mall's dealer directory flashed on-screen.

"Him?" Lee said in astonishment. "The postcard guy?" The newscaster said investigators had yet to determine a motive for Mr. Marsh, but they did confirm Lindy was found locked in his basement dungeon.

"Guy lived just a couple blocks from here," someone said. "Some lonely old widower. Who woulda thought?"

Lee sat and watched TV in a daze. Periodically someone would come up and shake his hand; without Seymour around, he was the next best thing. Finally he belonged, he was not just tolerated but accepted and embraced. After all he'd done to ingratiate himself with the community, it was Seymour—elitist Seymour, who referred to the neighbors as "those Kansans," whose snobby East-Coaster persona Lee was surer and surer was not just an affectation, who had treated their move back to Wichita ("back for *you*, not me, sweetheart," he'd said) like a prison sentence—who'd won their approval.

Veronica had been on the phone for a while by then, talking to her contact in the police department. Periodically she'd set the receiver down and mute the television to make an announcement to the din of cheers and hollers. And whoops.

"No signs of sexual abuse!"

Keith Stoller stumbled into the room, raised his beer, and said, "I'll drink to that." He chugged till the bottle was empty, then reached into a nearby cooler for another. When he saw Lee, he collapsed onto the couch, put his arm around him, and leaned in to his ear. "Where's that guy of yours? I could plant a kiss on his smacker. You ever feel like things are finally starting to go your way? You ever notice that good things only happen when you've given up all hope and are considering—seriously considering—faking your own death for the insurance money?"

Veronica returned with an update: "No signs of significant physical abuse!" She was like a campaign manager on election night. Seymour would love this; it was burlesque. Lee wished he, too, could find the humor in it, or moreover could share it with Seymour.

They used to have such fun. What happened to them? Whose fault was it? They were each miserable but expected the other to jolt himself out of his own misery, if for no other reason than only one of them should be allowed to be miserable at a time. Seymour had first attracted him with his easygoing sociability, his eagerness to go out and do things, and above all to be seen doing them. That joie de vivre had given way to curmudgeonliness as they grew closer and older. "I'd think you were embarrassed of me," Seymour said one drunken night, "but the truth is worse: you're boring." He was probably right, but Lee had bit his lip and inhaled his own accusation: Seymour was shallow.

Yet look at what his boyfriend had done. Lee snaked free of Keith's grasp, rose from the couch, and headed out the door, ready to explain that the man of the hour was probably looking for him. But no one asked.

The phone was ringing when he got home. He regretted answering as soon as he picked up—it was probably some reporter hunting for a quote. What was he supposed to say? He held the phone to his ear but didn't speak.

"Hello?" A tentative voice answered itself. "Is this the residence of Lee Fallon?"

"Hello."

"Lee Fallon the musician?"

It had been a long time since he'd played music. "This is Lee Fallon," he said. "Who is this?"

"Simon Kurtzman." Lee knew the name, but he had trouble connecting it to a person. "Sluggo."

Of course, Simon "Sluggo" Kurtzman, onetime lead guitarist for Tears in the Birthday Cake. Sluggo had been known more for his stage presence than for his musical ability, at least at first. Iggy was his hero, and in the early days when the band had only four songs, he'd extend the set with an impromptu jam in which he'd strum his Les Paul with his erect dick. It was gimmicky, reckless, desperate in theory but awe-inspiring in practice. Sluggo was one of those gifted few capable of performing with a total lack of self-consciousness, who really did not care what the audience thought of him, and wasn't just good at acting like it. (Seymour claimed to this day that the dick strumming had been *his* thing first, that Sluggo had copied his idea after seeing Foxy Nazi, but Lee insisted that playing a theremin with your dick and playing a guitar with your dick were two separate things.)

"This is Lee Fallon," he said again.

"I guess you can guess what this is about." The voice on the phone was both familiar and unfamiliar, marked by years passed, not gravelly or aged but different, devoid of Sluggo's usual stoned drawl.

Oh god, Lee thought. He's gone Jehovah. Or Scientologist. Or he had an STD—he and Lee hooked up one night early on, before Seymour. But that was so long ago—there must be a statute of limitations on that sort of thing. "Just tell me."

"You never told us you were in a band with Mickey Gordy! Jesus, me and the guys, our minds were blown when we found out. Shit, back in the day you shoulda been hounding him to give us some opening slots."

Was this one of Seymour's pranks? If so, it only confirmed he'd developed quite a cruel streak. The last thing Lee wanted to talk about with his ex-bandmate was Mickey fucking Gordy. "It's kind of a bad time—"

"Aw come on, man. We don't need an answer right away—well, we kind of do, actually. After the Mickey Gordy thing they won't stop calling. My email exploded. How's it been for you?"

"*Who* keeps calling? *You're* the one calling *me*."

"Everyone," Sluggo said, exasperated. In the background, children's voices whined for Dad. Sluggo ignored them. "Mickey's big publicity tour for the new album. He's been name-dropping us left and right since it came out. *Rolling Stone* a couple weeks ago. The feature on *Pitchfork*. Even NPR, if you can believe it. Don't tell me you don't keep up with the music press anymore, you old fogy."

Now Lee was getting annoyed—or he'd been annoyed from the moment he'd answered the phone and he was just now realizing it. This was no prank call but it felt like one. "Sluggo"—the name felt heavy and awkward on his tongue—"what the hell are you talking about?"

"They want Tears to get back together." He went on, explaining that Mickey Gordy had dug a copy of the Tears record out of a two-for-a-dollar bin at a flea market and fallen in love. It was the main influence on his latest album and he'd been extolling them in interviews ever since. Bootleg copies (they'd only been able to scrape together enough money to press three hundred) were blowing up the blogosphere. Sub Pop wanted to reissue it along with a bonus compilation of demos and live tracks. Now Gordy was offering the band a tremendous amount of money to reunite for his TrashRiot music festival in Atlanta. It wasn't a Morrissey-Marr-level payday, but it was plenty more than Lee had ever expected to make off his short stint as a semiprofessional musician. "I haven't spoken to him directly, but Mickey's—what do you call 'em? his people or whatever—they say Mickey wants you. He won't do it without you. You know his mystic tip. When he found out you were in Tears *and* his first band way back when, he flipped, says it's fate or kismet or whatever. Hey, I found some Sodashoppe Teens tracks on YouTube—Christ, they're awful." Lee barely listened as Sluggo filled him in on the where-are-they-nows of the other Tears alumni. They were all either lawyers or teachers. "And *you* were the hardest to find. Where the hell have you been keeping yourself? Oh, and I forgot to say, depending on how the TrashRiot show goes there's talk of a tour. We're convening here in Mass.—I'm outside Amherst—for practice in about two weeks. You in?"

Lee looked at the door, hoping Seymour would burst in. He didn't. "Can I call you back?"

"All right," Sluggo said, disappointed. "Listen, do yourself a favor and Google 'Tears in the Birthday Cake.' Read the thing in *Pitchfork*. You'll see what I mean. Would you ever have imagined—"

"Okay," Lee said and hung up.

He went upstairs to the record room. The Tears album, all ten copies (most still shrink-wrapped) in plain white sleeves with hand-written track listings onto which Seymour had pasted collages of old porno mag scraps, were still sitting out from when he'd compared his discography with Mickey's the night before. Lee hadn't played it in decades, and listening to it up here, with the full fidelity of his rig, in the intimacy of this room, would be too much, so he took the opened copy—it smelled like beer and weed—downstairs and plugged in the portable toy Osmond Family–branded record player. The volume turned as low as a whisper, he dropped the needle and listened.

Not bad, pretty good even. Good enough that he could forget for a moment here and there he was listening to his own band. He was surprised from the opening chords that he remembered the names of each song—"Sorry to Die," "Refractory Period," "Her Stitches"—and moreover the choruses, the lyrics, each and every note were tattooed somewhere deep in his brain.

The front door swung open as Lee was really starting to get into it, fingering the keys of an imaginary saxophone. As quick as he could he flicked the record player off and slammed the lid shut. Donny's dimpled face smiled up at him. He'd have preferred to have been caught masturbating.

Seymour looked exhausted, bags under his pallid eyes, sweat stains dampening the armpits of his shirt, a bizarre plastic lawn ornament slung over his shoulder. He'd always had a taste for the ugly, but this was something else. "I don't wanna talk about it." He dropped the lawn ornament onto the floor; it made a hollow noise like an out-of-tune flute.

"You're home." Lee could think of nothing more to say. He ran his fingers through Seymour's moist blond hair and wished he hadn't; Seymour could use a shower. "Where'd you get it?" He pointed at the giraffe and its jockey.

"No, you're off-script. Who cares about that? Little Lindy Bobo? My daring rescue?"

"You said you didn't want to talk about it."

"Don't ask. It's nothing. I was out for a walk. Wrong place at the wrong time. Or right time, I don't know. It was that batty Barbie bimbo. Don't ask."

Lee didn't, although Seymour was clearly waiting for him to.

"Anyway, I'm sure Veronica Samples will be pleased. I'm the neighborhood hero. *I* kicked the door down. You should've seen this weirdo's basement. He had his own little talk show studio."

"I saw on the news. What kind of sick shit was this guy into?"

"Who knows? One of the reporters said the staff of the *Eagle* have been arguing over what to call him. They haven't had such a hit on their hands since BTK. Apparently—" Seymour craned his neck. Following his nose like a dog, he shoved past Lee and went right for Donny. He flipped the lid—"Ha!"—and found the record sleeve behind a table lamp, holding it between two fingers like a tossrag. "Who knew? Even Lee gets the nostalgies."

Recounting the call from Sluggo was tedious. As he listened to himself speak he marveled at how depressed he sounded. It was a dream come true burdened by the many years that had passed since he'd given up on it. "It's called TrashRiot. They want us to play, but I don't know."

"Shit! This is fantastic. I mean, shit."

Lee had almost forgotten about this part of Seymour, his genuineness of feeling, his generosity of pride. There was no envy in him. Back in the day, Lee had considered Seymour's band a rival. Art was a contest and success was in limited supply; every show another band booked, every favorable write-up in a zine or alt-weekly it garnered, every clap of applause for someone other than him, diminished his own opportunities. Seymour talked the snob in public, but in truth Lee had never known a more generous appreciator of art. He believed in goodness for goodness' sake, that good music and good art should be promoted because it was good, not because it was cool, that there was no cost to someone else's success. No one would ever demand a reunion of Seymour's band. They were awful. But Seymour didn't care.

"I don't know," Lee repeated. "We're broke."

"Exactly. People call this sort of thing a windfall. People are supposed to be happy about this sort of thing."

"It's not that easy. Who knows if the money will even come through, or when? And we're supposed to up and leave without knowing what will really happen."

"Fuck money who cares you're doing this." He said it like it was one sentence. It was what Lee wanted, what he needed Seymour for: to be persuaded to do what he wanted to do but was too afraid to. "I haven't touched a sax in years. And what about the house and—"

"Fuck it, we'll abandon it if we have to. We'll sell everything. We're doing this. We're starting over." He picked up the lawn ornament and slammed it into the floor. "We'll sell it all. I hate this stuff. It's stuff. Fuck it." He wrapped his arms around Lee and tried to lift him. He was not strong enough, or Lee was too heavy, so he grabbed Lee's butt instead.

"Lumpy mashed potato butt," he whispered in Lee's ear. "Fuck it. We'll get rid of everything. Fuck it."

"Everything?"

"Everything."

SUNDAY

THE NIGHT BEFORE

KEITH

Keith felt at this moment that nothing could be better than having a sit-down dinner in the company of his family, a ceremony of life-enriching acts of kinship and love, the conversation and food providing not only reinforcement of already-strong familial bonds but also decompression after another long day on this lovely planet we called Earth. He had prepared a cheesy potato-and-cornflake casserole (it was only slightly burned) with microwaved vegetable medley (it was only slightly mushy) for the occasion, and what a pleasure and honor it was to share this handmade meal with his wife and beautiful daughter.

Things were finally looking up, all was well, his vision of the future was boffo, and the incredible hangover acquired at last night's celebra-tion was only a reminder of his great fortune. Last night, once he'd finally convinced the late-working intern to forward his call to a real person, Keith pitched it as a human interest story: it was two of the mall's own dealers who had come to Lindy Bobo's rescue. (He left out the fact that a third dealer was involved as the kidnapper himself.) The producers were thrilled. Mark and Grant would love it. The TV shoot was back on, baby!

Even the unhappy silence emanating from his wife and daughter as they sat together in the dimly lit dining room of his beautiful, overvalued Eastborough home would not dull Keith's optimism or curb his appetite. Stacey scraped food around her plate like the morose teenager her daughter actually was, biding her time till the end of another online auction. Ellie, meanwhile, had been sulkier than usual, her dreams of the reward money, though she'd done little more to locate Lindy than meander about the neighborhood with headphones on, quashed by the telegenic heroism of Seymour and Delores. And yes, she only grunted when Keith asked how her day had been and pretended not to hear when he asked her to pass the ketchup. But that she had joined her parents at the dining room table at all, when ordinarily she ate alone in her bedroom, often in the middle of the night while watching television on her laptop, Keith counted as a win.

Nope, nothing was going to go terribly wrong, not as long as Keith could help it. There was no way, for instance, that the producers could call and announce they'd canceled the taping owing to the Heart of America's unseemly association with a(n alleged) local child-napper. He'd already thought of that and had arranged to have every trace of the man excised from the premises. Nor was there a chance that this feeling of tightness in his chest was a terminal heart attack, because he'd thought of that, too. It was just those most unfamiliar of feelings: Hope! Excitement! The absence of his customary black drowning dread!

He scraped a gob of casserole into his mouth whereupon tongue and teeth met a slick nonfood substance. Without registering disgust, he spit the object into his palm and held it like a magician who'd pulled an improbably long handkerchief from his sleeve. It was a plastic-wrapped whistle, presumably from the cornflakes box, in the shape of a cartoon monkey he recognized from a program Ellie watched as a girl, about an intergalactic princess and her cadre of sapphic girl-servants. "Wow," he said, almost smiling, halfway jolly at the pure, random surprise of it. "I didn't think they put prizes in cereal boxes anymore."

He tossed the whistle to Ellie, who ignored it, curled her lip in disgust, and pushed her plate to the center of the table. She crossed her arms but remained seated, did not, as Keith assumed she would, go sullenly up to her room.

"You sure are chipper tonight," Stacey said as she emptied the remains of her plate onto Keith's.

"What's not to be happy about? Tomorrow's the big day."

"The filming of the Mark and Grant show," she said unnecessarily.

"Mark and Grant," Ellie repeated.

"Mark and Grant," Stacey said back, like they were playing a game in which Keith was not a participant.

Ellie said, "Mark and Grant are dead. Mutual erotic asphyxiation." After a moment she added, "It means jerking off with a belt tied around your neck."

Stacey took a sip of orange drink. "And you thought you wouldn't learn anything in community college."

The phone rang. Probably it was the producers calling to hammer out the details for tomorrow. Keith leapt out of his chair and answered hello, spewing potato and cornflake crumbs into the mouthpiece.

"Jimmy Daniels calling," Jimmy Daniels said. Birds chirped in the background. "I know tomorrow's a big day for you, so I wanted to clear the air."

Keith licked up some of the crumbs and said he didn't have time right this minute.

Jimmy continued anyway: "Figures to me I've been doing you a favor, sticking around as long as I have. So you won't take it personal that I'm saying adios to the Heart of America."

By way of response Keith burped, a tentative taste of vomit in the depths of his throat.

"Yep, got a new thing opening up in Delano, and you'll never guess, it's a co-venture with Margaret Byrd. Never got that glass stuff myself, but old ladies suck that shit down like red cream soda."

This was fine. Nothing could spoil Keith's newfound hopefulness. He wouldn't let it. Sure, Jimmy was the Heart of America's single most profitable dealer, often its *only* profitable dealer, but what did that matter? Filming tomorrow would go off without a hitch, Mark and Grant would make a generous offer on the mall, the light at the end of the tunnel, the rainbow after the storm, if you can see it you can be it, etc. Nothing at all to worry about.

"Way I see it, it was past time, this being my day job and all. And don't take this personal, but your place kinda gives me the creeps now that they found out about the old man child molester. Business is business, know what I mean?" The deliberate silence that followed was undermined by cheerful bird chirps.

Keith said yes, he knew what Jimmy meant. The casserole, of which he by himself had eaten the majority, recongealed into one dense, cancerlike mass in his stomach.

"I know you're in a bind, brother, so don't worry, I'll still be there for the taping. Give you some of that Jimmy Daniels charm. Consider it my parting gift." Jimmy, of course, wouldn't fail to mention on-camera his new private venture. "And listen, do you know anyone looking to buy a pet bird? I don't know what breed, but they're very decorative. Bought a lot of antique birdcages at an auction in Omaha—didn't realize they came with birds. They're pretty exotic but I could get you a good price."

Keith hung up.

Back at the dinner table, Stacey asked who called.

"No one," Keith said.

"It didn't seem like no one."

"It wasn't anybody."

"Stacey. Mom."

"Don't worry. Everything's going to go off without a hitch."

"Dad. I'm trying to tell you guys something."

"Who's worried? Is something wrong?" Stacey said as if it had occurred to her for the first time ever that something was wrong.

"Hey! Listen to me. You never listen when I'm serious," Ellie said. She was never serious.

"It's fine. Everything's fine. Tomorrow's the big day."

"This is important. I made a decision."

"You look anguished. Is your ringworm acting up again?"

"Keith. Dad. Come on."

"Can we not talk about this when I'm trying to enjoy dinner with my—"

A shrill noise pierced the air. Ellie spit out the whistle and said, "*Now* are you listening?"

21

ELLIE

What Ellie had been trying to say at the dinner table was: *Goodbye, I can't take this anymore, I'm leaving, not just the room and this oppressive goddamn family but Wichita, forever and for good, right now.* Instead she yelled, "Fuck this shit," and stormed out the door. As she merged onto I-135 in Keith's Bonneville, the exhilaration of escape vanished; she had no money (she'd forgotten her wallet), no clothes but the paint-flecked hoodie, paisley bell-bottoms, and men's combat boots she was wearing, nothing packed at all, nowhere to go, and no place to stay when she arrived.

She ended up at the Professor's studio apartment and there, on his pillowless sofa bed, she experienced what the addicts and depressives on exploitative reality shows referred to as "bottoming out" or "hitting rock bottom." It was as the Professor, shirtless and wrapped in a stained sheet, described the central argument of his dissertation using his Troll dolls as visual aids that she saw how unglamorous self-destruction could be, how predictable and boring. What had brought her there was desperation. What she needed if she was ever *really* going to get out of Wichita was resolve. She was going to do something, not just to get a reaction or to see what would happen, but because she herself had decided she wanted to. She was going to be a person. "I'm done," she'd said in the middle of the Professor's point about common misconceptions of the term *art brut*, then got dressed and left.

"You're still going to show my dolls to Mark and Grant, though, right?"

"I thought you said they weren't dolls," she'd replied and slammed the door.

Now, back home in her bedroom, she clicked "send" on a one-sentence email asking the Professor for a letter of recommendation and to otherwise never contact her again. What she would do next she did not know. There were many actions, both responsible and not, to be taken toward liberation—filling out scholarship applications, scouring the web for sketchy private loan companies the government had not gotten around to shutting down that did not require a cosign, phone-banking her limited social network in search of a friend dumb enough to let her sleep on their dorm room floor for an indefinite period of time—but each offered dispiritingly slow or unfavorable results.

She lay in bed staring at the glow-in-the-dark stars that had been stuck to the ceiling for as long as she could remember, until Keith knocked on the door. She knew it was him because her mother never knocked. The door creaked open. The yellow light from the hallway gave him a sallow complexion, or maybe that was just the way he naturally looked, his beady eyes sunk under dark bags, his teeth tiny and dull, his thinning hair tinged with dusty gray.

"Don't come in," she said.

Without a word he shut the door and moped away.

MONDAY

CLOSING TIME AT THE HEART OF AMERICA

22

MARGARET

There was stalking and there was tailing, Margaret Byrd thought as her car idled in the parking lot of the strip mall where the yoga studio sat between a musty used bookstore and a dimly lit bakery. Stalking was something criminals and lovelorn psychopaths did with the intent of making their presence known, of intimating threat. Margaret had no interest in such histrionics. Even "tailing" was not quite right. What Margaret was up to (and she wasn't, not really, "up to" anything) was more akin to—what was the word?—a kind of *escorting*, accompanying Patricia from one place to another, practically by mere coincidence. Margaret happened to find herself outside of Patricia's yoga studio just as her Monday three o'clock class was ending. And if she happened by chance to bump into Patricia on her way out, and if they happened to get to talking and things happened to be just like they used to be, then, well, Margaret would surely be inclined to "go with the flow," as Patricia would say.

Men and women began to file out of the yoga studio, sucking grotesquely on water bottle nipples and clutching rolled mats in their clammy armpits. Just the thought of the smell of strangers fresh from exercise nauseated Margaret. She turned up the air conditioner. After a few minutes, the initial flood of people had all gotten into their cars and left. A few stragglers stood in the parking lot chatting, but Patricia was nowhere to be seen. Maybe she was onto Margaret. Not that there was anything to be "onto," so to speak. Margaret just happened to be here, that was all.

And what was the harm? This—whatever it was that Margaret was doing—was at the very least less intrusive than the phone calls, which she did sincerely regret. She didn't know what had come over her, the things she whispered before hanging up and calling again and again.

Margaret was not ready for Patricia to emerge from the yoga studio door, to appear before her in the hyper-detail of real life. Even from across the distance of the parking lot, it was too much to take in. She had no photographs of Patricia (she cursed herself for taking no photographs, but she was not one to carry or own a camera, to squint through a viewfinder and demand a pose or smile or an utterance of "cheese," and she had never owned or felt the need to own a smartphone), so for the past weeks her only images of her old friend had been in her mind. To see her now—so casual and yet somehow so elegant, in a neon-pink tank top to match the scrunchie that held her flaxen hair in a ponytail that draped against her slender, tan neck—was thrilling but also a painful reminder: Patricia had continued to exist and thrive and be Patricia despite her absence from Margaret's life. It wasn't fair that Patricia didn't seem to need Margaret the way Margaret needed her.

Margaret started the car. Patricia lingered by the studio entrance. Holding the door for a soccer mom with severe bangs, she tilted her head, ponytail swaying, and laughed at something the woman said. Finally, the woman waved farewell, but not before Patricia touched her shoulder with the tip of her fingers and the two hugged briefly, chastely, for a period not exceeding more than three seconds, and went their separate ways.

Margaret squeezed the steering wheel till her knuckles popped. This woman, with her bangs that she probably thought exuded a charming air of insouciance but which really, in Margaret's informed opinion, were plain sloppy, a pathetic imitation of Patricia's deceptively laissez-faire earthiness—what could she even have to offer Patricia? Margaret had never seen her at the Heart of America. Perhaps she was not even a collector!

Margaret supposed it was for the best that Patricia had left #1-146. She'd be packed up and ready to move into Margaret's new store, where she could have the pick of the lot. After all, it wouldn't be called Pretty Patty's Antiques Shoppe for nothing. Margaret could scarcely wait to tell her the news. Over the weekend she'd met up with Jimmy in Delano for an inspection of the premises. Although small and rough around the edges—the wood floors hadn't been washed in decades and a heap of videotapes, many of them pornographic, remnants of the building's previous tenants, lay abandoned in the corner—it showed tremendous potential; Jimmy hadn't lied about the natural light. As she looked about, aisles and displays and exhibits of the finest antiques sprang into being, the sun through her glass casting a kaleidoscopic glow not just upon the floor and walls and ceiling but the very air—every molecule—within the building itself. In her mind, she stood before the threshold on grand opening day, her hand in Patricia's as she threw open the doors and a crowd of collectors—true collectors, bespectacled from years of poring over research books, bedecked in long skirts and serious tweed—shuffled in to admire the redesigned space lit by Spanish chandeliers. And meanwhile, across town, the last unfortunate dwellers emerged bleary-eyed, under GOING OUT OF BUSINESS banners, from the failed Heart of America, Seymour and Lee among them, as the very building, perhaps under the psychic weight of so much accumulated *junk*, literally collapsed into rubble. "Well, it ain't big enough to fit a Saturday-night orgy," Jimmy said, spoiling the reverie, "but it's sure as shit all ours." Before Margaret could register her disgust, Jimmy pulled from his coat pocket the rolled lease contract. Any hesitation she felt dissipated upon seeing the words PRETTY PATTY'S ANTIQUES, LLC.

Patricia was now pulling out of her parking spot in her Volkswagen with the bumper sticker advertising a local craft microbrew her ex-husband had started. (It was permanently affixed, virtually irremovable—Margaret had even tried her patented solution for dissolving the residue off unseemly price stickers, eucalyptus oil and rubbing alcohol, to no effect.) Margaret *escorted* from a distance of three or four cars.

Ordinarily—that is, before their misunderstanding—Patricia and Margaret spent Monday evenings on the phone or at one or another's houses watching the new *Antiques Roadshow* together, but it didn't start until seven o'clock. Margaret didn't know what Patricia did in the hours between yoga and the program's airing, and she could only guess where Patricia was now headed. It wasn't toward her home on Seneca Street, a spacious three-bedroom Victorian she'd gotten full ownership of after the divorce, decorated with the same elegant sparseness as her booth. Margaret loved being there, admiring Patricia's aesthetic—little things Margaret could never have thought of, like a shelf of bell jars filled with different colors of glass marbles—but sometimes she'd notice something out of place, a pair of men's work boots in the closet or a mismatched light switch plate in the upstairs bedroom; these things were artifacts of Patricia's ex-husband, she knew, and Margaret hated him, not just for the ways he'd made Patricia suffer but for the history he shared with her, for the parts of Patricia he knew (not in a crude way) that Margaret never could. Margaret was not proud of it, but she felt the same rancor toward Patricia's sons, all three high-school-aged and indistinguishable in their thick-necked, brooding reticence. Surely they took after their father. Margaret preferred them to not be around. She didn't like to think of Patricia as a mother.

Margaret wondered if Patricia was on her way to pick them up from school. No doubt they'd be coming from some kind of sport practice, dirt-caked and stinking. But she drove right past the high school and onto Highway 54, accelerating nearly twenty miles over the speed limit. She was a speedy driver but not a ruthless or impatient one. Heavy-footed or absentminded, more like. A few times she'd missed the exit to an estate sale as Margaret fretted over all the glass that was surely being snatched out from under her as they dawdled their way back.

Margaret was a nervous driver. When she slowed to observe the posted speed limit, a hulking RV merged into the space between her car and Patricia's. Her heart racing, she turned on her blinker, changed lanes, and prepared to pass. But every time she accelerated—she'd never before in her life brought the pedal so near to the floor—the RV's speed matched hers and she could not overcome it without ramming into the slow-chugging pickup truck before her. She drove alongside, intermittently tapping her horn, for what seemed like miles before finally the RV yielded enough that she could maneuver her vehicle unsteadily into the opening behind Patricia's Volkswagen.

By now it didn't matter. She knew exactly where Patricia was heading. She could tell by the tableau before her—the familiar triptych of a QuikTrip gas station, a Spangles fast-food restaurant, and the burned-out husk of a Dairy Queen—and by the life-size beaming bearded faces of Mark and Grant from the hit series *Pickin' Fortunes*, reproduced along with the Home Channel logo above the windshield on the RV she'd just passed.

Of course: she'd been so focused on escorting Patricia, she'd entirely forgotten. Today was the day they were filming at the Heart of America.

Patricia slowed, her eyes in the rearview widened with recognition. Margaret, feeling Patricia's gaze and not knowing what to do, raised her hand and waved. With that brief distraction, her foot pressed the gas pedal it thought was the brake, and she collided into Patricia's car, sending it nose-first into the ditch. Behind her, the RV screeched and, unable to halt its forward momentum, swerved into the shoulder, skidded off the road, and toppled onto its side with a terrifying but understated *thud*.

23

KEITH

Mark and Grant were very busy people. They were just late, Keith had insisted as the first wave of dealers shuffled off around five. They'd been due to arrive by three and it was now nearly closing time.

How he longed for the solace of his usual emotional numbness! This rapidly dissolving driblet of hope—that the Mark and Grant show could fix everything—was too volatile for his clunky old body. Being surrounded by old things all these years, day in and day out, some chemicals or an aura or curse had contaminated him. Who knew? If not for the Heart of America, his life could have been different. He could have kept his job at Boeing, picked up an innocuous hobby like bowling or making love to his wife every Wednesday night, raised his daughter without too many mistakes before sending her off to an expensive out-of-state college the fall after she graduated high school, and then, an uneventful span of years later, died content in the bliss of desireless ignorance, mortgage fully paid.

When the door jingled, Keith struggled to hope that he'd look up from the counter and find Mark and Grant's beaming bearded personages as if they'd just stepped out of the television screen. It was only Delores, but he barely recognized her at first in jeans and a baggy sweatshirt, her hair down, without makeup. "Delores Kovacs, one of the Heart of America's local heroes. I'm sorry to tell you that Mark and Grant are running a little behind. It seems we may—"

Delores made a noise that somehow perfectly translated to *don't bother me* and went straight into Hall Two.

Keith sighed. Who could blame Mark and Grant for standing them up? A stink permeated the Heart of America—not just the actual flatulent aroma that Keith, try as he might, could never Lysol out of the area surrounding Pete Deen's booth, but that of scandal, defeat, and abandonment. So many dealers had dropped out over the past year that entire aisles of the mall were bereft of merchandise. Light bulbs had burned out in the ceiling and no one had bothered to replace them. (Keith supposed that was his job.) A pile of dishes had been sitting unwashed in the back room's sink for weeks; a family of silverfish had taken up residence in them.

He could imagine the looks on Mark and Grant's tan, telegenic faces if they did show up, what they would say: *We came all the way to Wichita for this? This half-abandoned dust bunker that smells like burned hot dogs? This sad repository of chipped Precious Moments and leaking Beanie Babies? This is the Heart of America? And you, Keith Stoller, you consider yourself worthy of Mark and Grant's Antiquarian Pickporium franchisee status? Don't make us laugh our charismatic TV-ready chuckles, supercilious twinkles in our deep brown eyes, as we kick up dirt on our way—laughingly—out of what you have so hubristically deemed the Heart of America. Ha! we say, Keith Stoller, you failure of a husband, father, and business owner, ha!*

Keith caught his reflection in the service bell. He didn't look so strange—in fact he resembled his memory of his own father, a career bureaucrat who in his free time wrote letters to bridge columnists—but there was something wrong with him, some crucial defect hidden away undiagnosed in a body cavity that had prevented him from developing into an ordinary person like the rest of humankind.

At least Ellie would evade the Stoller family's congenital deficiencies. Keith would see to that before he sent her on her way. He felt he'd gotten to know his daughter better than ever over these past few months. Not that they talked so much. But there was a lot you could learn about someone through observation. Ellie had grown into a smart and self-possessed young woman. Her ruthlessness was, from a certain vantage, admirable. You needed to be a tough bitch to get by in this world. Otherwise you'd end up like Keith.

She sat at her perch at the other end of the counter for the last time, duffel bag at her feet, waiting for Seymour and Lee to finish up and take her away. Keith had always thought that by the time she reached this age, their relationship would have evolved into one of mature love and understanding, they'd no longer be father-and-child but father-and-adult-daughter, she'd understand she had as much to teach him as he had taught her, etc., but she acted today as she had since she was thirteen, saying as few words to Keith as possible, shutting down his every gesture toward conversation or tenderness with an icy stare or shake of the head.

The phone rang. Who could it be but the producer calling to apologize for the delay and reassure him that Mark and Grant would be there shortly? But before Keith could pick up, Stacey emerged from the back room where she'd been hiding from the disappointed dealers and answered herself.

"The Heart of America. Yes, certainly."

"Is it them? What are they saying?"

Stacey shushed him and withdrew into the back room. After a few endless minutes, he could take it no longer. He got up and followed her, but by the time he reached the doorway she returned to set the receiver in its cradle.

"So what did they say?" Keith asked. "Is it still on for today or are they going to reschedule?"

"What did who say?"

"The producers."

"You heard from the producers?"

"No, I mean—who was on the phone just now?"

"Nobody. The bank."

"Which one?"

"There's more than one?"

"What did they want?"

"Nothing important," Stacey said. "I mean, it is important. But we can talk about it later."

"What did they say? The bank people?"

"You seem agitated right now. I don't want to upset you. Anyway, it is what it is." She raised her palms as if it were out of her hands, which Keith supposed it was, and disappeared into the back room, probably to check the status of an auction on the computer. He envied Stacey's ability to never worry about money matters—except insofar as they pertained to her need to shop for collectible pottery, which at least partway explained the Heart of America's gradual, probably at one time preventable but now hopelessly inevitable, failure, which was not to unfairly discount the impact tolled by Keith's own ineptitude as a business owner and human being.

Keith returned to his stool and studied the creases in his palms. It was impossible to tell how much time passed before the door swung open and Jimmy Daniels walked in holding two birdcages in one hand. "Hidey ho, Mr. Stoller. How goes it?" He set the birdcages on the counter. "Shame about Mark and Grant. Guess you won't be a TV star after all."

"They're just running late," Keith said.

Jimmy's grin was unwavering. "Didn't you hear? The crew's RV drove off the road and rolled over. On 54. Thank god nothing happened to Mark and Grant. They travel separately. Took hours to get up and running. Whole production schedule's shot. One thing's for sure, they ain't coming back to Wichita."

"That's not good," Keith said, the familiar black balloon of angst swelling in his chest. Hope had never worn well on him. It was in the face of failure he felt most himself, and he had never been more himself than in this moment. In the span of a day—the day that was supposed to have solved all his problems—the Heart of America's fate had become irrevocably fucked. First, Jimmy called to inform him he and Margaret, two of the Heart's most loyal dealers—among the few who could be counted on to pay their rent on time—were striking out on their own. Then Seymour and Lee, the only new blood the Heart had seen in years, reneging on their lease. Now, on top of everything, no Mark and Grant. Without them, the Heart of America was done for, and so was Keith's last remaining unlikely chance at personal and financial redemption.

Jimmy chortled. "Bad luck, huh? Anyway, I wanted to ask if you could let me have the extra key so I can move out after hours. I got a couple transactions to complete before I go." He picked up the birdcages. "Guy in Hall Two is trading me an Al Kaline rookie card for these. I know a Tigers nut who'll pay top dollar for it."

He couldn't find the spare in the register, so Keith had to give him his own. It made no difference now. "What did you end up doing with the birds?"

"Had to toss 'em."

"You just let them go?"

"No, of course not. I killed them. Sold their feathers to this costumer I know. I said, 'Here, make necklaces out of them. Dream catchers or some shit.' " Jimmy strolled off to Hall Two.

Well, if the Heart of America was going belly-up, if Keith was destined to default on his home loans and lose everything, pretty much every last thing for which he had worked so hard—well, maybe not *that* hard, but work was work—was there really so much shame in that? He'd run a business—not particularly well but not so poorly, for the most part—for two full decades plus. Forget about their debt and their mortgage and dead-endedness. What the future held for him and Stacey, Keith did not know and was not particularly curious to find out. Ellie was all that mattered now. As he gazed down the counter at her, a little bit of poisonous air dislodged from the black balloon. It was time for an incredible gesture of selflessness he was pretty sure he would not regret.

"Ellie, I have something for you," he said as he embarked on the long journey from his end of the counter to hers.

"Dad," she said in the tone with which she'd address a fly about to be swatted.

He wanted to say to her all that had been on his mind, to explain why he was the way he was, to impress upon her that yes, she was right, he was a failure and a dumbass and a loser, etc., that she was already at her age smarter than he'd ever been and more interesting and good-looking and perceptive and talented. He wanted to tell her what she meant to him without having to brace himself for her caustic reply, to say, "I love you," without it sounding rehearsed and insincere, but instead like the words were new to them both and actually meant something. He didn't even care if she said it back.

But he didn't say anything. He reached into his back pocket and brandished the envelope of cash, all that he could scrounge up from the cash register, the store safe, the cigar box in his sock drawer. It was not as much as he owed her and not as much as she deserved, but it was all he could manage on short notice.

The moment was not as tenderhearted and climactic as he'd imagined. It felt like a ransom drop-off. She accepted it without a word, as if he were only delivering a payment she was owed. She did not smile, but without meaning to she lifted her head, and her eyes—fish-like, lined with scaly green mascara—met his. The saliva in Keith's mouth made a smacking sound and a cloudy look of dread settled on her face.

He couldn't blame her for the way she saw him. He was after all an old man, and like all old men he was disgusting. Only when he added, "Don't tell your mother," did the slightest smirk play on her thin lips. She zippered the envelope into the duffel bag beneath her stool. She did not say thank you.

"It's a start," she said, adding, when Keith continued to stare without moving, "Is this a bonus for all my hard work?"

"No," Keith said. "You're fired." He opened his arms to embrace her, but Ellie refused.

"This is getting a little Disney Channel, Dad."

The intercom screeched. Stacey announced that the mall would be closing in fifteen minutes. "Please finish browsing and pay for your purchases at the front counter at your soonest convenience." But there were no browsers left, and even though tomorrow Keith would wake up at eight thirty, drive from his exceedingly overvalued home in Eastborough and open up for business as usual, it felt at the moment like the last day at the Heart of America.

He walked unsteadily back to his stool, feeling a lot lighter without the cash weighing down his pocket.

"Hey, Dad," Ellie said. He turned. "The mall is closssssing." Her impossibly white young teeth flashed behind a curled lip, as close to a full-on smile as he'd seen from her in months. She was mocking her mother's sibilant *s*. It was a thing they used to do, whenever they passed one another in the hall or when Stacey left the room, because it was funny and because they had nothing else to talk about.

"Yesssss, it issss," Keith said. "It ssssure is. The mall is closssssing," he continued, prolonging the joke well past the point of amusement. He didn't care. He was having—he hoped he wasn't just deluding himself—what might be called a "moment" with his daughter.

24

RONALD

It was closing time at the Heart of America, but that made no difference to Ronald, presently locked alone in the interrogation room of the
police station across town while Detective Skinner, the lady policeman,
transcribed his confession. An interrogation room, just like in the movies: concrete walls, a bare light bulb dangling from the ceiling, venetian
blinds covering the windows. Venetian blinds! Who was he, John Derek
in *Knock on Any Door* from the old movie channel's noir week programming?

Detective Skinner had been a touch brash with him at first. His wrists
still smarted from the cuffs, but the physical pain was nothing compared
to his anguish at the name-calling: *kiddie diddler, pervo, sick f-word,
creep.* "And we found your little movie studio," she'd said accusingly.
"That'll help us put you away for a good long time on CP charges." No
no no, Ronald had explained. She had the wrong idea.

And what do you know, once the two of them got to talking she
softened right up. It was a lot like Ronald's show, only this time *he*
got to be the guest. Ronald had of course waived his right to counsel;
he knew what he'd done was wrong, even if it all started with a silly
misunderstanding—even if his intentions had never been malicious—

and he took full responsibility. Besides, having a lawyer present would have interrupted the flow of the conversation. He'd really been on fire, the words pouring out like never before. He could not have asked for a more captive audience. Though Detective Skinner received his anecdotes with stoic professionalism, he could swear she'd cracked the slightest smile during his bit about *My Secret Princess*.

Detective Skinner returned carrying a Styrofoam cup of coffee and a thick sheaf of papers. She set the papers on the table and handed him the cup.

"Don't suppose you have any hot chocolate?" he asked. "I've never been much of a coffee drinker myself. The one time I managed a full cup, I was practically jitterbugging all over the house. Why, I've heard tell that there's a village in France where they brew a cup so strong—"

Detective Skinner shoved the papers so they hit Ronald in the chest. "What happens now is you read what's on there aloud. Every last word." She sighed and rubbed her temples. "Talk fast. When you're done, if you take the words to be truthful and accurate, you sign your name." She offered him the pen from her pocket.

"Yes, ma'am!" Hoo boy, that was a lot of pages. And it told the whole story from beginning to end. He had seen enough movies to know where he was headed. The future held things both inevitable and uncertain. One thing he was secure in knowing, however, was that when he was released, his Heart of America booth would still be there for him; a while back, the nice boy at the bank had helped him set up automatic monthly transfers to the Stollers, and with his modest lifestyle he had funds to spare. It wasn't about having a home for all his postcards, though. On the contrary, what comforted him as he prepared to make official his confession was a newfound understanding of why Melinda had always ribbed him about his collection. People were what mattered, not silly objects. It was through the many relationships one fostered throughout life that a person made his or her mark and, in so doing, continued to live even after death. And there was no person that mattered more to Ronald than Melinda. His harebrained pickle with Lindy had been nothing but a way of distracting himself from the loneliness of life without her.

Well, there was nothing left to do but get on with it. He cleared his throat and began: "On the evening of—"

He coughed.

"On the evening—"

He coughed again, his sinuses sandpaper-dry. He tried to continue, but the words stuck in his throat.

Detective Skinner drummed her fingers. "Don't tell me that *now* you're gonna cry."

But it wasn't that. Ronald had talked so much, he'd lost his voice.

25

LEE

"Aren't you going to regret it?" Jimmy Daniels said as he hauled away the last vestiges of the record collection from Lee and Seymour's Hall Three booth, leaving behind only a patina of dust marked with footprints and a single cardboard box filled with the leftovers even Jimmy wouldn't bother with, namely nine copies of *Whipped Cream & Other Delights.* The house on Waterman was empty (even the stalwart Sansui 9090 that had helped him land Seymour was gone), their car packed with the saxophone and two suitcases that now comprised the entirety of their earthly possessions. All that remained to do before leaving was help Jimmy with the last few boxes of junk in Hall One—he refused to hand over the cashier's check until it was all securely in his truck; "Past experiences," he'd said, "have challenged my naturally trustful disposition." His offer was surprisingly fair considering the value of the individual pieces, but nevertheless incommensurate with the pricelessness of the collection as a whole—not the sum lot of physical objects but rather the decades of life Lee and Seymour had spent acquiring them.

There was something dreadfully Sisyphean about it; they'd brought it in just a few days ago and now out it all went. Was Jimmy right? Would Lee regret it? Did he feel different, was he happier dispossessed of the historical weight of the collection? Or was this just a paroxysm of the belated midlife crisis that had led to the failed shop in Cambridge and the move to Wichita to begin with? At the very least he felt lighter, a touch youthful even. As a fan he'd always regarded band reunions as desperate cash grabs by enfeebled has-beens, and frankly he couldn't say it would be any different with Tears in the Birthday Cake, but in a way it was cooler to succeed after already having given up, kind of like in school when you aced a quiz just by guessing.

For his part Seymour was approaching the purge with shocking enthusiasm. Presently Lee found him in the lobby sitting cross-legged on the counter poring over the sales computer with Ellie. As Lee approached, he read off the screen: "'And just when the shambling charm of it all threatens to implode in "European Son" levels of indulgence, that saxophone breaks out as reliably as acne on a teenage James Chance's upper lip. Chaos and structure haven't had such a tuneful marriage since *Loveless*—and this came out years earlier! Probably the last un-lost classic of the Internet Age.' Damn! I always thought they were good, but *that* good?" He turned to Lee and motioned at the monitor. "Robert Christgau's blog."

"Christgau's a pretentious turd," Lee said.

"Then take your pick on a second opinion." Seymour clicked through countless browser tabs, flashing past over-the-top headlines hailing the momentous rediscovery of the Tears in the Birthday Cake album, each illustrated with old band photos in which Lee looked, compared to today, prepubescent. "I tucked away our OG pressings in your sax case. It's cracked the Discogs Top 30. Once we get to Mass., I'm going to make a killing unloading them on some unsuspecting collector scum."

To think, back in the day Lee couldn't give the record away with a free case of beer. By the time it was pressed the band was all but broken up, the scenesters had moved on to other darlings, many of whom Lee would recognize on *120 Minutes* just a few years later. Most copies were sent to uninterested record companies and the rest were divided between band members. They never even played a release show. Its failure had been so raw that over the years Lee had convinced himself it was perfectly rational; no one liked the album because no one heard it, and no one heard it because it was no good. Now, twenty years later, it was being heralded as a masterpiece by the hipster cognoscenti. It made no sense. Success was stupid, sometimes deserved but rarely earned.

"This one's my favorite," Seymour said as he double-clicked. The wordless moan that opened "Her Stitches" tremoloed out of the tinny computer speakers.

At least ten thousand people were expected to attend TrashRiot. Lee couldn't imagine there existed even a tenth that many Tears fans—and who could they be? Would he be playing to a crowd exclusively made up of geriatrics like him? To Ellie, a conveniently proximate representative of hip young people, he asked, "What do you think?"

She exhaled through her nose—never had Lee known someone who could express derision through such a multifarity of gestures—and said, "Well, since you're giving me a ride, I think whatever you want me to think. Long-lost classic. A real mind-bender. Right up there on my desert island list with the Velvets and Milk 'N' Cookies."

"I've been educating her on the canon," Seymour said.

"Really, though," Lee said with a twinge of desperation. Fortune had been so arbitrarily bestowed upon him, he needed someone he barely knew to confirm it wasn't all a mistake.

Ellie shrugged. "I mean, it's okay, I guess."

"Don't listen to her," Seymour said. "The fact that she acts too cool for it means it *is* too cool."

"I like it," Keith said. He'd been eavesdropping from the other end of the counter. "It's catchy."

"The fact that *he* likes it," Ellie said, "means it can't be cool."

"It's very punk," Keith said. Ellie rolled her eyes.

"See?" Seymour said. "Who needs Christgau when you've got Keith Stoller, the people's critic?"

The door swung open. Jimmy Daniels walked in and joined them at the counter. "Hey, fellows, Hall One awaits. Sorry to rush ya," he said, "but it'd be stellar if we could wrap this up right quick. I got an appointment with the widow of a tin lunch box collector. Lucky thing: this guy offed himself for some reason or another and now she's giving me the whole kaboodle for gratis. Too many painful memories to keep around, she said. Hell, I've made money off worse tragedies."

"It's a public service you provide, Jimmy." To Lee Seymour said, "I'll go. You should bask in the glow of your online fame." Seymour followed after Jimmy, leaving Lee to stand around and avoid eye contact with Ellie as "Her Stitches" played to the end.

Lee had never been one to make friends or develop a rapport so easily as Seymour. Watching the slow procession of the waveform on the monitor, he said, "It sounds better on vinyl," and immediately cringed at the cliché.

"Sounds best to me when I don't have to pay for it."

Hot blood flooded Lee's face. "Oh, no," he stammered. "I wasn't trying to sell you anything. Sorry."

Ellie's lip curled in a way that could be construed either as a smirk or a snarl. "Jesus, Lee. I didn't mean it that way."

Lee was strangely touched; he sort of assumed she didn't even know his name. "It's just, it never came out anywhere but the record. How did you ever find this song? The internet?"

Ellie stared at him in disbelief for a long moment, as in: *Are you kidding?*

No, not kidding, he said with his silence; he was indeed a clueless old luddite who used a flip phone, watched movies on VHS, and had always let Seymour handle the computer side of the business.

She rotated the computer monitor so he could see and showed him a website all in Russian that, she claimed, archived for streaming or download virtually every recording in the history of man.

"Is it legal?" he asked.

"Ha!" She set the keyboard before him on the counter. "Whatever you're looking for, it's there."

Seymour trailed Jimmy in and out of the Heart of America unloading the last of their Hall One booth box by box, while Lee, oblivious, poised over the keyboard testing the breadth of the site's incredible inventory, pausing only to minimize the pornography banners that popped up with every click of the search button. Though divested of the collection, he could never—thank god—shake the music itself. It turned out that what he needed to reenter the sweet zone was not the best possible copy of an album or the most comprehensive or conscientiously curated collection or a restored vintage sound system but a *new* way to listen. They had the complete uncut *Headquarters Sessions*. They had bootleg editions of *Abbey Road* reconstructed with demos and alternate takes. They had Dave Clark Five's entire discography including obscure B-sides, sparklingly remastered Tommy James & the Shondells singles compilations, 5.1 surround sound mixes of *Pet Sounds* and *Skylarking*.

A sidebar whose header Lee guessed translated to "You may also like . . ." offered links to recommended albums and artists. While he trawled the Tommy James stuff, a familiar name caught in the corner of his eye: the Sodashoppe Teens. Thoughtlessly he clicked it and was taken to a page that listed all ten tracks, not in the order they appeared on the album but according to the results of some arcane ranking, complete with line graphs and a series of numbers whose meanings, because they were described in Cyrillic, Lee could not make heads or tails of.

"What does this stuff right here mean?" he asked.

Ellie yawned. The wonders of technology did not impress her. "Total streams and downloads. I think the graphs chart track or artist popularity over time or something."

As far as Lee could suss out, the Sodashoppe Teens were in the lower percentiles of popularity with only a couple thousand streams and a few hundred downloads, all Mickey Gordy completists no doubt. "And they have this information for everything?"

"Yeah. Just click the icon on top of the artist page."

He slid the cursor back to the search box. *Tears in the Birthday Cake*, he typed. To search for his own band felt like checking himself out in the reflection of a store window, but he had to know. According to

Sluggo, and based on the stuff Seymour had read, Lee's old band had been subject to an unprecedented critical and popular reappraisal, but it all remained intangible. Deep down he didn't actually expect the official TrashRiot offer to come through, for the band to reconvene for practice without disrupting into the same arguments and pettinesses of decades past. Nothing had ever worked out for Tears before; why should it now? Mickey Gordy liked the record, so what? The music was exactly the same now as when it had come out in 1987, and back then it had led to nothing.

Clicking the artist stats link, Lee waited while the page-loading icon rotated endlessly. Across the globe, diligent Russian algorithms scanned an infinite metaphysical repository for every digital trace of his greatest achievement. He had shouted his name supplicatingly into the all-encompassing godless void of technology, and finally the void answered.

Not until months later, when he stood atop the TrashRiot main stage cradling his sax, looking not out into the crowd screaming at Beatle-maniacal decibels, not at Seymour backstage mouthing the words to every song, but at Sluggo wielding his guitar like an epileptic dance partner, waiting for the little nod that reminded him the instrumental break of "Sorry to Die," Tears' traditional opener, would hit in three . . . two . . . one, would Lee know how it felt to offer the world your art, with little ambition but no modesty, and have a small piece of the world—in the grand scheme, a very tiny piece—thank you for it.

For now there were only the numbers, but that was enough.

26

DELORES

Skipper was gone.

Saturday night, after she and Seymour busted the door down and disarmed the old pervert, after the authorities arrived and carried the criminal efficiently away and she'd answered all their questions with Skipper's coached responses (she just happened to be outside when she heard a sound like a scream from the basement, she said; it was pure chance: right place, right time; she'd always had a strange feeling about the man), Delores ran off to take refuge from the news crews and reporters and neighborhood lookie-loos under the shadows of a neighbor's tree. There she stood gazing into Skipper's unblinking eyes, waiting for her to tell her what to do next.

After an interminable silence, Skipper said, "I'm proud of you, Dolly. You've finally proven that you're all grown up. And now that you're grown up, you know there comes a time when a young woman puts away her childish things, her games and toys and dolls, and turns to the grown-up world. Do you understand?"

A policewoman carrying the blanket-shrouded girl-victim approached. "The family is overwhelmed right now, ma'am, but they wanted me to thank you for your heroism. Lindy, too."

"You're welcome," Skipper said.

The girl-victim, known as Lindy Bobo in the press and on the fly-ers, poked her head out from under the blanket, her eyes widened and trained upon Skipper. And in that instant, Delores understood. Lindy could hear her, too. She reached out and—

In an action that superseded thought, Delores handed Skipper to Lindy.

"We're going to be great friends, aren't we?"

Lindy nodded.

"Isn't that sweet?" the policewoman said as she carried Lindy back to her family waiting before a police vehicle.

The last thing Delores heard was, "Bye-bye, Dolly." Then there was silence—not total silence but a kind somehow more pervasive for all the inchoate noise that filled its space. All her life she'd searched for Skipper, and now there would be no getting her back. Yet she felt no regret. She was so tired she could think of nothing else but going home, where she found herself, for the first time, alone. The Barbies did not greet her upon her arrival, not even to chastise her for the run in her stocking. No one said a thing.

She'd come to the Heart of America now not to meet Mark and Grant—without Skipper, she had nothing to show them—but to make sure it was true. And it was: the empty silence filled her booth in Hall Two as well. She spun around and studied the contents of her shelves, as lifeless and quiet as inanimate objects. Not a peep from the bubble cuts or flip 'dos, Sunset Malibus, the Fashion Queens, the Miss Americas, the Color Magics, or the Dramatic New Living Barbies. Not a word from Midge or Stacey or PJ or Steffie or Jamie or Francie, nor Ken, Allan, Brad, or Curtis. Not from Teen Talk Barbie, not even when Delores pressed the button on her back. Barbie and friends were here as they'd always been, but not really. The voices were gone.

And yet, Delores hadn't noticed till just now that so, too, were the pinch in her spine and the tension in her stomach she'd carried for de-cades like matching accessories. Could it be that without Barbie, she could finally, for the first time since they'd met, relax? Maybe it was simply her ensemble. There had been no one to tell her what to wear that morning, so she'd rolled out of bed and without even showering thrown on an old sweatshirt and a pair of blue jeans she hadn't even known she owned until she found them in the back of her closet in a box she'd been meaning to donate to Goodwill. Anchored in flats—not, for once, tottering high heels—she luxuriated in the generous embrace of gravity.

Now she caught her reflection in the plaque that read IF YOU DON'T SEE WHAT YOU'RE LOOKING FOR—ASK. I'VE PROBABLY GOT TWO OF IT IN STORAGE, but didn't cringe, didn't scour for flaws in her face or body or hair. She merely observed—in fact, admired—what she saw. Barbie had always been there, and so Delores never bothered to wonder what she herself thought or wanted or felt. Now that she had the freedom not just to think or want or feel, but to listen to herself think and want and feel, she took a long hard look and what she found was that she was beautiful. Not immaculate, certainly not perfect, and best of all, not plastic.

27

ELLIE

Lee had finished waxing nostalgic about his band days and had gone to help Seymour and Jimmy with the last of the boxes, leaving Ellie alone once again with her father. She'd put in this one last session at work not because she thought she owed it to her parents, not even out of a sense of routine or nostalgia for what she hoped would one day be remembered as merely an amusing anecdote about a truly miserable time in her life, but because she felt like it, because maybe at the very least she could carry with her this reminder of the hell she was about to escape so that no matter how dire things in her life got, she knew she was strong, she was brave, she would only tolerate shit for so long. And maybe, just a little, because this would be the last time she had with her father before she took off.

She made the mistake of glancing in his direction. Instantly his eyes met hers and he said, "Sssorry we're clossing," forcing a chuckle. He didn't know when to drop it.

Ellie wanted to be merciful. She understood that a parent who tried too hard was better than one who tried not at all. She appreciated the money, was in fact deeply grateful for it. She forgave him his failures, in a strange way was impressed by the notion that there were parts of her father that existed unseen and independent of her narrow perception of him, albeit parts that were mortifying to see expressed publicly or privately. Ellie tried to be merciful, really she did, but he was being such a dork. She shook her head and said curtly, "No, Dad. It's done."

He tried to turn a grimace into a smile. She felt bad enough to apologize, but luckily Seymour strolled up to the counter just in time.

"Well, since Mark and Grant stood us up, looks like we'll be heading out in a few."

"Those guys are pathetic. You actually wanted to be on that show?"

"No, not really, but your dad said he wouldn't penalize us for breaking our lease if I played along."

Lee plodded out of Hall One carrying an armload of boxes up to his eyeballs. Jimmy Daniels followed holding only a single box out of which stuck the bulbous green head of a Herman Munster hand puppet.

His arms quavering under the weight of his load, Lee said, "This is the last of it, right?"

"Sure is," said Seymour. "So how about that check, Jimmy?"

Jimmy set his box on the counter, looked Seymour up and down as if appraising his trustworthiness, then reached into his shirt pocket and handed him a cashier's check with a number on it big enough to almost cover one year at the expensive private college Ellie had lied to her parents she was going to attend. "You're the shrewdest negotiator I ever dealt with, I'll tell ya that. A man with nothing to lose."

"Nothing to lose now that it all belongs to you." Seymour sounded strangely sad.

"You're lucky we don't charge you for the labor," Lee said from behind his boxes. "It occurs to me, now that my arms are rubber and my hernia is on fire, that we could have just moved this stuff into your booth."

"Keith, you didn't tell them?" Jimmy said. "What's the matter, you insulted by a little friendly competition? I'm afraid that no longer does Jimmy Daniels reign over the Heart. Someone else can be Dealer of the

Month, for once." He took a stack of cards from his pocket, gave one to Seymour, one to Ellie, and tossed one to Keith, who tried to catch it and missed. JIMMY DANIELS, it read, CO-OWNER, PRETTY PATTY'S ANTIQUES SHOP, LLC. "Margie Byrd and me are going into business together."

Seymour gasped. "You mean all this junk is going to share shelf space with Margaret's precious glass?"

"Priced to sell. She's got her customers and I got mine."

"Jimmy, I say with maximum sincerity that I will be devastated to miss your grand opening."

"Touched, man. I'm truly touched. Here. Something to remember me by." Jimmy drew from his box a headless MC Hammer doll and handed it to Seymour. "Even I can't sell this."

Lee shifted his weight to steady the boxes. "Can we get a move on? I'm about to collapse and I'd prefer not to be killed by the weight of a passel of Jayne Mansfield water bottles."

"Jeez, Seymour. Your guy's a vicious taskmaster."

"I know it."

Lee followed Jimmy out the door.

"Shall we proceed?" Seymour pointed the onetime pop-rap superstar at the exit.

Ellie stood, duffel bag strapped to her shoulder. This was it. She was leaving. Finally. This was what she wanted and she was excited, she told herself. Right now, she was excited, really, even if she knew that on the way there she'd second-guess her decision. As if it were so simple. As if *where* she was changed *who* she was. Wherever exactly *there* would be. Most of what she'd told her parents was a lie. She had no plans beyond getting out. Once they were on the road she would figure it out. Either that or realize how bad an idea it had been to leave with no plan whatsoever other than to crash with two virtual strangers in Boston until she decided what to do or they kicked her out.

Keith stood, took one step toward her and one step back, raised his arms uncertainly. "Ellie, you're leaving."

She hugged him, quickly but tightly. He felt smaller than she thought he would. "'Bye, Dad. I'll send you a postcard, I guess."

"Don't. I've seen enough postcards for one lifetime. Sprained my back hauling Ronald's out to the dumpster."

"An email, then."

He hugged her again and wouldn't let go. He started to cry. For once, it wasn't annoying. It made her love him more. Or she loved him as much as she always did but for the moment she was less embarrassed on his behalf than usual. This was the man who raised her, the one person who found her mom as annoying as she did. This was Santa Claus in a fake beard on Christmas, the hand that doled out allowance, the arms that pushed swings higher and higher, the fingers that gently rubbed the back of her neck as he and Stacey broke the news about her college fund. This was her father.

Stacey appeared in the doorway to the back room, a vacant look in her eyes. She watched Ellie and Keith. "You and your father have always made such a powerful little team," she said, standing stock-still with her arms at her sides. Like an inanimate object.

Ellie felt sorry for her, but the warmth she felt for her father in that moment couldn't extend to her mother. There was no use in her dwelling over a failing business and marriage and her estranged daughter, Ellie guessed. These things were intangible constructs, and all that mattered to Stacey were the things you owned, the things you could hold in your hands. Or maybe it was simple: Stacey just didn't like Ellie that much, at least not as much as she liked her collection.

Ellie gave her father one last hug. He basically blew his nose into her shoulder.

"Later, Stollers," Seymour said. "I'll, uh, make sure she wears her seat belt."

But just before they made it to the door, Pete Deen caught Seymour's shoulder in his hammy palm.

"That is *mine*," he said, grabbing the MC Hammer doll by the parachute leg.

"Not so fast." Seymour held tight to MC Hammer's other leg like it was a wishbone. "It's come back into our possession, you know how these things happen."

Ellie could see Pete's heart pounding through his unseasonal Christmas sweater. A lock of his greasy hair dripped sweat as he struggled to maintain his grip. "What do you want it for, anyway? It's not even your style."

"If you really want it, we'd be willing to sell."

"Not necessary when it's already *mine*." Pete's grip tightened. His wrist veins pulsed. A lifetime of frustration shone on his face: every spurned advance, every lonely night in front of the TV, every unmarked box on the checklists he'd compiled of his most desired toy lines. He yearned for the warm feeling of acquisition. He raised his fist in the studied position of a Rock 'Em Sock 'Em Robot and—yelped upon seeing the brown plastic nub like a baby's penis where MC Hammer's head was supposed to be. "It's not mint!" He released his grip and pivoted, fighting back tears. "It's incomplete!" He ran into Hall Two.

"I guess he doesn't want it?" Seymour said.

"Guess not," Ellie said. She could feel her father's gaze on her as she opened the door, but she did not look back.

And so, MC Hammer in hand, they went: Out of Wichita. Out of the Heart of America.

28

MARGARET

There were accidents and there were mishaps. There were crashes and there were bumps. There were bumps and there were taps. And what Margaret had done—rather, what her vehicle had done—had been nothing more than a tap, a love tap even, a peck between bumpers. How presumptuous of the airbag to activate itself.

On the other hand, an accident was what had happened to the RV adorned with the faces of the TV hosts Mark and Grant, though *that* was no fault of Margaret's. She ought to get out and survey the scene, check to make sure no one was hurt. But she couldn't take her eyes off the back of Patricia's head. Her ponytail shivered in what appeared to be a sigh. She shifted and, like an afterthought, the car's emergency lights began to blink. Margaret triggered her own emergency lights, clicked them off and then on again, trying to synchronize with Patricia's. The door opened and Patricia stepped out on the soft soil of the roadside ditch. She appeared undazed, perfectly kempt save for a red mark on her forehead from the impact of the airbag. She began jogging, cellular phone to her ear, down the road toward the overturned vehicle.

"Patricia, wait!" Without consciously thinking to, Margaret had exited her own car and was struggling in high heels to catch up. Patricia stopped and looked back. "Patricia." Margaret was already out of breath. "I'm so . . . happy to see you. How . . . have you been?"

"Are you crazy? People could be hurt." Patricia kept her ear to the phone. Behind her, a door flew open and a man climbed onto the RV's flank. Into the phone she said, "Yes, there's been an accident . . ."

"Of course . . . anything I can do . . . to help," Margaret said, but Patricia wasn't listening. The best she could do was stay out of the way. She sat in her car and watched as her friend took charge, helping the RV's occupants exit safely, checking to make sure no one was seriously hurt, running to the gas station for drinks and snacks while they milled about and waited for the tow trucks. Most of them sat in the grass and shouted into their cellular phones. When they squinted their eyes and gazed into Margaret's car, she tried to send them a sympathetic look. She was here if anyone needed her, but Patricia had control over the situation. A few appeared injured, bruised or limping or cradling flaccid arms. Besides that, they were indistinguishable, sweatshirt-wearing men with dark hair and pale skin, and a couple women Patricia stood around and joked with as the police and trucks and medical personnel made their rounds. Although she did not care for their show, she was disappointed to see neither Mark nor Grant in the crowd.

The only person she talked to was a police officer who took down her story—though *story* wasn't quite the word for it, as Margaret spoke only the pure unvarnished truth—after the RV had been hauled away and the TV crew with it. He seemed convinced—though why should it take any convincing?—of her faultlessness. It helped that Patricia corroborated her every word. Was that a look of complicity she flashed over the policeman's shoulder when he looked down at his pad of paper?

It had taken a couple hours, but order was restored. Patricia's car had been towed along with the RV, and Margaret's heart nearly shot out of her mouth when she overheard Patricia decline the policeman's offer of a ride. They were alone now.

This was what she had yearned for, finally, or was close to it: a face-to-face reunion with her best friend, a chance for reconciliation. There was opportunity and there was action. Margaret had the former and the *intention* for the latter, but she'd been through it so many times in her mind that now, faced with the reality of it, she didn't know where to begin. Patricia stood with her hands in her pockets. There was nothing, no one, to look at but Margaret.

"Shall I drive you home?"

Patricia pulled at the stem of her ponytail, a gesture Margaret recognized as an indicator of annoyance or distraction. "My son will pick me up." Beyond her, Margaret thought she could make out the faintest impression of the Heart of America, a beige speck in the distance.

There had been a time when in Patricia's presence Margaret was as unselfconscious, as playful or silly, as a girl. Now she approached her best friend as uneasily as she would a stray dog. "Patricia," Margaret said, "you were on your way back to me." When Patricia said nothing, she added, "To the Heart of America. Booth one-dash-one-four-six." She was getting ahead of herself, but so what? The hope that sounded from her own voice was both embarrassing and exhilarating. All this time without Patricia, she'd had nothing to lose. She'd had nothing. She searched her friend for any tiny movement or expression she could interpret as an invitation for embrace, for taking one step closer. Cars sped by on the highway, blowing autumn air into her ears. Even from out here, even above the noise, she heard—she knew she was only imagining it, but that didn't matter—the near-silent chime of her glass collection, waiting peacefully down the road.

"I came for my china doll," Patricia said quietly. "I've got a table at the flea market now."

Margaret staggered backward, then forward. "No, Patricia, no." This was where she ought to announce her plans for Pretty Patty's Antiques Shoppe. This was where she should explain away all the confusion about that day. Instead she only stepped closer, but not close enough to touch.

Patricia smiled toothlessly and shook her head—it was the same look she'd once given after Margaret explained that a clueless housewife had just sold an exceedingly rare, though cracked, Theresienthal bowl to her for a few dollars at a garage sale. "It never bothered me what happened. It was how you reacted."

"Let's not talk about that. It was nothing."

"You know what I mean."

"Sure. It was nothing. A misunderstanding." Margaret shrugged. "You broke my jar. I was upset. I overreacted."

"*That* was nothing. That's not what we're talking about." Patricia looked deeply into Margaret's eyes. "I want to hear you tell me what happened."

Why should she have to? They both knew, why bother with rehashing an irrelevant little incident like that? It was unseemly. Margaret would have been mad if she didn't already feel so hurt. Why couldn't things just go back to the way they were before? "We're friends, Patricia."

"You're being dishonest, Margaret. With yourself more than with me. I already knew how you felt about me. That's not what scared me away."

"What scared you, then?"

"That you were so scared. So damn afraid and *ashamed*. You're not good at hiding what you feel. Maybe you're just bad at knowing it." Patricia brushed a stray hair from her forehead. "What do you think I am to you?"

"You're my only friend. I'm not like you. It's not easy for me to say." Margaret took another step closer. She had already lost Patricia once, and now she was losing her all over again. If she had never met Patricia she would have been fine. Her life would have been as it always had been before. But now that she had had Patricia, and known what it was to *not* have Patricia, she had no life without her. "You're Patricia. I—I love you." Her voice wasn't her own. The words had crawled out of her mouth from some place deep in her chest where secrets were kept. It was the voice of someone Margaret wished she could be but who she was not. Not yet.

Patricia narrowed her eyes. "How do you love me?" Her words were penetrative but her tone and expression uncharacteristically flat. Margaret felt as if she were being given a pop quiz. "What am I to you?"

"Everything."

"What do you want from me?" There weren't words for what Margaret wanted from Patricia, not even in the space deep in her chest. Patricia's stance relaxed ever so slightly, her shoulders dropped a millimeter or two. She had barely moved, but something about her softened, a threshold for embrace opened, and all Margaret had to do to reach her was lift her leaden feet and drag herself through it.

And then she was watching her own hand cup Patricia's cheek, warm and a bit moist. It was the opposite of glass: fleshy, supple, yielding to Margaret's gentle touch. Underneath, Patricia's jawbone was sturdy and unfragile and her teeth shone—in a wince, not a smile—like decorative pearl embellishments. She did not remove Margaret's hand. Patricia was patient. And Margaret was patient, too. She could stay like this forever.

But that would not be fair. Margaret had something to say, to herself as much as to Patricia, a truth pure and unclouded by shame or judgment. It was something better said in action than in speech. A hand— she wasn't sure if it was her own or Patricia's—pulled her forward. Her face was close enough to see the impressions of the impact of the airbag. Between them they shared a breath, wheaty and a little sweet, redolent of Nilla wafers and lipstick. Patricia's lips were parallel with her own. The texture and taste of those lips had never left Margaret's sense-memory. They were impossibly soft, slick-wet, absorbing Margaret's own like a tissue dropped in a puddle. She longed for them to envelop her once again.

Patricia tilted her head and narrowed her eyes. An earthquake could strike at that moment, sending all of her glass shattering against the hard ground, and Margaret wouldn't care. She had acquiesced to desire. She wanted only one thing, and it wasn't made of glass. She wanted to kiss the woman she loved.

But before she could, a heavy plastic object came sailing through the air, the purple parachute cloth swaddled around it glinting in the sunlight. In the blinding white flare of pain as it struck her square in the eye, Margaret knew exactly what it was and whence it had come.

29

SEYMOUR

It had been an immature thing to do, Seymour admitted, chucking it at Margaret Byrd. But what use did anybody have for that headless MC Hammer doll? Not even sticky-fingered Pete Deen wanted it. Nor did Ellie, in the backseat next to Lee's saxophone case, screeching with laughter, not just at Margaret's favorite rapper being returned to her, but at the sheer exhilaration of leaving home.

And leaving unencumbered, at that. There were just three bags between them, not counting the case containing Lee's sax and the suddenly priceless original pressings of the Tears in the Birthday Cake album. He'd sold the rest: his records and stereo; his antiques and curiosities; most of his wardrobe; his accumulated kitsch, camp, crap; his whole collection of collections, to Jimmy Daniels. He was rid of it, free. Life stretched out before him—not as far as it did for young Ellie, but far enough.

All the things he'd bought and owned, his mania for collecting and completism, his belief that a person was only as interesting as his possessions, had damaged him, his love of objects superseding his love of Lee, his love of life itself. He'd been happiest when he was young like Ellie, too broke to own anything of value, not comfortable enough to want anything other than the people and experiences that were freely, newly, and abundantly available.

This Seymour knew now only because he'd sold it all.

He also knew, as he watched the Heart of America shrink, fade, and disappear in the rearview mirror, that not a day would go by for the rest of his life that he wouldn't regret it.

ACKNOWLEDGMENTS

This book would not exist without the support and/or influence of:

Mary South.

Sean Manning, David Litman, Marysue Rucci, Jackie Seow, Daniel Benayun, Lake Bunkley, Yvette Grant, Carly Loman, Heidi Meier, Jonathan Karp, Richard Rhorer, Elizabeth Breeden, and everyone involved at Simon & Schuster.

Richard Klein, Woody Skinner, Ian Golding, Brent Stroud, Becca Hannigan, Daisy Carlsen, Chelsie Bryant, Liz Stetler, Justine McNulty, Bess Winter, Lindsey Simard, and Jason Teal.

Jack Pendarvis, Leah Stewart, Michael Griffith, Chris Bachelder, Roxane Gay, Barbara Lowenstein, the Oxford Conference for the Book, and the Sewanee Writers' Conference.

My teachers and peers at the University of Cincinnati, the University of Wisconsin–Oshkosh, and Wichita State University.

The Cincinnati Public Library.

My family.

Steph Barnard.

ABOUT THE AUTHOR

LUKE GEDDES holds a PhD in comparative literature and creative writing from the University of Cincinnati. Originally from Appleton, Wisconsin, he now lives in Cincinnati, Ohio. He is the author of the short story collection *I Am a Magical Teenage Princess* and his writing has appeared in *Conjunctions, Mid-American Review, Hayden's Ferry Review, Washington Square Review, The Comics Journal, Electric Literature,* and elsewhere.